To A

STOLEN YEARS

Best wishes

Rita Bell

Fiction is the truth
inside a lie

STOLEN YEARS

Rita Bell

© Rita Bell, 2016

Published by Danior Publishing

All rights reserved. No part of this book may be reproduced, adapted, stored in a retrieval system or transmitted by any means, electronic, mechanical, photocopying, or otherwise without the prior written permission of the author.

The rights of Rita Bell to be identified as the author of this work have been asserted in accordance with the Copyright, Designs and Patents Act 1988.

This is a work of fiction. Names, characters, businesses, places, events and incidents are either the products of the author's imagination or used in a fictitious manner. Any resemblance to actual persons, living or dead, or actual events is purely coincidental.

A CIP catalogue record for this book is available from the British Library.

ISBN 978-0-9935548-0-3

Book layout and cover design by Clare Brayshaw

Cover image © Dmitry Kandov | Dreamstime.com

Prepared and printed by:

York Publishing Services Ltd
64 Hallfield Road
Layerthorpe
York YO31 7ZQ

Tel: 01904 431213

Website: www.yps-publishing.co.uk

Chapter One

1971

Tess walked into Lena's hovel carrying a briefcase – she walked out carrying a briefcase and a baby. Lena's rasping voice resounding in her ears. 'Okay, you toffee-nosed bitch. You think you can do any better with this bleedin' kid? 'Ere, you 'ave 'er then.' Tossed like scrap in a skip, the scraggy infant dumped in her arms, the door slammed. She settled Jade, an eighteen-month-old baby, inside a half empty box of sample nappies. What would you have done? Contact Social Services? Call in at the local police station? Tess did neither, she drove straight home. Placing the precious box carefully on her grey tweed sofa, she slumped down beside it. Only then did the enormity of what she had just done overwhelm her. Trembling beside the sleeping baby, she felt the strength slowly sucked out of her body.

'Mary, Mother of God. What have I done? What came over me? Why didn't I take the baby to the police station?'

1946

At seventeen, Tess, was cloistered as a postulant in an English convent. Her parents in Ireland, promised Father Conran, that two of their daughters and one son, would enter holy orders. The priest told them, 'To dedicate one child to God is a privilege. Two daughters for the convent and a son in the seminary, God will bestow a great blessing on your family.' Her school friends were cynical. 'Huh! Some parents are not t'inking of God's blessing. They are t'inking what a blessing that will be, two less mouths to feed.'

'Yes, two weddings your Da doesn't have to pay for,' said another.

Tess admired the nuns at her school and wanted to follow in their footsteps. Despite an overwhelming ambition to train to be a teacher, it was not possible. Taking holy orders, with its vow of obedience, her own desires were denied. The religious order arranged for her to train to be a nurse. On entering a hospital ward, it held a certain familiarity. At the convent, and at school, women also wore white headdresses and were addressed as Sister; but it was the vow of poverty and relinquishing of all possessions she found most difficult. The bracelet her grandfather had given at her confirmation. The little box engraved with her name that her brother had lovingly carved out for her, in his woodwork class. The most upsetting was her mother's hand-embroidered cushion she had sent for her birthday.

'Don't forget to write to your mother and thank her for it.'

'Yes Reverend Mother.'

'You know of course you cannot keep it. It will be raffled at the church bazaar.'

To commence her general nurse training, she was sent to a London Teaching Hospital, followed by training to qualify for a community midwife.

1969

It was five o'clock, Tess was about to leave the ante-natal clinic when the phone rang. It was the Catholic Adoption Society to check up on a new adoption placement. The society had asked her to give the new parents any advice, or assistance they might need to cope with a new baby. As she opened the clinic door a surge of swirling fog greeted her; switching on her cycle lights she made her way to visit the adoptive parents. I'm sure I'm the last person they want to see today, she muttered. She decided to call in as it was on her way home to the convent. Jeanette and Felix as future adoptive parents, had not dared to speculate or hope for a young baby. When Jeanette opened the door, the midwife found herself catapulted into the house.

'Oh! Thank goodness you've come Sister, I didn't dream I'd get such short notice. I only had two hours to pick up the baby from hospital. By the time I got home, the shops were closed. My husband doesn't even know yet. We didn't think we would get a young baby. As soon as I heard, I rang my sister at work. She left early and is going to come down from London with some baby stuff for us.'

Jeanette covered her eyes, her forehead showing worry lines under her wispy brown fringe.

'Relax Jeanette, calm down. Where's the baby?'

'Over there in my bedroom. In a chest of drawers, I emptied a drawer. He's in there.'

'What about feeding him?'

'They gave him a feed in the hospital and gave me some Cow and Gate milk and bottles to take home. But I haven't a clue. We didn't expect a tiny baby. He was premature too, he only weighs five pounds. Once his weight reached five pounds, the hospital discharged him.'

Jeanette heard her husband's key in the door, she called out and rushed to greet him. Felix had arrived home unaware of the drama taking place. He ducked down to allow his towering frame through the door of the cottage.

'What's the panic?'

"I tried to ring you, you were in a meeting and couldn't be disturbed; we have a baby!'

'What? When?'

'Like NOW!'

'Wow! Great. Where is it?'

'It, darling… is a boy.'

'Fantastic. How old?'

'Six weeks. But wait a minute Felix, he's very, very tiny. I've had to put him in a drawer until we can go and get a cot, a pram and all the things we need. Sheila's on her way from London, bringing a carrycot and baby blankets.'

Little did Tess know, one day she too would identify with Jeanette's feelings of panic. Nor could she have possibly guessed, how in later years their paths would cross in a most remarkable way. The baby had been named Jason, by the midwives in the hospital. Not because he had been wrapped in a golden fleece; he was wrapped in a school pullover. Pinned to the pullover, was a Catholic medal. Discovered on Christmas Day abandoned in a bus station. The police had issued an urgent message for the mother to come forward. Being on holiday, allowed the 'gymslip mother', as she was called, to disappear without her absence from school being brought to attention. After helping Jeanette to feed and settle the baby, Tess cycled in the fog to the convent. Unaware she too would be confronted with a shock.

'I'm sorry Sister, we have given your room to a visiting missionary. I have made arrangements for you to go and stay at another convent.'

Tess was shocked and angry, she couldn't believe it. The convent had been her home for more than twenty years. She was distressed that Reverend Mother could suddenly treat her like this. She had no choice but to make her way to the sister convent. On her arrival she was befriended by Agnes, who also thought the sudden move to another convent was unkind. It took time for her to settle into a different congregation.

One night she heard the cell door creak. She sat upright in bed. It was forbidden for nuns to lock their doors. A shaft of light illuminated a shadowy figure.

'Agnes?' she whispered.

She suddenly felt the movement of someone sitting on her bed.

'Agnes?' Agnes's cell was next door.

'Ssh! It's Brother Andrew.'

'What are ye doing here?'

Brother Andrew was a monk from the nearby monastery. Rarely would nuns and monks meet, or even take Mass together and when they did, they were not permitted to look or converse with each other.

'Calm down Sister.'

'What do ye want?'

'I'm not going to hurt you.'

He stroked her face. Instantly she pulled away cringing. She could not remember the last time a man had touched her skin. Even the nuns were instructed not to touch each other.

'Get away. Leave me alone.'

He started to touch her breast, over her nightdress.

'What do ye think you are doing? Get out. **Get Out**!' Cold hands tried to remove her nightdress. She clung on to it. It was useless. Brother Andrew's broad, farmer-sized hands, swiftly ripped it off.

'Help, **Help** someone help me!' Her voice echoed down the corridor.

'Ssh. Ssh. No one will come in.'

'I'll report ye to the Abbott,' she cried.

'You're wasting your time. The Abbot has given permission.'

'Liar – Help – **HELP!**'

'Sister, believe me. No one will come. They all know why we are here.'

The monk had stripped off. He made sure to hook his cloak over the small peep-through window, on the door of the cell. He closed the door.

'Get off me. What are ye doing? I don't believe a word about the Abbot.'

'Huh! You should do. He came with me. He's probably with one of the other Sisters.'

She tried to cover herself with the blanket and coiled herself up into a ball. When she tried to scream, the monk stuffed a small piece of cloth into her mouth. He pinned her to the bed. Lay his naked body on top of her and violated her body. He removed the cloth. Ignored her distress and got dressed.

'We both took a vow of celibacy,' she sobbed.

'Don't worry Sister, sex between two religious cannot desecrate our vows of celibacy. You forget I am your superior. Remember the saying of Ignatius, *all should give themselves up entirely to their Superior. As a dead body allows it to be treated in any manner whatsoever, make yourself into that body. Your own will and feelings must be broken. Only then can God work through you.*'

She lay in bed, shocked and shaking. Angry that the monk would use a theological argument, to persuade her that what he had done was not a sin. She wanted to scrub every inch of her body to rid herself of the evil that had devoured her. She felt dead inside. Her body like an empty shell. As she lay trembling, over and over she reasoned to herself, who will believe me? Who will believe it was against my will?

At first when she awoke, she thought it could have been a dreadful nightmare. Then terrible pain and soreness. It felt as though her whole lower body had been ripped open. She dragged herself out of bed. It was then that she noticed the blood-stained nightdress and bed sheet.

After Lauds, the early morning liturgy in the chapel, she found a quiet corner to talk to Agnes.

'Something horrendous happened last night.'

'I know. I am so sorry. I wanted to help you. I got up and made for your door. I was stopped by the Abbot.'

'I'm leaving Agnes, I'm not staying here a minute longer than I have to.'

'You look dreadful.'

'I feel sick, sick too of this place. I don't even want to go back to my own convent now.'

'I know how you feel.'

'Do ye? Do ye know what happened?'

Agnes nodded. 'The monks seem to have sanction to do what they like with us.'

'Holy Mother of God. What happened last night was monstrous. I shall write to my father. Explain what happened. He will come over from Ireland and take me home.'

'You are wasting your time. Do you think Reverend Mother only opens incoming mail?'

'What are ye saying, she opens our letters for posting?'

'Oh yes. I've seen her going through the outgoing mail. Slitting open the envelopes. Reading our letters. Some I saw her tear up. Others she removed pages.'

'How do ye know this?'

'It was when I was in the recess arranging her flowers, she didn't notice I was there. When she did spot me, I quickly averted my eyes, gave the impression that I was oblivious to what she was doing.'

'What can I do?'

'You have your sister Maura living in England, she knows where you are, pray that she will visit you this month.'

'Did the monks come to ye?'

'Not last night, but they have been. I reported it to Reverend Mother. She couldn't or wouldn't do anything. The Abbot had told her that the young brothers must find some relief for their sexual frustrations. The Abbot being her Superior, she was forced to give in to his request.'

'I cannot believe it. They are treating us like prostitutes. Suppose I became pregnant, what would I do?'

'Oh, try not to think about that. It would be terrible.'

'I am asking ye what would happen to the baby?'

'I imagine they would give the baby up for adoption. At least I pray that is what they would do. Although I did see something in the garden the other day.'

'What?'

Agnes shook her head.

'**What** did ye see? Tell me.'

'All right. There is an incinerator. It is hidden behind some trees. I saw one of the Sisters carrying a paper parcel and disappear behind the trees. She didn't see me, I secretly followed her. She put the bundle into an incinerator. Then sat for a few minutes on a tree stump, she looked distressed.'

Tess knew it would only be lack of money that would prevent her sister Maura from visiting. She decided she would write to her father and remind him it was Maura's birthday, she felt sure she would appreciate money for her birthday. As Tess had not yet been in this particular convent for six months, she could have a visitor once a month. Time was running out. Soon all visits would cease and all regular letters home forbidden. The only letters allowed would be thank you letters on the receipt of a birthday or Christmas present.

She knew, if her sister received money for her birthday, she would not hesitate to buy a railway ticket with it.

It took a few weeks for her plan to work and for her to make the trip to the convent. On her arrival Maura was shocked to see how pale and ill her sister looked.

'Do ye get enough to eat?'

'Yes.'

'Ye are not looking so well. What's wrong wid ye?'

'Let's go out in the fresh air Maura. We'll have a walk in the garden.'

'She gradually explained to her sister what had happened to her.'

At first, Maura refused to believe it. She thought her sister must be losing her mind. Until she showed her the secreted incinerator. There was a half burned parcel in there. Maura prodded it with a stick and let out a yell.

'Jesus, Mary and Joseph. I didn't believe ye. I've seen it with me own eyes so I have.'

It explained her sister's appearance and withdrawn behaviour. This was something she could not have imagined. Unable to contain her emotions at her discovery of the sordid truth, tears streamed down her face. This wasn't something anyone could fabricate. Tess's face, was impassive. She appeared distant, detached from reality.

'Don't worry. I'm going to get ye out of here. I'll phone daddy straightaway.'

'Do ye think daddy will believe it?'

'I'll **make** him believe it.' We'll have ye home in no time.'

Maura went to give her sister a hug. Tess shook her head. Then, Maura having seen that they were unobserved, ignoring the usual observance, gave her sister what she hoped would be a warm embrace. She found her body to be cold, rigid with tension.

Once out of the convent Maura rang her father. She kept going over and over in her mind what had happened. It was unbelievable. How could this happen in a cloistered community? Who would ever believe that such violations were happening in a Roman Catholic Convent?

Their father made immediate plans for a flight to England. He booked a hotel and hired a car. Sean McCarthy knocked loudly on the heavy oak door of the convent. It slowly opened. He was ushered by one of the nuns into a panelled waiting area. It smelled musty and damp. Shadows flitted across the room from the small, high, oval window. A large wooden cross dominated the room, together with a painting of the Sacred Heart of Jesus, with a prayer underneath. Anger and guilt bubbled up inside him. Heavy shoes on stone floor – clink of crucifix – nun's rustling habit, heralded Mother Superior. Instinctively he stood up.

'Reverend Mother, I have come to…'

She raised her hand. In a sweeping fashion, beckoned him to sit down.

'Yes, yes, Mr McCarthy. I think you made your intentions quite clear in your telephone conversation last night. Although there was no need for you to be quite so explicit. Here are some papers for you to sign for the release of your daughter.'

The elderly nun sat opposite. Tight lipped. Hands folded. Sean read the papers. He hesitated. Put his pen down. He looked the Mother Superior straight in the eye, she could see he was furious. Before he could remove his daughter, he had to sign to the effect that he would not make any malicious statement, or complaint, against the convent. He was seething. He had no choice than sign the papers.

'Where is my daughter?'

'She will be with you shortly. She will come out of a side door. I suggest you wait outside the main gate.'

He felt if he uttered another word, he would explode with anger. He stormed out of the room.

Out of a side entrance she appeared, wearing the same clothes that she wore over twenty years ago. No longer would she be called Sister Bridget. She had left the cloistered life forever and reverted back to her name of Teresa, or Tess as she was known. He hardly recognised his daughter. Her clothes, hung on her emaciated body. Her face, the colour of alabaster. Instead of the neat, tailored, grey dress, it enveloped her like a shroud. Once outside, they fell into each other's arms.

'Oh Daddy, Daddy.'

'Don't be crying darlin'. Ye are safe now. Let's be goin' home.

On opening the front door for his traumatised daughter. Tess held out her arms.

'Oh Mammy.'

'God love ye. Ye look so pale. Come here darlin'. Kathleen hugged and kissed her. She lifted the corner of her apron and dabbed her eyes.

'Don't cry Mammy, I'm home now.'

This was a different daughter she was greeting. Not the one that left home as a cheerful, joyous teenager. Her face was wan, emotionless–eyes sunken–body wasted. Too upset to face the family, Sean retreated into the garden. He had held himself together the last couple of days for his daughter's sake. Now he was overcome with grief and guilt. This was a very sick woman he had brought home. He put his head in his hands and wept.

Within a few days Sean had assembled all his family together. The parents were anxious to gather them not only for comfort and support for Tess, but for Sean who had a very serious mission. Maura was first to arrive with her brother from England. Then the eldest son Kieran, a few days later from Canada. At first there was a feeling of a long-awaited family reunion. Sean did not mince his words. He explained how their sister had been raped by a monk. That this was not a one-off incident, but a regular arrangement that the Abbot had organised with the Mother Superior. She would allow the brothers from the nearby monastery to enter the convent and violate the young nuns. The Abbot was himself involved in this regular sexual activity.

After they heard what had really happened to their sister, they sat several minutes in stunned silence, unable to utter a sound. Sean broke the silence with a brief statement and proposal that could affect them all, possibly for generations to come. They listened intently. They were unanimous in their agreement. The whole family made the firm decision … to leave the Catholic Church.

Chapter Two

It was to be several months before Sean and Kathleen would see some improvement in their daughter's health. She refused to have any medication from her doctor, choosing instead to attend counselling sessions. The counsellor didn't offer solutions. She listened intently without saying very much. Her presence gave Tess a feeling that this was a warm, caring person that she could trust. After several months of one-to-one sensitive sessions, she found she could gradually open up to her. Over time, her feelings of guilt and blame began to evaporate, as well as her sense of shame. She began to relax, eat and sleep better. Instead of sitting staring out of the window for hours, she begin to take an interest in the outside world. She started to take the dog for a walk to a nearby park. She had difficulty in talking through her problems with her parents, often she would be found talking to Tinker, a scruffy mutt of unknown origin. The dog gave her the comfort she needed. Tinker didn't criticise her, tell her to snap out of it, as neighbours and friends had done.

They of course were unaware of the *real* reason why she had left the convent. They had no idea of the true story. Slowly she began to improve. It took a year before her parents recognised the lively, chatty daughter, they once knew.

'Mammy, Maura has asked if I would like to go and stay with her for a while. I've been thinking. I feel well enough now to return to England.'

Kathleen was pleased that her daughter was able to make decisions. At forty one, she needed to move towards her independence again. Although she knew she wouldn't find it easy. The convent had stolen twenty three years out of her young life. The Irish looked upon England as the permissive society, a land full of hippies, mini-skirts and the contraceptive pill. It was all about love, sex and rock and roll. The era of the Beatles, with their screaming fans. The Animals with their *House of the Rising Sun* and Dusty Springfield singing about stealing kisses from the son of a preacher man. Although Tess had worked in the community previously, she had been cocooned from the reality, of what it was really like to live in the world. What would she make of it, going back to England without the protection of a nun's habit? It was to be a culture shock.

Kathleen hoped it didn't show how worried she was for her daughter. Both Sean and Kathleen were concerned as to how their daughter would cope. During her teenage years when she would have been going out with boys, that era had been forfeited for a cloistered life. No pin-ups of boys in *her* bedroom. No mirror to check *her* hair. Hers was a bare room in the convent. A simple cross, a bed, a hand basin and a chair.

Her first convent in England where she had been happy, sent her a letter. They noted with sadness her feeling of necessity to leave her religious calling. Enclosed was a sizeable cheque. This the letter explained, was in respect of her vow of poverty. It represented all her accumulated earnings, whilst working for the National Health Service.

'As a qualified nurse and midwife, I could get a little part-time job to start with.'

'Would ye not be thinking of getting a job here?' asked her mother.

'Not in our home town. Face all the people I once knew? No, there would be too many questions, too stressful. In England, I would not have to explain anything to anyone. They would only need to know my qualifications and where I trained.'

Letters winged back and forth to Maura, living in Essex. Tess held her ticket to freedom, a freedom she had little knowledge of. She had tasted a little, when working with the other nurses, but always her habit was prohibitive and would impede any light-hearted banter amongst the staff. They might have a joke or tale to tell about a doctor or patient. They did not feel comfortable in including a nun in their cosy little group. She felt as though she was peering through a window like a child, looking at a scene that she was not allowed to belong to. This time it would be different. She could put those cloistered years behind her. She would step confidently out into a world that she had shut herself off from, for all those years.

What she hadn't thought about, was how the world had changed during that time. How was she going to be able to adapt to modern life? There was a huge gap in her understanding of the sexual revolution. Her knowledge of men, love, romance and sex, was non-existent. She could only relate back to a teenage crush that she once had when she was fourteen. She would find that her naïveté would act like a magnet to attract men to her, something that she was not prepared for.

It was a delighted Tess that boarded the ship to England. Maura had arranged to meet her at Liverpool docks. Tess gazed out of the lounge window as the seas swelled on the high tide. The waves battered the windows, glasses slithered across the tables. The voyage was a roller-coaster journey; she was glad of the barley sugar her mother had slipped into her handbag in case of sea-sickness. Tess settled down to read the recruitment page in an Essex local paper that Maura had sent her. Was this really happening? She felt the need to pinch herself.

A smartly dressed man in his mid-forties sat down beside her.

'Going far?' She looked up to see a freckled face smiling at her.

'The other side of the world,' she grinned.

'And where might that be? China, Australia?'

She smiled. 'No. No, just coddin, back to England. Only at the moment it seems a million miles away from home.'

'I know the feeling. 'Tis nice to come home to Ireland, but sometimes 'tis good to get back to work.'

He held his hand out. 'I'm Brendan.'

She blushed at the formal introduction. 'I'm Teresa.'

His eyes alighted on the Nursing Recruitment page. ' You're a nurse?'

'Yes.'

'Been nursing long?'

She nodded and smiled. She noticed Brendan had taken some papers out of his briefcase, so she settled back to her recruitment page. One advert stood out. It was at an Essex hospital. It was something she was really interested in. They were sponsoring qualified nurse/midwives to train for health visiting. Three magazines and a bundle of documents later, the Captain made his announcement.

'Ladies and gentlemen we will shortly be arriving at Liverpool docks. Please make sure you have all your belongings with you, before we disembark.'

Brendan turned to her, 'Well here we are. If you're ever feeling in need of a bit of company with someone from the old country, get in touch.'

He reached into the inside pocket of his immaculate navy-blue suit and took out a business card.

'Good luck. Who knows, we could meet again?'

Taking the card, her face reddened. She felt its warmth.

'Thank you, I'll put it in my change purse.'

Maura was waving in the distance. They took a taxi to the railway station and after a quick cup of tea and a sandwich at the station café, made their way to the correct platform. Her sister chose what she thought to be a respectable compartment, with a lady reading a newspaper. Tess glared in disgust when she realised the woman was reading the *news of the world*. It was still in publication at this time; it was banned in Ireland. It didn't stop them finding their way across the border. Nor did it stop determined men crossing into Northern Ireland, not only for the 'scandalous' paper but to visit a barbers to get their regular supply of *something for the weekend*.

Maura's husband met them outside Southend Station. As Tess relaxed in the rear seat of his Ford Cortina, she glanced at Brendan's business card. His occupation was enough to give anyone a warm glow. Senior Sales Representative. Jameson Irish Whiskey Distillers.

Chapter Three

She stayed with Maura for a few weeks. On the day of the interview, she felt nervous as she approached the hospital and made her way to the Community Nursing Offices. Fortunately the convent had enclosed her nursing certificates. References, too, had been obtained from her Community and Midwifery Managers.

'We are very pleased with your references, Miss McCarthy. I see they refer to you as Sister. Were you a Midwifery Sister?'

'No, it was a religious title.'

The panel looks surprised. Tess's heart quickened. Maura's husband had briefed her what to say.

'May I ask why you decided to leave the religious life?'

'By not being subjected to the constraints of the religious life, I felt I could serve the community more effectively.'

She hoped it didn't sound too rehearsed. They seemed satisfied with her explanation. It was reasoned that if she was accepted for secondment, she had to serve at least two years as a qualified Health Visitor. If she wished, she could eventually become a triple worker in a rural area. District Nurse/Midwife/Health Visitor. That had little appeal, at the beck and call of everyone in the village. She could visualise going out on a delivery all night, then having to do her other visits during the day, with a baby clinic thrown in.

It hadn't occurred to her that there might only be one baby born per year in a village.

She was told she would have to make her own applications to the nearest universities. They pointed out one or two colleges known to be sympathetic to mature students. Following success in her university entrance examination and interview, she was accepted and able to start her studies in September.

Tess soon found the public often had a stereotype of how social workers and health visitors would look. Even social workers and health visitors themselves, had their own ideas of how each discipline would dress or appear. On the first day at college, they sat with social worker students and both disciplines were asked to describe the other. Both had stereotype visions. Social work students when asked to describe a health visitor, would often visualise her dressed in twinsets and pearls, tweed skirts and sturdy, laced-up shoes, the style of a woman seen on the front of a fifties issue of the *Women's Weekly* magazine. The health visitor students when describing a social worker, said hippy clothes and Jesus sandals; the men having beards, long hair and jeans. Afterwards, they had to stand up and face each other. They were surprised how wrong they were about each other.

Before the introduction of school nurses, Tess found she may have to go into schools, where she would bear the familiar nickname of *Nit Nurse*. Health visitors and school nurses were later able to instruct parents how *they* could deal with this problem and how to get the necessary treatment from their local chemist.

Once a week, Tess as a student health visitor went out into the community under the guidance of a senior health visitor. Once satisfied, she was allowed to spread her wings and do her own home visits. This took place in an area some distance from the college, not on her home patch. After she had sat her exams and qualified, she would be moved to her own area. Health visiting in the community, she was told, would be to care for all ages from the cradle to the grave. She soon found this was only possible in rural areas. Most of her visits were dominated by babies from ten days old, until they went to school.

Having received her NHS money from the convent, Tess was soon able to find a suitable flat.

'Haven't ye finished splashing out on fancy furniture and stuff yet? I think the delivery van must have a special parking permit for here. Every time I call something else is being unloaded. What is it this week? Saints preserve us 'tis only a pink chaise longue she's having delivered.'

'No doubt Maura, ye will be the first to stretch out on it.'

'That I will, in fact, I'll try it out for ye now. Ah ha, this is the life, Tess. Sure I'm only coddin, I'm pleased for ye really.'

Having been used to an austere and sparsely furnished accommodation for many years, Tess was determined to have all the comfort she could afford.

'It feels really strange to have my own place.'

'I thought ye would miss the company of the Sisters, after all those years.'

'In a way. But I'm beginning to appreciate my own company. It's as though the huge cloud that enveloped me, has gradually dissipated. I am able to think, eat, dress and say what I like. It's wonderful. I didn't think I would ever be interested in men, now I have several dates.'

Maura looked shocked. 'What do ye mean several dates?'

'I went to a party with one of the other students. Several men there asked for my phone number. In case they don't turn up I've made special arrangements.'

'What sort of special arrangements? Tess, for God's sake be careful.'

'First there is Joseph, then Roger and Trevor. Joseph, I've arranged to meet at half seven, outside Brown's the bakers shop. Roger, fifteen minutes later by the Town Hall. Trevor at eight, by the post office, near the cinema.

'I don't believe it, ye are playing games like a school kid.'

'I know…'tis fun. I had a date with Brendan the other day. Ye know the lad I met on the boat coming over. He gave me some whiskey samples. Not my type – a mammy's boy.'

Joseph turned up on time and drove her in his luxury Jaguar car.

'Lovely car Joseph. Really comfortable.'

'It's a poor man's Rolls Royce.'

She noticed him glancing in the mirror at his greasy hair. He smoothed it before driving off. Tess wasn't into *gussing herself up*, as her mother would call it, before going on a date. She had the minimum of make-up and wore in trepidation one of Maura's dresses. She thought it was too revealing. It had been too late to change. It showed rather too much cleavage for her liking, although it definitely appealed to Joseph's liking. He put his arm around her shoulder in the cinema. As soon as his hand began to stray, she sat upright, fumbled in her bag and brought out a bag of sticky toffees. It would take two hands to unravel the sticky papers.

By the end of the date, Joseph would have been unable to recall the deep blue colour of his date's eyes. His own had been downcast – or to be more explicit, cast down, in one direction all evening. As he drove her home she asked him,

'What do ye do for a living?'

He thought for a second before answering. 'I'm an engineer?'

To be able to run such a flashy expensive car, thought Tess, he would have had to have had a civil engineer's salary. Just as she thought, it transpired he was a car mechanic. The expensive car no doubt belonged to a client, which he had 'borrowed' in order to impress her. Tess was not impressed. Once home, his foot was swiftly placed in her door.

'Aren't you going to invite me in for coffee?'

She guessed this must be a requisite of the dating procedure, to provide coffee after an evening out. Following coffee and biscuits, Joseph seemed reluctant to leave.

'Tis midnight. Shouldn't ye be going home?'

'I'm quite comfortable here.'

'I thought ye had to be up early tomorrow?'

'It's all right, I've put an overnight bag in the car.'

'What! Oh no. Oh no. Away wid ye. I don't know what your game is, but ye are not staying here.'

Tess, grabbed his coat and threw it at him. He struggled to find the openings for his arms, in his now screwed up, black leather coat.

'So after paying for the cinema and the meal in the restaurant, that's all the thanks I get?'

'I am not ungrateful Joe…so I'll say it now. Thank ye very much – now go.'

One of the students laughed, when Tess related her evening.

'It was not at all funny.'

'I can see you need a few tips on men's body language and how to read what's going on in their mind. You have no idea how to handle men. You are so innocent any one would think you have come from a different planet. Are they all as naïve in Ireland?'

She had no intention of letting her know, where she had been for the last two decades.

'When I was younger, we used to warn each other said one of the students, if we found a lad with arms like an octopus. We used to tell all our friends if the boy belonged to the WHC.'

'What's that?'

'Wandering Hands Club.'

'Joseph was a founder member, an opportunist.'

'Do you come from a large family, Tess?'

'Oh, yes there are hundreds of us. Well no, not quite. Nine kids altogether. And ye?'

'Just my brother and me. Although I would love to have a big family. I've been married three years. We keep trying, but no luck so far. Did you never want to have children?'

'I never thought about it until recently. Not until I saw all those babies in the clinic. I picked up a little baby last week. He took my hand and smiled. I had the strangest feeling come over me. Then a knot in my stomach.'

'Ah ha, the old maternal instinct voiced a fellow student. The hormones must have gone into overdrive.'

The likelihood of having children now she thought, would be remote at her age. Besides she needed to find the right man. She hadn't met one yet. People kept saying that you know when it is Mr Right, when there is that spark of attraction between them. If she found her 'spark', they could adopt a child.

Then she remembered the social worker she'd met the previous week, who had turned down a lovely couple in their forties, for being too old to adopt. That left fostering. She didn't need a man for that. But how could she fit that in with health visiting? She smiled as she realised that in order to think like this, it must mean she had put the traumatic events of the past behind her. It was the end of a dreadful chapter. She had closed that chapter and started a new life – one that promised to be full of hope and excitement.

Chapter Four

The baby awoke to the feel of warm soapy suds enveloping her and screamed. After the initial shock, she started to gurgle and smile.

'Well me darlin', it looks as though I have done something right.'

'Like hell ye have, what a stupid thing to do.'

Although her sister Maura was angry, nevertheless she had responded swiftly to Tess's phone call to bring baby clothes, milk, bottles and anything else that she thought would be needed to care for an eighteen month old baby. Not that Jade looked her age. There were no dimpled cheeks on this skinny baby. After her bath, she sucked hungrily on the bottle that Maura had prepared.

'Sure I don't know what the hell ye were playin' at… Happy Families? Ye could be accused of kidnapping and find yerself behind bars.'

'Aren't ye getting carried away? Wasn't I after doing the mother and child a favour? Besides, they won't be finding out, I told ye, I'll be having her brought back on Monday.'

'What will ye do if she won't take the child back?'

'Course she will, she just didn't like taking advice. Or the fact I hadn't any children of me own. Who was I to give advice? What did I know? She'd been drinking. There was a man in her bedroom. She got angry. 'T'was on impulse.'

'Hope ye are right.'

Monday, Tess took the baby back, along with her raggedy old clothes that had now been washed and pressed. The new ones that had been bought for her were roughly ripped off, as soon as mother and baby disappeared through the open door. Lena would sell the new ones. This became the Monday morning routine for Lena and Tess.

'So, thank ye for looking after her then?' asked Maura.

'You're coddin, 'twas, 'ave 'er again on Friday and the door slammed.'

'Jesus, Mary and Joseph what are ye going to do? Tess, what about the risk?'

'Oh be shutting up Maura, don't ye t'ink I know that? Don't ye realise I'm sick to me stomach with worry. Can ye imagine how I was sweating, when Miss Brigham phoned me this morning and told me to report to her office tomorrow afternoon? Sure I was tishing meself. She wanted to discuss Lena and baby Jade from Basildon. What am I going to say?'

Maura tutted and shook her head disapprovingly. Maura had always been bossy. Not because of her age, it was because she towered over her diminutive sister. Shortly after arriving in England she got married to a Cork man. It was a family joke that she had to travel all that way, when shortly after she left home, a handsome, bachelor from County Cork moved in next-door.

'Miss McCarthy, I expect you know why I have called you to my office? Miss Brigham looked stern. 'I have some serious concerns regarding the care of baby Jade out at Basildon. In the past, I have asked several health visitors to look in on this family without success. They all say they were unable to gain access. That is, until Friday. Miss Anson, one of our health visitors was allowed in, only to discover that the baby was missing.'

Tess felt her lunch rise ~~up from her stomach.~~

'You have gone very pale, would you like a drink of water?'

'Er … yes please Miss Brigham.'

There came a tap on the door. The door opened and a uniformed head peered in. She felt faint… it was a police officer.

'Miss Brigham?'

'No, she's not here at the moment.'

'I'll wait outside then.'

Her heart pounded then fluttered uncontrollably. It felt like a trapped bird, anxious to get out of her rib cage. She wanted to make a run for it, but knew she had got to stand firm. It was no good. She was going to have to face facts and confess where the baby was. This would be the death knell to her qualifying as a health visitor and future job prospects. The General Nursing Council would strike her name off the register. That was the least that could happen. It was obvious why the police officer was there. He had come to caution and arrest her. How long would the courts give her for kidnapping? All these thoughts tormented her mind; they were interrupted when Miss Brigham brought in a tray of tea and biscuits along with a glass of water. Would this be the condemned prisoner's last meal?

'Help yourself to tea and biscuits, I have to speak with someone first.'

Tess took the glass of water. She felt sick with anxiety. Maura was right after all. She started to consider the possibility of spending a night in a police cell. Her hand grasped a few biscuits and placed them in her pocket, she might get hungry during the night. There was a muttered discussion going on outside, before Miss Brigham returned to her office.

'Now,' she fiddled with her owl-like glasses, tangled in her white peppered hair. 'I'm waiting for your comment about baby Jade?'

Tess shivered. It did not go unnoticed. Miss Brigham stood up and closed the window.

'Well, I'm waiting for an explanation as to why the baby wasn't there?'

'When…er… when I went to see her Miss Brigham. Lena was…was very, very angry. I thought she might harm the baby.'

'Yes, yes I know about that. According to Miss Anson, Lena told her, a friend had taken the baby. She was tired and her nerves were bad, she needed a break and so she gave the baby to a friend to look after. Is that right? Were you there when the baby was taken?'

'Yes that's quite right Miss Brigham.'

'Good. That's confirmed then. Now, I would like to know how you get on with this family. So many others have given up on her. Are you able to give her advice?'

'Oh yes. I have been able to give her advice.'

Don't ask me Miss Brigham, she thought, if she has ever taken any?

'Not an easy family by all accounts. I am pleased to learn that you are able to gain entry and interact with the family. Very good Miss McCarthy, I'll leave this family then in your capable hands. Well done.'

Before leaving the room, Tess could hear a cough and a shuffling of feet outside the door, indicative that the police officer still loomed large. She felt compelled to mention him.

'Miss Brigham, a police officer was looking for you earlier.'

'Yes, yes I saw him. I've spoken to him.'

She hesitated. Then decided to tell Tess the reason.

'A man was seen earlier rifling through staff lockers. Inspector Rainer has come to tell me that they have apprehended a man and arrested him. He is going to show me a photograph of the man, in case I've seen him before.'

Tess left the office feeling emotionally drained.

'So how did ye make out with the boss?' asked Maura.

'Quite well, my notes were acceptable, written up as before, omitting weekends of course. Not that I'd be visiting normally at weekends anyway. I'm lucky I'm still a student, and my fieldwork training is in a different area. If I'm seen with Jade, I'm not known as the health visitor for that area, so no one knows me. As soon as I am qualified, I will have to go back to Southend. Neighbours seeing me pushing a pram, would probably think I was a relative.'

'That's not what I asked. Did she know who'd taken the baby?'

'Fortunately Lena had told another health visitor that a 'friend' had taken the baby to give her a break.'

'So I s'pose ye're the friend?' There was no answer.

Every time she took the baby back home, a different man was sleeping there. Men were coming and going all the time. Most looked rough and were uncouth. Lena was not exactly purporting to run a high class brothel. Smart business types, or commercial travellers did not frequent this sex industry. Her clientele matched the home. Sordid, scruffy and smelly. Lena never hesitated in saying how she hated Jade. She had been in prison for theft, after her release she was raped by a friend of one of her punters and became pregnant. Then of course there were her regular male friends, any one of whom, could be the father. Not, that any one of them would have shown the slightest interest. Tess could believe that. One such individual was Ken. He spoke like a Romany, but was not a friendly individual. His lips curled in a permanent snarl, with an equally permanent roll up, poking out of his nicotinic stained beard.

'Can't you stop that bleedin' chavi screaming? I'll ring its bleedin' neck in a minute.'

She reached to lift the baby out of her cot. It was evident how he had retaliated and projected his anger on the baby. The room, already littered with discarded dirty nappies, scattered half-eaten food, was now smothered in a blanket of coloured fur and cotton wool stuffing. He had taken the knife attached to his belt and ripped up all her toys.

'Never mind darlin,' Tess whispered, Aunty will buy you a lovely big teddy.'

This time the soft toy would stay at *her* house and would not be returning home with the baby. It would be kept safe, ready for her to play with, in a home where she was loved.

Chapter Five

1950

Lena, could not conceive what it must be like to have a loving home. She had been placed in care of the local authority, following an angry attack on a pupil, with a wooden rule.

'What you in 'ere for?'

Lena did not reply to the girl's question. She sat on the bed, knees under her chin and started to rock to and fro.

'Leave her alone, she's only just come in,' called a voice from across the dormitory.

Later, one of the house mothers, took Lena to the bathroom for bathing and inspection for any injuries or head lice. She had both. Wheals, resembling an imprint of a wooden coat hanger, together with three-inch burns were clearly seen on her body. The house mother drew the injuries on a body map, and wrote her notes in the admission book. It had been late evening when the 'on call' social worker, made her decision for Lena to go 'into care.'

The children at Applefield Lodge were already in bed. Once bathed and in clean pyjamas, Lena was taken back to her bed in the girls' dormitory. A younger child missing home could be heard whimpering in the corner, with an older girl trying to comfort her.

'That little one has only just arrived today.' said the house mother. 'You will both soon find friends here.'

Friends? Lena didn't know what it was like to have a real friend, most had shunned her at school. Children refused to sit next to her on account of her filthy clothes and continuous head scratching. She was constantly bullied. Despite being unable to make friends, school was the only place where she found refuge. She hoped this too would be a safe place and that they wouldn't send her back in the morning. They won't find *me* crying to go home, she thought.

After the children had washed, dressed and made their beds, they filed into the sparsely furnished dining room. Some, having endured long periods of starvation, had voracious appetites, unable to appreciate that the food would no longer be snatched from them. Many of the children looked at life with empty eyes. Their body language and behaviour spoke a thousand words of their home life.

Like Lena, Jo was ten years old when she arrived at Applefield Lodge. Jo had difficulty at first to sit on a chair. She was not familiar with chairs, she had been found tied up on the floor of a shed. In comparison, the family's two Pekingese dogs, kept in the house, were beautifully groomed, cuddled and constantly pampered.

Because many of the children had been sexually abused and forced by their perpetrator to continuously tell lies, they found it difficult to distinguish when it was safe to tell the truth, even over the simplest facts. One of the house mothers noticed Eileen, tucking into her third breakfast that week, of baked beans on toast.

'I see you love your baked beans Eileen.'

'No, Miss, I hate them. This is the first time I've had them.'

On Saturday, Lena, pulled the sheet over herself and refused to get out of bed. Any attempt to forcibly remove her, gave vent to an hysterical outburst.

'For goodness sake Lena, come on, get out of bed, you haven't even been in the dining room for breakfast. The tables are cleared now. You must be hungry, shall I bring you some toast?' asked a staff member.

Lena shook her head. Lena refused to eat or speak. This continued throughout the day. At first it was thought she must be ill. The resident nurse sent for the doctor.

'She doesn't appear to be physically ill. No pyrexia – temperature's not raised – tonsils not enlarged. Have tried to check her for pain, hard to tell. She refuses to speak. I'll have a specimen of urine sister, when you can get one. The bed linen and pyjamas need changing too – she's wet the bed.'

Every Saturday it was the same. Yet the rest of the week Lena was fine, helping to lay tables, making her bed, and was generally happy and cheerful. At school, the only difference her teacher had observed, was on a Friday afternoon. Lena found it very difficult to concentrate and after school, she hung around outside the school gates. To the staff and doctor at Applefield Lodge, it was a mystery.

Shortly after Lena was taken into care, she had a visit from her father. Respectably dressed in his business in the city, pin stripe, he was laden with chocolate and sweets for his daughter. He briefly kissed her on the cheek, then left the confectionery on her bedside locker. In another paper bag was a pair of innocuous-looking heated curling tongs, together with a photograph of Minnie, her kitten, which he left on her pillow.

The house mother walked over to Lena. 'That was kind of your father to bring all those sweets. Fancy him remembering your curling tongs too and photo of your cat?' Lena did not reply.

Over many months, the doctor, nurse and psychologist tried to unravel the mystery. But Lena remained mute. The staff tried to reassure her that she could tell someone what was wrong and that she wouldn't be harmed.

One Friday, Rosie, the cleaner at the home, found Lena curled up crying in the broom cupboard. Rosie, not in any particular hurry, made her an orange drink and sat down beside her in her locker room, where they would not be disturbed. She put her arm around her in an attempt to comfort her.

'Come on darling, tell old Rosie what's upset you?'

Gradually between sobs, Lena blurted out her dreadful secret.

'It's Saturdays.' Followed by a long pause.

'What darling, what happens on a Saturday? You can tell me Lena, Rosie won't let anyone lay a finger on you, you know that.'

'Mum goes out with her boyfriend,' she sniffed. Rosie handed Lena a handkerchief.

'Dad's friends,' Lena started to shake, then blurted out, 'they all play poke.'

'What happens then?' asked Rosie, gently prompting her. Lena became hysterical. It took sometime before Rosie could calm Lena and enable her to continue.

'Okay, sweetie, calm down and tell Rosie what they do? They play cards do they? They play poker. They play cards and then they play poke. What do you mean?'

'Dad's friends all come in my bedroom.'

On Saturdays the father used his wife's long-standing affair, as an opportunity to invite his friends round for a poker evening. A game of poker wasn't the only activity on the agenda. Every Saturday it took the form of an identical routine.

'Dad's friend Tom,' sniffed Lena. 'Saturday's for whisky – poker – and a poke with Lena. When it's poke, I don't sleep.' She pointed, 'I hurt down there. Blood in my pyjamas too. I hurt all over,' she sobbed.

Each man in turn entered her bedroom and she was gang-raped, from the age of six years, until she was ten.

'I hate my Mum.'

'Don't say that darling.'

'But Rosie, why won't she stop dad? I tell her and she shouts, 'Liar' and hits me.'

'What with dear?'

'Coat hanger.'

Lena had only been taken into care when her mother couldn't handle her behaviour and her teacher reported she had lashed out at a child with a wooden object and damaged the child's eye. If bruising or burn marks were visible on Lena's body, she would be kept home from school. The curling tongs left on her pillow, had nothing to do with curling her hair. They were used as an implement of torture. They were used if she tried to refuse her father, or his friends' sexual demands, or threatened to tell someone their secret. He would heat them up on the gas ring and use them on Lena's back. For Lena his other reminder of the threat, that he left on her pillow, the photo of a cat, that was far worse. Her father's voice echoed with the photo.

'You dare breathe a word to anyone and I will drown that wretched cat of yours.'

Rosie was shocked at Lena's revelations.

'Rosie, would he really drown my cat Minnie?'

She couldn't answer, she felt a huge lump in her throat as she fought to hold back the tears. Lena started to cry again and whispered to Rosie, 'I really love Minnie. When she licks me and purrs, I think she's saying she loves me too.'

Chapter Six

1972

'Take your kid down casualty and the next thing you get is some bloody interfering old cow on your doorstep.'

Edna stood arms akimbo, outside her flat. Her spikey hair resembled grated carrots. She was defiant.

Having qualified as a health visitor, Tess found she was thrown into the deep end on her own patch. She wondered what had happened to, *I think all you girls are angels and I don't know what I'd do without you,* style of greeting that she was used to as a midwife? When she did her midwifery training, she was in holy orders. Having left the convent and eventually qualifying as a health visitor, she missed the buffer provided by her nun's habit. This was different territory. People could be hostile, rude, even violent. The caseload she had inherited, bore little resemblance to her clinic observations. Health visiting on her patch was going to be stressful. Her GPs, were new in their practice. It meant they had to build up their numbers, it made it difficult for them to raise any objection to a particular family that had signed on their list.

'Can I come in?'

'Huh, s'pose so.' Edna gave a quick glance at her watch. 'Not long, I've got business.'

Tess could see it would take more than a smile or a grin, to win over the confidence on this case load of families. The woman scowled. Her face at thirty, revealed a coarse, wrinkled skin, the legacy of a heavy smoker. She led the way up the narrow staircase to a flat over a betting shop, lit a cigarette and pointed to the little girl's bedroom.

'She's in there.'

The pretty fair-haired girl sat motionless on the bed. With one arm around a rag doll, the other encased in plaster of Paris. Tess checked the hospital notes. That day was Crystal's third birthday. Yet the room was devoid of any festivity. No sign of any wrapping paper or presents.

'Hello Crystal, how's yer arm?'

Her mother glowered – framed in the doorway – cigarette dangling from magenta lips.

'Does it still hurt?'

The child glanced up at her mother, searching her face for clues as to how to respond. Tess sat on the bed next to the thin, pale-faced child. The child's response in the negative, was barely audible. She clung to her doll for comfort.

'There you are, I told you she was alright. She's just clumsy.'

'I need to ask ye a few questions Edna.'

'What sort of questions? I haven't got all day.'

'How did Crystal break her arm?'

'Like I said, she fell down the stairs didn't she?'

'Did she?'

'You calling me a liar?'

'No, I'm just asking ye how it happened.'

'And I'm just telling you.'

They were interrupted by the shrill ring of the telephone. The woman grabbed it quickly.

'Yeah okay. I've got someone here, five minutes right?'

As Tess took down a few details, the phone rang again.

'Make it half an hour then. I'm busy. No, the woman from the clinic.' Then a muffled, 'No stupid, of course not.'

Minutes later they were startled by a shower of small pebbles hitting the window. Edna opened the window and leaned out. 'I told you when.' She added a coded message, that only made sense to her and her caller and closed the window. Tess gathered up her notes.

'I'll call back, when ye not so busy.'

As she made to leave, she noticed a tiny discarded plaster of Paris on the sideboard downstairs. Strung up in a teenager's bedroom smothered in signatures and cartoons, this would not have raised alarm bells. This seemed sinister. Was it used as a warning to Crystal? It was not difficult to imagine Edna's voice shrieking, *Shut up Crystal, or you'll get another one of these!*

Whilst building up their numbers, doctors in this position, would attract drug addicts, neurotics, alcoholics and families with children on the Child Protection Register. The families with such children were often 'on the move.' As soon as the situation started to hot up with searching questions from health visitors or social workers, they would often *do a moonlight*. She drove to the surgery, as she needed to notify the GP of her suspicion's regarding Crystal, and the course of action she intended taking. Several unruly drug addicts were sitting on the wall outside the surgery, or pacing the pavement anxious for the surgery to open, so as to get their prescriptions. As soon as the receptionist opened up, they intimidated the other patients waiting outside, shoving them out of the way as they rushed through the open door.

As a nun and community midwife, Tess often needed to call into a clinic to collect dressings. She observed the health visitors prancing up and down in their white coats, weighing babies, talking to mothers, or pen pushing in a comfortable office, whilst she and her colleagues were out in all weathers, day and night. They seemed to have the rough end of working with families in the community. Two incidents made her change her mind. One afternoon a community physician called in the clinic with an emergency. He had permission to take a nurse with him to inoculate several children against polio in the community. All the health visitors were out on visits or in clinics. He decided to take Tess.

As the doctor drove to the first house, he explained that some mothers had been very lax about polio immunisations. Because this disease had been practically eliminated in this country, they felt immunisation unnecessary. It took an unprecedented outbreak of poliomyelitis, to send the community into a panic. Tess soon observed the anxious, tear-stained faces of the mothers and felt the tension in each home. All this panic and anxiety what for? Tess could not understand how parents could refuse to have their child undergo such a simple procedure. She knew that vaccinations and immunisations couldn't be made compulsory, but realised that polio was only rare, because of the unstinting health promotion by health educators. It worried her when parents decided against immunisation for their child, not only for the risk of their child becoming infected, but that they left a child with reduced or no immunity, in constant danger. For the first time, she had witnessed the unseen value of health visitors and health education. This was just one disease where many lives had been saved, or a life time of disability avoided.

A few weeks later when she went into the clinic soaked to the skin, one of the health visitors had heard about her visits with the Community Physician, and approached her to ask if she had ever considered health visiting? She pointed out a simple example of the different practice between a community nurse and a health visitor.

She asked. 'What course of action would you rather do for your mothers for constipation? Advise them about a healthy diet, or call round and give an enema?'

Put so succinctly, she had to admit health visiting had a certain attraction. Further conversations with the health visitor left her feeling, yes, here was a profession that would appeal to her. However it was not one that that she could approach Reverend Mother with. An easier life of her own choosing, was not one that would meet with approval. Her nursing career had not been her own choice within the religious life. She soon discovered that any choice of her own would not be granted. A nun's life was one of obedience and needed to be dedicated to take a more difficult journey.

Once having left the convent, it then became possible with her nursing and midwifery qualifications for Tess to make her *own* decisions regarding her career. As a newly qualified, health visitor, she wondered what skills she could bring to this job. Filthy, cluttered homes. Homes where her feet stuck to the floor. No – that didn't faze her. To be faced with child cruelty, that was something unimaginable.

Back in the office, she found another file on Crystal, from a previous health authority. Only the year before, when Crystal was two years old, the mother had taken her to a different hospital with the same story of a broken arm. On that occasion the diagnosis was a spiral fracture. This type of fracture is induced by manual twisting of the arm in two different directions. Tess immediately rang the social worker.

'A tough morning Tess? Coffee?' whispered Lyn, a colleague. She returned with a steaming mug of coffee. She placed the mug on a coaster advertising a pharmaceutical product.

'Yes, I suppose it was a bit grim.'

'You can always ask me for any help, just give me a shout.'

'Thanks, I'm sure I'll be taking ye up on that.'

She was in no doubt she would be looking for advice. It was one thing being steeped in the theory of health visiting practice; quite another dealing with it.

'They always give that case load to a new person. Loads of kids on the Child Protection Register.'

'I guessed as much,' sighed Tess.

A hurried case conference was convened and Crystal was eventually taken into care. The mother did not admit injuring her child. With the evidence, it looked as though it could have been one of her clients. Crystal's behaviour and injuries did not appear to be an accident. Her blank unemotional expression. The stillness of her body. The searching of her mother's face. Watching her every movement. This phenomena was something the lecturer at Tess's college had pointed out. He had said that once seen, she would recognise it immediately as...frozen awareness. Tess could vouch this was true. What she had witnessed was a child frozen-detached and in despair. This ugly scene, would forever haunt her. A person, thought Tess, that cannot care about the life of an innocent child, cannot care about anyone.

Chapter Seven

'We don't treat our kids like you people do.'

'What do you mean?'

'Hurt 'em, burn 'em. Rom don't do that. I keep him quiet with sweets.' Drina pointed to a swarthy boy of about five years. 'I buys 'im one pound of sweets every day.'

His jaws crunched on a boiled sweet as a way of demonstration. Lyn wasn't sure if Drina meant a pound in sterling, or in weight. Judging by his khaki grin, the sweets had already left their mark. Drina wanted Lyn to give her a lift into town.

'You can stop 'ere.' They hopped out of the car to go in the courthouse.

'Will you be alright?'

'I have to pay some money,' she shouted back. 'If I come to the clinic later, can you 'elp me with something?'

'Yes of course, I'm in the baby clinic with Tess this afternoon, we'll see you there.'

The clinic was over, when Drina and her friend appeared. Staff were stacking chairs and putting away the tables. They hovered in the doorway. Lyn beckoned them over.

'Where are the children?'

'Grandmam has them. I need your help Miss.'

She took them into a separate room so that they could talk privately.

'How can I help you Drina?'

'I want you to find out how old I am?'

'When Drin went to 'orspital,' related her friend, 'the nurse called out *Mrs Cooper*. She read out some numbers and asked if it was her? Drin didn't know did she? She says, yes anyway. A woman called out that it was 'er name, 'er name was Cooper like Drin's. The woman was going to be cut open Miss. That could 'ave been Drina.'

'Hells bells! Drina, that could have been dangerous!'

'I know.'

'First you will need to give me some information, then I'll see what I can do.'

'She's legal Miss, she were born in the 'orspital.'

'Do you know which hospital?' Drina nodded.

Lyn was surprised. With their nomadic lifestyle, often forced eviction and with it, reduced access to health care, it was very unusual for Romany and Traveller babies to be born in hospital. She also knew that they had the highest rate of miscarriages, maternal and infant deaths. As a health worker, she was well aware, of a certain hostility and lack of trust of health professionals. This plus lack of ID or evidence of personal residence, made it virtually impossible for travelling families to register with a doctor or register the birth. Lyn had found that they were unable to claim any state benefits, as they do not possess a National Insurance Number or even open a bank account.

One traveller, she remembered, on seeing a house for sale, in a rural area that he liked, called on the owner and handed him a huge bag of money to purchase the property. The owner managed to persuade the man to go with him to the bank. At the bank the traveller tried to explain to the bank manager, that he had the money to buy the house. Upon which he promptly emptied the sack of money on the manager's desk. The manager and the owner eventually persuaded him to open a bank account. The owner took him to see a solicitor. After that the owner invited him back to the house to have a look around. He was surprised to learn that the man wasn't interested in seeing *inside* the house. His interest was in its location and huge garden. Sometime later, after he had moved in, he set up his stall outside the house, selling flowers and vegetables.

Drina's father happened to be a porter at the hospital at the time when his wife went into labour. Because he was an employee, she was admitted to the maternity ward. Lyn was hopeful that a birth certificate could be obtained for Drina. Drina's mother could remember someone coming to the ward, when she was there, writing down the names of the babies born there. This sounded as though the Registrar had been to the ward. Within a few weeks, they had a birth date for her. When Drina arrived in the office, Lyn and Tess were excited for her.

'You will be able to celebrate your birthday soon.'

'Yes it will be ye eighteenth birthday next month,' said Tess.

Drina was not excited, she looked puzzled. She was silent. Her brow furrowed. She shook her head in disbelief.

'What's wrong?' asked Lyn.

'I thought I was older than that.'

'It's grand. Ye're younger than ye thought.'

Drina shook her head. 'No. That means I were only thirteen when I had Dodo.'

'Phew, I suppose it does,' said Lyn. 'There isn't any point worrying about that now.'

Drina sauntered out of the office in a daze. She lived with her extended family on a recognised site. With close family support in her community, neither Drina nor Dodo, were any worse for her having had her first baby at thirteen years.

'She's gone. Taken the baby with her.' Noah, was distraught. They had four children, the baby was only six weeks old. The Roper family didn't seem to associate with other travelling families. They preferred to live in a caravan on farmland.

'Any idea where Ellie has gone?' asked Tess.

'Left two days ago with some gorja. She's gone off with him to some drug squat.'

'Where is it?'

'About twenty miles from here.'

'What do the police say?'

'Shadogs? (*police*) I'm not telling them about the children.'

Once Tess contacted the police, her phone never stopped ringing. It was either a police officer or a social worker wanting a description and details. Later that day the phone rang. It was the familiar cheerful voice of the police officer.

'I've found the baby. But not the mother.'

'That's grand. It was the baby that was the biggest worry.'

'Me too.'

'Where is the baby, I'll go and see it.'

'On your own? No you can't do that.'

'Why not?

'Even I wouldn't go there, not without a senior officer going with me.'

'Why?'

The police officer looked at his watch. 'I've got to go now, I'll ring you back.'

She busied herself catching up on her notes and reports. The telephone rang again.

'I've been to see the baby. He's fine and the other children are there. They are with the grandfather. He's feeding the baby with a bottle and the children are having something to eat, they look fine.'

'That's a relief. So ye managed to get someone to go with ye then?'

'No I went on my own.'

'I thought ye never went unaccompanied?'

'Oh I didn't go in.'

'What do ye mean, ye didn't go in? How do ye know the children are all right then?'

'I peeped through the window.'

'Ye peeped through the window! Saints preserve us,' she sighed. 'Ah well, s'pose tis better than nothing. In case I need to contact ye again what's yer name?'

'Sergeant Michael King, and yours?'

'Tess McCarthy.'

'Seriously Tess, I suppose I'd better explain. I wouldn't dare go in. I was the officer responsible for getting the grandfather sent down for seven years. He's not long got out.'

'What did he do?'

'He had a row with his son over drugs and the old boy went after him with a shotgun. He found him in the barn and shot him.'

'Killed him?'

'No, made a mess of him. Tess, don't ever upset a Roma, they've got long memories.'

'Is that so.'

'They will never forgive and forget. When I looked in the window, I could see he had the shot gun propped up against the wall inside the caravan. Believe me, if I'd gone in, I'd have ended up with more holes in me than a block of Swiss cheese.'

Two Romany children were awakened to the sound of heavy traffic. Cars and lorries tooted their horns. Unity was fetching water from a nearby hotel toilet. When she got back she was greeted by Local Council and Education Officers.

'Who are you? What are you doing in my trailer? What do you want?'

'I'm Mr Gardner, from the council and I want you to move your caravan. This is Miss Martin. Miss Martin would like to know why your children are not at school?'

'Mr Gardner, I'll move my trailer when you find me a house.'

'You can't stay here, you are parked on a public highway. What is more you are parked on a roundabout.'

'Find us somewhere to live and we'll move it.'

The council officer licked his pencil and wrote something on his clip board.

'I'll be back.'

After he had left, Miss Martin asked to see the children. They were cowering under blankets.

'Mrs Cox, it is against the law to keep your children away from school. Don't you want your children to learn to read and write?'

'Yes I do. When I 'ave running water and can wash my kids proper. 'ave clothes that I can dress them like you people, I'll send them to school. I'll not 'ave your kids calling 'em dirty or nasty names.'

Mr Gardner called back later that day. He had a sheaf of papers that he thumbed through.

'Right,' he sighed. 'Mrs Cox, if I allocate your family a council house, will you promise to move the caravan?'

'When I 'ave a key.'

'I'll warn you the house is in a bad state.'

'That's all right, my man will soon clean it and make it right.'

'It's a deal. You come with me and I'll show it to you.'

'I don't need to see it. I'll 'ave it thank you.'

'You will need to pay rent every week.' He mentioned how much it would be and Unity fumbled in her skirt pocket and gave him enough for a month.

'Lyn I've just been to see Unity. She's on my patch. Ye should see her house now it's spotless. Her man took up all the floor boards and cleaned them, then he went up in the loft and did the same. He's painted inside, it looks grand. Before it wasn't fit to keep a hog in it. They never complained they just got on with it. The children have started school. They came in looking smart in their school uniforms. Unity's having a problem with the younger one Mirella. Terrible thirst, quite apathetic. I got her to give me a specimen of her urine.'

'Diabetic?' asked Lyn.

'Looks that way. Sure we'll have one hell of a problem with that one, if she is. Neither parent can read or write.'

The following day the GP referred Mirella to the Children's Diabetic Clinic. When Tess went with Unity and Mirella to the clinic, it was confirmed that the child was indeed diabetic.

'I've got to think of something easy to help the family cope with a diabetic child.'

'How about a scrapbook?' said Lyn.

'Great idea, we could cut pictures out of a cookery book.'

'How about a cockerel crowing for morning,' suggested Lyn.

'And a bed for the evening.'

They both spent an enjoyable morning 'working' on a suitable scrap book. Dad soon learned to draw up the insulin from the vial, with a marker at the side of the syringe. He was instructed how to give insulin and the different sites he could use. As for Mirella, there was no holding her back. She was soon telling the dinner ladies what she could and couldn't eat.

Once the Diabetic Nurse was involved, Tess didn't have to visit so often. This particular morning when she called in, she was taken aback by Unity's request.

'You people know these things. We want to get married proper'. Now I'm in brick and got the kids off to school, I want to do what's right. My sister wants to as well. Her sister peered around the door. Tess called her in.

'We've been told 'aven't we Unity, that we can't get married in church,' she blushed.

'So we wants to get married in that office place.'

'Ye mean the Registry Office.'

'Yeah.'

'Why can't ye be married in church?'

'Cos none of us is christened. The church refused to do it.'

'Ye are probably right about the church, but don't worry, I'll tell ye what I'll do. I'll get ye some information. I'll come back and we can go through it together.'

Unity grinned, excited at the prospect. The two sisters had already discussed what they wanted to wear and had decided on a joint wedding. Although they were already 'married' when quite young, by Romany custom, this was not considered legally binding. A few weeks later, Tess was shown the wedding photos. A very different wedding to the norm. One wore a black suit with white accessories, the other a white suit with black accessories. They looked very smart.

Unity grinned, 'Now we are proper married, like you people.'

Tess smiled. The only marriage *she* had wasn't legally binding either. As a nun she was escorted down the aisle with her parents either side. She received a ring and became a Bride of Christ.

Chapter Eight

A few weeks later when leaving the flat of a teenage mother, Tess met up with Michael King, the police officer. He had received a tip-off, that the mother's boyfriend had been dealing drugs.

'Tess, did you notice anything when you went in?'

'There is something going on. She never opens her curtains and there is a peculiar smell in there. Michael, ye don't think she's buried someone under the floorboards?'

'You've been watching too many horror films Tess. What you can smell is probably cannabis. If it's as strong as you say, he could be growing it up in the loft.'

'Do ye need me to hold your hand to go in?' she teased. 'Only I know how nervous ye are when there are babies around.'

'Cheeky devil. I could arrest you for undermining a police officer in the course of his duty,' he smirked.

'You may be surprised to learn, that I know a lot about babies. As a single dad, I had to look after two of my own. They were quite young, when my wife left. Of course they are grown lads now. My mum helped out, but I've done my share. Adam, is nineteen and at university. Alex, is twenty-one on Thursday. He's supposed to be getting married next year. Do you have any kids?'

'Not exactly.'

'What does that mean?'

'I'm not married. But I have a little girl that I foster weekends and holidays. She's almost three and goes to nursery in the week.'

'Sounds as though you've got your hands full. Well, I'd better go in. If I'm going to find that corpse, I'll have to start taking up the floorboards,' he grinned.

Tess sat in the car and started to write up her notes. Michael turned back and tapped on the window. She wound it down.

'By the way, are you doing anything Thursday evening?'

'I don't think so, why?'

'I wondered if you might like to come to our small family get together, nothing big. My sister is bringing a cake. As I said, it's Alex's birthday, just a quiet evening. Saturday will be his own mad celebration – out with the lads.'

'Mm. I'll think about it.'

He scribbled his address and phone number on some notepaper and handed it to her.

'Thanks, I'll let ye know.'

Back at the office, she confided in Lyn.

'What do ye think?'

'I've met him a couple of times. He's a sergeant with the drug squad isn't he? He seems a decent enough guy.'

'Lyn, I'm in my forties. I've had a few casual dates, but usually after one date, I've lost interest.'

'Yes, I remember one of your dates. The one with that wine merchant,' she laughed.

'It wasn't funny, it could have been really embarrassing.'

'Oh Lyn, I'll not forget that night. He'd already bored everyone at the restaurant, especially the wine waiter. Constantly showing off his extensive 'vintner knowledge', as he kept calling it. I invited him back to my flat for a coffee.

All evening he pontificated on different wines, regions, their bouquet and so on, ad nauseum.'

'I am really a connoisseur of wines. These days, of course, I'll only drink the best.'

'The only thing that I knew about wine was its colour. I'd bought a bottle of white from the local off-licence. I was just coming into the sitting room with a tray, clinking two glasses and the wine, when he reached the point and heard him say…'

'The worst wine of all, is one from the Rhine district. It tastes absolutely disgusting, it's called Liebfraumilch.'

'I checked the bottle. Ye can guess what I read on the label. Did a swift about turn and emerged yawning from the kitchen. He took the hint and left.'

'It's not the first time Michael has asked me out.'

'Goodness, you kept quiet about that. Now's your chance then.'

It wasn't the only thing she had kept quiet about. Only the boss knew about her former life. She had told her boss, that after twenty years, she had come to realise she wanted her freedom. The real reason was only known to her immediate family. She was very apprehensive. How would she cope? Michael seemed serious. Could she do a *strong line*, with him, as they used to say in Ireland. By what she had seen and heard, couples didn't go courting any more. One man asked her, 'What planet have you come from? Courting? Nah, that's old-fashioned. Today it's, *Hi yer honey – and hop into bed.*'

She didn't think Michael was like that. He had invited her to his house to meet his son. His sister would be there too. Hardly a situation for anything improper to take place… or was it? That evening Tess rang Michael. He wasn't in, she left a message with Alex, his son, that she would like to come on Thursday.

Her hand shook as she rang the bell. In the background she could hear his young nephews, squealing and laughing. Michael greeted her at the door. He looked different out of uniform, younger, more handsome. She hadn't noticed his bright, emerald eyes before, or his curly, auburn hair hidden under his hat.

'Come in, come in. Love the dress. Wow! Tess, you scrub up well, you look lovely.'

Earlier Lyn had come round to the flat to 'sort her out.' She had with her an above the knee, pretty blue dress that she had promised to loan her. She curled her hair with some tongs. Once the hair was styled, she set about giving her a make-over. Tess had never worn mascara, or high heels before. It was quite a transformation. She needn't have worried about going to Michael's place, the family made her feel very welcome and at ease. She got on well with Alex. Adam, his younger son, couldn't make it until the weekend. She met Michael's sister and her two boisterous boys of six and eight.

Michael was intrigued by Tess. He found himself observing her more closely. Apart from her gleaming russet-brown hair and hypnotic navy-blue eyes, he couldn't put his finger on it, but there seemed to be a huge chunk of general day-to-day knowledge missing. Major world events, seemed to have passed her by. Yet she could be very independent and capable of doing jobs that some men might have had trouble with. One day he saw her outside the clinic. The bonnet of her car up with Tess tinkering underneath. A sudden roar from the engine and job done. Another time she told him she was thinking of converting the cellar into a utility room. The walls needed plastering and the uneven floor, needed cementing over.

'I know a guy who could do that for you?' he suggested.

'I was thinking of going to buy the cement and the other stuff, and sort it out myself.'

He was lost for words. Left pondering, what sort of girl was this? She was unique. Where had she acquired her mechanical and DIY skills from? Other times she was so naïve, especially about relationships. The detective in him was curious about her lack of everyday knowledge. He felt she was holding something back. Even ex-cons he thought, just out of prison, were more clued up than she was. How could such an attractive girl remain unmarried? Was she a widow or divorced like himself? Michael's wife had taken off, for a younger model several years ago and were divorced three years later. Fortunately his sister and their mother were able to help out.

Despite Tess's sense of humour, he noticed some of it was a front. She seemed uncomfortable in the company of men. He remembered the words of a famous statesman that seemed to sum her up …a riddle wrapped in a mystery, inside an enigma.

He was very attracted to her but needed to find the key. She lived within walking distance. He wasted no time, when she was ready to go home that evening, to accompany her.

'I can't believe an attractive woman like you, hasn't been snapped up by one of those young doctors when you trained at the hospital in London?'

'Ye must be joking. No one would give me a second glance. Nor would it have entered my head to encourage any man to take an interest in me. Michael, it was totally different then. I was not in a position to even think such things.'

'Why not?'

'Why not?' Tess held her breath. She knew that one day she would have to reveal her past. She liked Michael, she had enjoyed the evening. She realised she would be happy if he decided to ask her out. If so, she knew she was going to have to be honest with him. At least, gradually reveal part of the truth about her past.

'I trained to be a qualified nurse and midwife then worked in the community. But I was not the same as the others.'

'In what way?' persisted Michael.

She paused then blurted out, 'I had taken holy orders Michael, I was a nun. My home was with the other sisters, in the convent.'

'I *knew* there was something different about you. I couldn't put my finger on it.'

Wow, he thought, that explains so many unanswered questions.

'So you were really one of the untouchables.'

'Something like that.'

Tess knew what the next question would be. She was not prepared to answer it. Not now, so she quickly asked him a question.

'What about ye? Did ye always want to be in the police force?'

'My dad was in the force. I admired him and I decided to follow in his footsteps. At first I thought it might prove difficult. Then he got moved to the Met, that made it easier. At first like most bobbies, I was pounding the beat. I have to say, I miss the beat.'

Outside her flat, his arms encircled her and they kissed.

'Thank you for coming tonight Tess, do you think you could brave it again with me next week? I'm off on Monday, we could go out for a meal somewhere?'

Tess found it difficult to answer him, not because she didn't want to. Her heart was beating so fast she had difficulty in breathing. Is this what happens, she thought, when you find that *spark* I hear people talk about?

'Is that a nod of agreement, or a no thank you?'

'I'd love to,' she whispered.

'Great. I'll pick you up at seven. He chanced his luck and gave her a long, lingering kiss, before walking home, light of step, despite his size twelve shoes.

Tonight, it was his heart that pounded, and missed the beat. He was convinced that there was a definite chemistry between them. Common sense told him, he would need to tread very carefully with Tess.

Chapter Nine

'Tess, can you believe it? I've just come from the Patel's, it's been crazy. Two brothers married two sisters. For the time being they are all living in the same house. One of the brother's is waiting for a mortgage. As you know, the boys take the father's surname, the girls the mother's. Recently they were persuaded to *all* take the father's name. So now I have *all* these children for development checks, *all* in one house, *all* with the same surname Patel!'

Tess started to laugh. 'Why not colour code each family? Take a couple of different coloured pens. Ask the mothers to line up their children either side of the room from youngest to oldest and colour code their files.'

'Brilliant, why didn't I think of that? Are you still thinking of learning Urdu Tess?'

'Yes. I definitely don't want another drama, such as we had in clinic the other day.'

'It was madness. Fancy the mother thinking it would be twice as good for her child to have her immunisation at the GP surgery in morning, then turn up again and let her have it again in the afternoon at our clinic.'

'Look at the panic it caused,' said Tess. 'That little girl was very lucky. It's so difficult when the mother cannot speak English, that's why I am starting lessons tonight at an Asian lady's home.'

'What happened to the Urdu evening class at the college?'

'I did go for a while. I had to learn how to write various phrases from right to left. It was disastrous. I put the dot in the wrong place and found I could be swearing at someone. As soon as the tutor mentioned a linguists exam, I took off. I just want conversational Urdu. Our interpreter, is lovely, but every conversation takes twice as long.'

'Not the one I had Tess, with Mrs Kaur. Her conversation with the interpreter was far too short. Afterwards I asked her, did you ask about contraception? She threw up her hands in horror. 'Certainly not. Not in front of the mother-in-law.'

The Urdu lesson was strict and took place in the lady's front room. She made it clear from the start that English was not to be spoken until the end. Then they could ask questions. She started with a box of vegetables and fruit. Naming them. The 'students' wrote them down phonetically. Then they had all the various greetings. Whether in Urdu or if the person was Sikh or a Hindu, they were taught the correct way to greet them.

They followed the lady into the kitchen to make some pakora. All the spoons of flour had to be measured and counted out aloud in Urdu. At the end of the lessons they were able to eat the pakora and ask relevant questions according to their various professions.

'It's a great way to learn a language Lyn, using food. Of course we all had our questions ready at the end. I wanted, *have ye had your injection*? A librarian asked for *put that book down*. For the teacher, it was, *sit down and be quiet*. The last one was a probation officer who wanted to know how to say, *you are a liar*.

The teacher shook her head, she was adamant, 'No, no you cannot say that.'

The probation officer explained that when she went to see her client in prison, she needed him to know he lied in court. She didn't get the phrase she wanted. She got something similar to, stranger to the truth.'

After attending for six months, she managed some of her visits without the interpreter.

'I'm thinking of buying one of those colourful, heavy, Indian duvets, Lyn. There's an Indian shop I've seen that sells all sorts. I am going to try out my Urdu.'

After rehearsing her lines, she ventured in the shop. There were several women there, not buying anything, just chatting to each other; a women's social get-together. When she walked in all heads were turned, conversation halted, the shop fell silent. She plucked up courage and asked in Urdu, 'Do you sell Razzia's?'

'Explain more,' indicated the young girl behind the counter. The shop remained silent. All were waiting to hear the reply.

'I don't want a double I want a single.'

Hardly had the words left her mouth, than the women started to giggle. If she had learned nothing else working with Asian women, she'd learned that they were great gigglers. The proprietor tried unsuccessfully to stifle her amusement but soon began giggling with the other women. It was infectious and Tess found herself laughing, but with no idea what she was supposed to be laughing at. It took a while for the laughter to simmer down and for the owner to try again with,

'Explain more.'

She began haltingly, 'I understand Indian men wrap themselves up in them at night.'

With that, the whole shop rocked with laughter. One of the women was practically hysterical. Granny who was supposed to be dressing the window, fell against the interior of the glass shop front, rocking with laughter. The young woman went out into the back room to bring in her husband to enjoy the joke and listen to this absurd Irish joker. By now people had tears running down their faces, holding their bellies and shrieking with laughter. Tess was still unaware as to what had caused all the hilarity. She was unable to stop laughing too. In the end once everyone had exhausted themselves, she remembered that one of the interpreters had written the word Razzia on a piece of paper. Having fished it out of her bag and handed it over the counter. Once again the young girl started to laugh. This time out loud. She circulated the paper around the shop to the women that were gathered. Just when no one thought that they could laugh any more they roared again. It took several minutes for everyone to recover. The manager explained that the word had been pronounced incorrectly. It was supposed to rhyme with desire.

'I thought you were trying to say that you wanted a brassiere. A single one and one that men wrap themselves up in at night.'

It was to be a long time before anyone in that shop would forget the incident. Tess only had to wander past, for the owners to grin and beckon her in, to join them for a cup of tea.

After that experience, she became more careful when using Urdu in the community. As with trying out any new language, new students hope that the person is going to reply with a stock answer. Such as, 'Yes thank you, baby slept very well, thank you.'

No… that was not how it worked.

Hearing a few words of their mother tongue, the mother would be delighted. She would expect the person to be fluent in Urdu and would reply in her native language such as,

'I've had a terrible night – the baby wouldn't stop screaming – he wouldn't take his feed – he was sick all over me!'

After the words terrible night, the rest of the reply to Tess, would be a mystery. All she could do was nod in agreement. She persevered in readiness for another client. There was a note on her file, in bold letters:- NO ENGLISH except seven-year-old son.

She sat outside in the car, studying her translation book. The young boy would be at school. It was important that the message was delivered correctly. Contrary to the usual advice, the mother had to *stop* breast feeding, as the doctor had prescribed steroid treatment. Tess had got to be word perfect. Twenty minutes later having gone over and over what she needed to say, she rang the bell. To her astonishment a smart, grey-suited gentleman opened the door. He spoke in impeccable public school English.

'Good afternoon. You must be the Health Visitor. Do come in.'

Back in clinic, on weighing an Iranian mother's six-month-old baby, Tess could see the baby was grossly overweight. Not wishing to discuss this in front of the other mothers, she decided to see the baby at home later that week.

'I'll call round about lunch-time.'

The mother greeted her warmly and showed her into the dining room, where a long low table was laden with a colourful buffet.

'I'm sorry were ye expecting some guests?'

'No, no… this is all for you. You mentioned you would come at lunch-time.'

What could she say? She had meant midday. The mother insisted she ate as much she could. How was it going to be possible to discuss the baby's weight now? She had planned on discussing nutrition. All the time there was constant prompting and insistence for her to eat more and more food. To refuse, she knew, would cause offence. Yet not one morsel touched the lips of the mother. How could she approach the subject of healthy eating; when she was about to waddle out of the front door, having stuffed herself with enough food to last the week!

Chapter Ten

When she first met him, he was in a drug- crazed stupor. It was hard to see what Alison, an intelligent mother, could see in him.

'Honestly Tess, when I first met him he was such a lovely guy.'

She was determined to find that same individual again, so much so, that she decided to lock him in the bedroom for three weeks to go 'cold turkey.' There was a lot of banging and shouting, but he eventually emerged to be the man she once knew. She was right…a lovely guy.

It didn't last long, before he was 'shooting up' again in the bathroom, until there were more blood blobs on the walls than stars on the American flag.

One morning the police raided the place. One arrogant police officer, grabbed Alison's arms searching for needle marks.

'What drugs do you take?'

'I don't. I've got more sense with a two year old child to look after.'

'How do you get your money then, on your back?' he shouted.

'How dare you! How dare you! I demand to have your number. I'll report you for that.'

Later the police officer, was suspended for his rude behaviour.

Alison stood out as an usual type of girl. Not one to normally get involved in a sordid sort of drug scene. Tess enquired about her parents.

'My father, is headmaster of a well-known public school. He threw me out when he found out I was pregnant. No daughter of his was going to live in his house and have a baby out of wedlock.'

Alison, had three A levels and wanted to be a dentist. As long as she could remember they had always lived in a school house; it went with the job. When she was thrown out, she had nowhere to go. She didn't know anyone in the area. After a short period in a mother and baby home, once she had the baby, the council gave her a flat. She was shocked to find that most of the other residents in the block were drug addicts.

When Tess called on Alison later that week, she took her some baby food samples and nappies. She made it a principle not to give anyone money.

'How ye getting on?'

'Not good. I was in court last Monday.'

'What for?'

'I found a benefits book, they say I stole it. It's not true. But I did try to use it. I got caught. No previous, so I got probation for eighteen months.'

In a way it was a stroke of good luck; the probation officer could see that Alison had potential. She managed to get her a new flat in a different area and her son was placed in a day nursery. She was taken to museums, theatres and encouraged to apply to get into university. It was a pity that Alison had to commit a crime, to get the help she needed, to enable her to turn her life around.

Other families such as and John and Carol, both of whom were involved with drugs, would not be so lucky.

The couple were both heroin addicts, although as soon as Carol realised she was having a baby, she took advantage of a Drug Rehabilitation Centre offered to her. She tried to persuade John to do the same, but he was convinced he could come off drugs without help.

'I can do it this time Carol.'

'I'm desperate to do it John, for the sake of our baby.'

'Don't worry. You'll see when you come back from rehab, I'll be clean too.'

Everyone was delighted that Carol, with help and plenty of support, was off drugs before the birth of the baby. John once again had tried and failed.

On the tenth day after the birth, Tess did a new birth visit. Carol looked really well.

'I can breast feed him. He feeds well, he's a hungry baby.'

'He's a fit baby too. Something he would not have been if ye hadn't come off heroin. Every time ye wanted a fix, he would have been addicted too and would have been screaming and restless. I am pleased with ye Carol. Ye have done so well. Yer baby is a good weight too. Ye didn't allow yer baby to suffer, on account of yer own problems.'

'John is terribly depressed. He wanted to be a good role model for his son. He's talking about leaving us. He keeps saying Social Services will take the baby when they find out his father is a smack-freak.'

John, with eyes glazed, shuffled into the room.

'Don't ye ever consider the risk to yerself John?' asked Tess.

'Not when I am so desperate for a fix, the danger and risk doesn't seem there. It drives me crazy when I can't get a vein and I'm in pain. After I've had a fix, I feel I can do anything. My mate says after his, he feels touched by God.'

'Look at yer son John. He's adorable isn't he? If ye want to come off, ye need to distance yerself from other drug users.'

Tess noticed he couldn't seem to get comfortable sitting in the chair. He fidgeted and soon left the room.

Three weeks later, Tess received a phone call to say that John had tried to hang himself. His brother had called, found him suspended by a rope from a hook in the loft. He grabbed a knife from the kitchen and cut him down. He still had a pulse with shallow breathing. He rang for an ambulance. Six weeks later, he was discharged from hospital. John had sustained a slight weakness down one side. But the best news was, he was off drugs. Carol was delighted. He was a different man. Eventually he was well enough to get a job and they both settled down to family life.

One night when he was coming off a late shift, he took a short cut down a narrow side road. Almost immediately, he was set upon by a gang of drug addicts. One pinned him down and another injected him with heroin.

A few months later, there were two calls for Tess. One call was from Carol, the other caller left a number for her to ring, but didn't leave a name. Carol broke the tragic news. John had deliberately overdosed and this time had killed himself. Listening to the heart-breaking news, she promised she would call round on her way home. In the morning she rang the unknown caller and was delighted to recognise the voice.

'Hello, it's Alison.'

'Where are ye?'

'I've moved again, I'd like you to come and see me. I'll tell you all about it.'

She sounded so different, really cheerful. She was living in Great Wakering a small village four miles from Southend.

Later that week she called in.

'My, what a lovely little cottage. It's semi-rural here.'

'Yes, guess what?... it's all mine. My uncle hadn't any children. He died. Left it to me.'

No wonder she was so pleased, her life had changed completely.

'Are ye still at university?'

'Yes, I love it. I am able to take Paul to the crèche there too.'

'Have ye found yerself a man? Tess put down her cup of tea on a small table, stood up to get a closer look at the photo of a handsome-looking man on the mantelpiece.

'Yes,' she grinned. That's Julian, we met at university.'

'What about yer father, did ye ever get in touch?'

'No, and I never shall. Not when I think of what he put me through. Although I have secretly been seeing my mother. My father has retired from education. They had to move out of the school house. They bought a house in Hampstead. According to my mother, my father now gives private tuition. I usually see my mother once a month. We started to meet in a coffee shop in town. Since I moved into the cottage, she has been coming here.'

'I am so pleased for ye Alison. Ye deserved to have some luck.'

'I thought you would like to see Tess, that we don't all end up on the scrap-heap.'

Alison was one of the lucky ones, able with help, to free herself from living with drug peddlers. At one time Tess, could never have imagined how Alison's life could change so dramatically. Very few of her clients, involved in the drug scene, had such a happy ending.

Chapter Eleven

As she drove home, Tess began to think how lucky *she* was. Meeting Michael was a turning point in *her* life. She had come to realise, just how deep her love was for him. That evening he had brought her to a hotel restaurant, where earlier he had booked a table. She looked around at the hotel's elegant setting, the dining room with its silver service, overlooking the sea. Her mind went back to her life in her first convent, with its simple life style. She mused how all this would be looked upon as the height of extravagance. After the meal, the waiter came to the table carrying a pink cake, on which was placed a red rose. At first it looked like a normal rose. Then in the candlelight she saw it sparkle. Before she could say anything, Michael had taken the flower off the cake and dropped to his knees in front of Tess and a restaurant full of diners. Being Valentine's Day, the majority of the couples in the dining room, were not quite so surprised as Tess. She stared at him in amazement.

'Teresa McCarthy, will you do me the great honour of becoming my wife?'

Tess stuttered and tried to speak in front of the now silent room. All patiently waited for her answer. Michael held his breath. They heard Michael say,

'Tess, please. Please say something.'

'Er um …yes… yes I will … I will.'

A loud cheer went up. People clapped. A pianist began to play the Wedding March and the wine waiter brought over a bottle of Moët & Chardon. Michael sighed, he was sweating,

'My goodness Tess you had me worried there for a minute.'

He removed the ruby and diamond daisy ring, from a special stem on the rose and placed it on her finger. At which Tess burst into tears.

'I hope they are tears of happiness and not of regret.' She shook her head and smiled broadly.

That evening, he told her that there was a Home Office house available for a married couple. After they were married they could move into a three bedroomed police house.

Later, he asked her,

'Now as my fiancée can you tell me why you left the convent?'

'Yes, darlin', but wait until we get back to my flat or it would spoil this moment.'

She had never dreamed she would get married. Couldn't believe Michael would propose to her. And on bended knee too. Back at the flat she reflected on the events that led to her leaving the convent. Michael sat quietly holding her hand, as she slowly revealed her story. And at what had forced her to leave holy orders.

Tess told Michael the whole story. In a low voice she explained how she had left home at seventeen to become a nun... By the time she had finished she was in floods of tears.

Michael was trying hard to hold back his. He threw his arms around her and held her tight.

'My darling I had no idea what you had been through. I had always thought yours had been a life a peace and tranquillity. It hasn't been easy for you to reveal all that to me. Darling, you've been through hell. Tess, to come out of that violent trauma, as you have done and start life afresh, as though nothing had happened, I think you are a very strong and courageous person. You're wonderful.'

'I love you so much Michael. I never thought I would ever get married. It seems a miracle.'

'My God, I love you Tess. You will never know how much.'

He took her in his arms and tenderly kissed her. To break the tension that Michael knew they both felt after Tess's horrific disclosure, he started to describe the house and suggested that they went to see it as soon as possible.

'Tess please don't tell me you want a long engagement.'

'No I'm happy to get married any time – any day – I'll be there.'

1974

Michael and Tess were married with a minimum of fuss in a Registry Office, with just two witnesses and little Jade as bridesmaid. Alex couldn't get away from his job in Scotland at short notice and Adam, they were unsuccessful in trying to trace him. Lena gave permission to take Jade with them for two weeks holiday in Spain. Once Jade was back at school, she soon came skipping out waving her drawing.

'Aunty, Aunty look.'

'Why that's beautiful. Did ye draw that seaside picture all by yerself?'

'Yes, my teacher didn't help me. She liked it.'

Dressed again in a dirty torn blue jumper and filthy leggings, she ran up the garden path to Tess and Michael's new house, she started to remove her jumper. She was used to the routine. She would remove all her clothes put them in the washing machine whilst 'Aunty' ran the bubble bath. She splashed joyfully playing with a wind-up fish that was skimming around the edge. Lifted out of the bath, wrapped in a warm towel, was how every weekend began. Clean clothes on, something to eat, then off to the local park. Once a skinny, malnourished, young child; now at five years she was beginning to thrive. She loved staying with Tess.

Nothing had changed back home with her mother. Jade was scared of all the men her mother had at the house. Jock most of all. If she didn't move out the way quick enough, she felt the side of his hand on the back of her neck. He never seemed to miss an opportunity to shout or hit her. Staying with 'Aunty' was a taste of heaven. This must be what other children had every day, she thought. Plenty of food, clean clothes and best of all someone who really loved them. She could not remember her own mother ever giving her a hug or a kiss. Yet she constantly saw her give plenty of hugs and kisses to all the horrible men of hers, before they went into her room.

Michael had become fond of Jade. Initially she had been very wary of him, not having ever experienced any kindness from men. Now she was happy for him to pick her up from school, carry her out of the car on his shoulders or take her to the park.

'I'm off this Saturday, why don't we pack a picnic and take Jade to Whipsnade Zoo?'

'How far is that?'

'Mm, about fifty odd miles, not far.'

They wanted to give her fun and freedom at the weekends, so that she had happy memories of their time spent together, as a contrast from her unhappy, neglected life during the week.

'Have ye heard from you son Adam recently?'

'Not since he and his girlfriend Melody, graduated and got their teaching posts. No it's all gone quiet. Alex was the same, the boys only contact me when they want something. Same with his wedding. Who was the last one to know the date Alex was getting married?'

After Jade was in bed and Michael had read her an animal story, he came downstairs and flopped down on the sofa beside Tess and cuddled up.

'I've been thinking, why don't we try to adopt her?'

'Could we?'

'Don't see why not. Especially as we have plenty of room. Lena doesn't really want her does she. She's always saying how she dislikes her?'

'That's true.'

'Jade and Lena's feelings seem to be mutual.'

'All right, let's try.'

'Lena didn't seem to mind when we took away for that fortnight did she?'

'I'll approach her about it on Monday. Are you sure you would be happy about adoption Michael? We're not exactly young parents are we? We are both in our forties.'

'We're coping. She's no trouble. I think she's a lovely kid. Nearly as lovely as her Aunty.'

'Ah away wid ye.'

He gave her a quick squeeze and kissed her. 'Forties? What do you mean darling? We are still kids. That means we should be in bed early, shouldn't we?' He gave her a knowing look. They cuddled up again on the sofa, hugged and kissed. Michael was powerfully built and towered over her. He lifted her up easily, like a baby and carried her giggling to the bedroom.

Tess spoke to Lena on the Monday. To her surprise and delight, she agreed.

'Keep her. I don't want her. She's nothing but trouble.'

She couldn't wait to get home and tell Michael. She wasn't allowed to ring him when he was on duty, in case something urgent was trying to get through. However he couldn't wait until *he* got home and in his break, rang Tess.

'Yes, yes, it's agreed.'

'Wow! fantastic. I'll be home early.'

Lyn put her pen down and looked up. 'You sound excited about something.'

'Oh it's just something we were hoping to get for the home.'

'What is it?'

'Must rush, I've got the baby clinic.'

All this time, the child had remained her secret, known only to her sister and her husband. She knew that Lyn would want to know all the grisly details. As the child didn't live in the area, or on her on patch, it was unlikely now, that any official seeing her with a young school child to be concerned, especially as she was married. When the child needed any medical help, Tess had to find an excuse to take off and take her to the GP that the child was registered with.

Michael hadn't cottoned on that she had been dicing with her career. To him it was no different to unpaid private fostering. Same as any other health visitor that had a child to get to school before starting work. Except that Tess had deliberately kept Jade, all this time, without notifying the authorities. Unlike a hospital nurse or district nurse, health visitors' hours were suitable to work around the care of a school-age child, as she only worked weekdays nine-to-five. It was difficult sometimes during the week to get her to go back home. This wasn't difficult to understand why.

Lena's lived in squalor. Filthy washing piled up in the bath. Ashtrays spilled over. Empty cans and bottles, used condoms, together with rotting food littered the floor. With Lena and most of the men in the house, worse for drink or high on drugs. Jade was intimidated by the sort of men that Lena had at her flat.

One day when she went to fetch Jade, she found the door ajar. She called out, but there was no reply. Thinking that Lena had walked out and left the child, she slipped in her bedroom and took Jade's hand. She was about to walk out, when she saw Lena through a gap in the door, cowering in the corner with two gunmen hovering over her. Drug dealers were demanding money owed. Tess crept into the kitchen with the child clinging to her. The men left after shouting a warning that if she didn't pay up they would torch the house. Once she was sure the men had gone, she found Lena in shock and shaking in the bathroom. She had cut her wrists. Tess quickly bandaged them up and sent for an ambulance.

'Don't worry about Jade. I'll look after her.'

She had hoped she could keep her for an extra few days, but Lena was discharged home the same day.

'Darlin' it would be grand if we could adopt her. To think that she wouldn't have to go back to that dreadful place would be wonderful.'

Chapter Twelve

It was not the first time Tess had been to the caravan site. Initially it had been set up as a holiday site; now it was like one large squat for drop-outs. Straining, snarling, salivating dogs tethered by their chains, frightened visitors if they entered the site, too near the vicious canines. The first time Tess went on the site, she misjudged the length of the chains and had to run for her life. The caravan site was a magnet for drug addicts, alcoholics and a variety of misfits in society.

One such misfit was Babs, a twenty-plus stone mother of five. Her children were from five months to ten years, with not a dry nose between them. All from different fathers, crammed into one stinking doss van. As she entered, Babs greeted her warmly, giving her a hug. Babs wasn't the only one excited at her visit. The whippet showed his excitement by peeing on the draining board.

'Where can I put the weighing machine Babs?'

Usually mothers would clear a small portion of the table. She had done this, but a dead rabbit had been strung up from the ceiling of the van and was dripping blood all over the table. She unhooked the rabbit and put it on the draining board, to marinate in the dog's urine. She grabbed the communal face cloth, with its indeterminable colour and gave the table a quick wipe and aimed that too onto the draining board.

'Shouldn't Wayne be at school?'

'Nah, 'e can't go to school. Not with 'is guts.'

'What's wrong with him?'

'Squirts. That's what, 'e can't go anywhere. 'e goes to the 'orspital. They give 'im medicine. They can't find out what's wrong with 'im.'

The paediatrician should do a home visit thought Tess. It would swiftly solve the mystery as to why all the kids had diarrhoea and runny noses. En route, she had the presence of mind to buy a newspaper, which she placed on the table and put the weighing machine on it. Whipping off the baby's sodden nappy, it was tossed by Babs, in the same direction as the rabbit. The baby was placed on the scales. One look at the arrow reminded Tess that this was when she should be giving the mother a pep talk on nutrition. She started to write down the weight of the baby. Where she mused, was that Persil white-coated health visitor, who gave *her* the pep talk?

'What would you rather do, give a patient a talk on nutrition or give an enema?'

She doubted 'Miss White Coat' had ever stepped inside a place like this. What sort of nutritional advice, she wondered, would she give here?

Babs interrupted her thoughts.

'Would you like to come to my wedding?'

She feigned deafness and continued writing up her notes.

'Would you like to come to my wedding in two weeks' time?'

Tess took in a deep breath, which she immediately regretted.

'Thank you, but I don't know if I can.'

'Oh please try. I've asked all the 'elf visitors. None of 'em can come.'

She was told the day, time and chapel where the wedding would take place. After some hesitation, she agreed to try and come. She hoped she could persuade her colleague to come with her.

'What! You must be joking, I've already told her that I couldn't go.'

'I know, she told me that she had asked everyone and that no one could come. Aw, come on. We could go together. Sure it won't be that bad. Her mother is doing the food.'

'Believe me that *is* bad. Okay, you win. If I get gastroenteritis, I'll blame you. Leave your car at my place and we'll go together.'

The wedding was in a tiny non-conformist chapel. Tess and Lyn sat at the back.

'Lyn, do ye recognise any of those people over there? They're sitting there with their notebooks, like a case conference.'

'Ssh! Yes. At least six of them are social workers. With all the kids on the Child Protection Register, they're hoping to get a glimpse of them. Save them visiting Babs' salubrious residence!'

'I suppose they can write down, all children looked well fed and cleanly dressed… for once. Babs said they were all going to be pageboys and bridesmaids.'

There was a muttering of voices in the vestibule. Babs raised voice, gradually became louder. They turned round and could see her through the glass door. She had squeezed her twenty-plus stones into a white wedding dress, giving the appearance of a parachute. She was struggling to get one of her girls to hold her train.

'Hold the bloody thing. Don't tread on it. It's got to go back tomorrow.'

Her voice resonated around the almost empty chapel.

There was no organ, just a piano. The pianist turned round and started to play an appropriate piece of music. If there was such a piece to fit the occasion. The groom made his entrance in an ill-fitting suit. Until now, Tess had only seen him in a string vest. The suit failed to disguise his scruffy appearance, his matted, spikey hair and beard. After several repeats of the same music, the pianist was at last able to play the Wedding March. The bride appeared with her entourage, smiling at the sparse congregation. After the usual vows, it was over. No bouquet to throw at the awaiting bridesmaid. No confetti. No photographer. No limo to drive the happy couple to their reception. The reception? That was at a walking distance, to be held over the top of an amusement arcade. In the far corner there was a bar. The bride's mother brought in some scruffy sandwiches and suspicious-looking cakes.

'Don't touch those cakes,' said Lyn. 'They could be cannabis cakes.'

'What! Drugged cakes?'

'Yeah, I've seen them before. Would you like a drink Tess?'

'I want something. I don't think I shall be eating anything here do ye?'

'Just a few crisps, I saw the mother open a packet and tip them in a bowl.'

'Same as you then, lemonade please.'

As Lyn walked over to the bar, the swing doors sprang opened and in sauntered a man in a smart white suit and dark glasses. The room hushed. Only the sound of talking money could be heard by the jangling jewellery on his wrists and neck. Lyn scurried back with some crisps and a couple of glasses on a tray.

'I reckon that's the Southend Mafia?' whispered Lyn.

'In case a fight breaks out, or police raid, I'm drinking this quickly and leaving.'

'Come on then.'

They left half full glasses and crisps and went back to Lyn's house.

'Do you know, I can honestly say it is the only wedding reception I've been to, where I couldn't eat a morsel,' said Lyn.

'They will *all* have difficulty eating any food there Lyn; they haven't got a full set of teeth between them.'

Lyn and Tess sat down to a meal of sausages, bacon, eggs and potato croquettes.

'Well thanks Lyn, that was lovely. I enjoyed that wedding feast. That's definitely one wedding we won't forget.'

Chapter Thirteen

At nineteen, Wendy was a pretty girl, small, waif like, with chestnut coloured hair. Yet another girl abandoned by her family at a time when she needed them most. Wendy was thrown out of her home by her mother, because she dared to become pregnant. This was such a hypocritical act; her mother being involved in the organisation Pro – Birth. She had even helped fund the setting up of one of the mother and baby homes. Then when her empathy should have extended to her own daughter, it was conspicuously absent.

'Here, take this.'

'What is it?'

'You can see what it is. A list of places where you can go. Sort yourself out and don't come back.'

She gave her daughter a list of suitable mother and baby homes. Most of the babies in the home were for arranged adoptions. Wendy was determined to show her mother that she didn't need her help, and endeavoured to cope on her own. Not easy when thrown out on the street. In her early pregnancy she managed to find a bed-sit over the top of a shop with a Saturday job. When she was near her due time, she was able to go into a mother and baby home. There she met Diane, a tall, lively character, full of confidence, who looked more mature than her twenty-one years.

'Oh it's not my first you know. My third, all adopted thank God.'

'I want to keep my baby.'

'What? With no family, how are you going to afford to do that? Let the state keep you both? I prefer my independence.'

'What job do you do?'

'I work in the community. After we've dropped our baggage, we must keep in touch. I could get you a little job? I could look after the baby for you part-time.'

'That sounds great.'

Already anxious about her rent arrears and other bills that were mounting up, to have a part-time job in the community sounded like a godsend. Wendy had already spent a considerable amount on a cot and a pram. There was still the bedding and a few more baby clothes to be bought. She was angry when she remembered how her married sister, was given all the big items, as gifts from relatives. No one in her family knew of her pregnancy, her mother had made sure of that. She who was the leading light in the Pro-Birth organisation was not going to have people point the finger at her. Wendy had brought shame on her family. Besides, it was at a particularly sensitive time for her. It was rumoured in her circles, that her name had been forwarded for a prestigious award, namely an O.B.E. This would be on account of her untiring work with underprivileged young girls.

When Wendy's girl was born, she called her Bethany. She didn't contact her parents. Due to their lack of concern, she hadn't spoken to her mother since she left home. Nor to the father of her child, a married man, whom as soon as the word *pregnant* was mentioned, scarpered.

Shortly after Wendy took her baby home, Diane called on her. She had bought her a beautiful embroidered, pink satin baby quilt, and two sets of baby clothes.

'Thank you so much Diane. You have no idea what a help that is to me at the moment. I thought it was bad enough before I went into the home. I have come home to find an eviction notice on the mat.'

'How much do you owe? Here, will this cover it?'

She produced a large wad of notes and peeled off more than enough to cover the rent arrears.

'I can't take all that.'

'Yes you can. We're friends aren't we? The extra can sort out any other outstanding bills.'

'I can't thank you enough. It will be such a relief to get out of debt.' She gave her a big hug. 'I hope I can help you one day. Another coffee?'

'No, I must go. Next time we'll talk about that little job. Are you are still interested?'

'Oh yes, if you can still look after Beth for me?'

'If I can't always do it, there's a nursery in town that takes babies from birth to five years. Anyway, I'll sort out a job for you and call in next week.'

When Tess visited Wendy for a regular check on the baby, she noticed how exhausted and on edge she seemed and wondered if she might have signs of post-natal depression. Wendy shrugged off any feelings of stress or depression.

'I'll give ye my phone number and the clinic times to come and weigh the baby.'

'I'm starting a job tomorrow and Beth is going into the Happy Smiles Nursery.'

'What sort of work is it?'

'Hotel work. Just part-time for a few nights. As well as the nursery, I have a friend who can babysit for me.'

'Are ye sure ye feel well enough to go back to work? Most mothers don't usually go back at six weeks.'

'I feel fine. My friend mentioned it would only be light duties.'

'Try and get to clinic when ye can, or give me a ring if ye have any problems.'

'Thanks.'

Hardly had she closed the door when Diane appeared.

'I waited. I saw you had a visitor.'

'It was only the health visitor, come to check the baby.'

'Did you manage to get the baby in the nursery?'

'Yes, I'm taking her there tomorrow morning for the whole day as you suggested.'

'Well, I have a client for you. He will be waiting at the Blue Moon Hotel 2pm.'

'What do I have to do?'

'First you'll meet him in the bar. Then you will go with him to his room.'

'I've never done this before.'

'I know. You have to start somewhere. It's not as if you're a virgin is it?'

'No, but sex with a stranger is different.'

'Come on now, this guy is very kind and gentle and you'll be paid for your services.'

'How much?'

'Much more than you think. That is why we get some students coming to our parlour. It helps to pay for their rent and other expenses. When they finish at university, they disappear into a new job. Some of them go into social work, teaching or counselling.'

'You had better give me some tips. What not to wear. What if I'm in danger? Or if he tries to force me to do something that I don't want to do? What if he refuses to pay me?'

'Slow down. I'll go through everything with you. First of all in escort work, always ring the hotel first, before you agree to meet. For this particular service, the gentleman's name is Mr Slawek. First you must ask which room Mr Slawek, is in? Has he booked in yet? Once you know it is genuine, ring your client and confirm the arrangement. For a new client, always meet in a public place, like the hotel bar or pub. Now, what to wear. Something smart, something simple. The fewer clothes the better. That way you have less things to keep an eye on and less to snatch up. You may need to make a quick exit. Make sure you're not wearing something that could be pulled over you, to lock your shoulders. The other thing, never wear a scarf or long necklace. Oh, and by the way, remove those earrings they could cause an injury. And don't forget to tie your hair up.'

'Should I wear a skirt or trousers?'

'If you wear trousers, take them right off. Just in case you have to make a run for it. Not easy when they're round your ankles. Oh, and decent shoes. Ones you can run in.'

'Do I need to take anything with me?'

'I'll start you off. Here are some condoms, lube and you'll need this safety alarm. Ring my number if you get into any difficulties and I'll come round straightaway, or ring the police.'

'It sounds more dangerous than I thought.'

'Not really, it's like the boy scout motto, *Be Prepared*.'

One thing Diane didn't tell her, was that sixty women in the sex industry, in the previous ten years, had been murdered.

Chapter Fourteen

When Lyn came out of the cinema late one night with her husband, he pointed out to her a prostitute leaning over a car, talking through an open window.

'Talk about lowering the tone around here, the police ought to do something about it. We can't even go and see a film without coming out and being accosted by someone like that, it's disgusting.'

She didn't say anything, but recognised Wendy, having recently done a hearing test with Tess, on her baby.

'Look Lyn, look at her, she didn't waste much time did she? She's just got in his car.'

'I saw her Tess, she looked dreadful. Thin, ill you would hardly recognise her.'

They both knew that the majority of street girls, would be on drugs and needed to sell their bodies to fund their habit. According to a Home Office report that they had read, the majority of women sex workers on the street used heroin. Sadly, it looked as though Wendy had become one of them. Worried about the baby, Tess called in at the nursery. The baby was poorly dressed and screaming. The staff were relieved to be able to discuss their concerns.

'Different people drop the baby off. It has been some time since we saw Bethany's mother.'

Social Services were contacted and a case conference was set up. Once all the facts were known, there was evidence to indicate a lack of basic care and obvious signs of neglect. Bethany was placed in the care of a foster mother.

Later when Tess had to do a developmental check on a young child, she met an older sex-worker's family which astonished her. The mother's other children were more than adequately cared for, they were both at boarding school. Her husband was quite happy to look after the children in the holidays, while as he put it, *the wife sets off on her nocturnal activities*. He had no qualms at all about his wife's 'profession.'

'The wife can earn more than I can. It pays the mortgage, we have two children at public school. I couldn't do that on my money.'

'Aren't ye worried about drugs?'

'No, she's never touched them. Seen too many girls addicted.'

'How long has yer wife been working in the sex industry?' He didn't say.

'She started out as an escort worker. Working the hotels. She's never worked on the street. She is an in-house worker. Works in a parlour. The Manager would swiftly step in if there was any violence, or if men were trying to force girls to do something that they had already refused to do. They have mirrors, so that the wife can keep an eye on the bloke. The staff are really vigilant. In-house workers, girls that work in saunas and parlours, have more control over their conditions, although there are strict rules. Drugs and alcohol are banned.'

'Don't ye ever worry about her catching venereal disease or other infections?'

'No, she is very careful. She always insists on them using condoms. They have regular health screening you know.'

'What about yer older children, don't ye think they wonder what their mum does for a living?'

'No they hear us talking about the parlour, they think it's a beauty parlour. Once the house is paid for, the kids left school, she can pack it in then.'

Tess was astonished at the revelation. She wondered how they had met. Had he been her pimp at one time? It was noticeable that he did all the talking. Tess was appalled at the lack of respect he had for his wife. She hoped her shock didn't show, when visiting clients on the seedier side of society.

At her next visit, she felt intimidated by a heavily tattooed man. He was stripped to the waist and filled the doorway.

'Yeah what the 'ell do you want then?'

'I've come to see the mother and baby.'

'Oh yeah and who are you? She's alright, we don't need anyone poking their nose in.'

'I am required to visit a baby on the tenth day.'

'What for?'

She began to think he was not going to allow her in.

'To make sure mother and baby are well.'

At this he turned his head to the right and looked into the front room.

He yelled. 'Brenda the 'ealth visitor is 'ere.' He raised his head and quickly jerked it to one side that indicated, *in there.* Reluctantly, he allowed a small space under his arm for her to squeeze through into the room. She nearly dropped the weighing scales. By all the banners stacked up and photos on the wall of recent protest marches, it was evident he was a member of the local National Front. He followed her in, whilst she weighed the baby. He was menacing. He amused himself by deliberately tossing live mice in front of her, into a tank which housed an enormous snake.

At the end of the visit, she gave Brenda a card with clinic times; she asked her to come regularly to the clinic. It would be the last time she would visit this house on her own. Next time she would make sure to bring a colleague with her.

The following week, she visited the home of a man she thought could also be scary. Bill had served time in prison for armed robbery. Had he been living in London, he would have been a small fish in a big pond. In Southend, he was considered to be a big fish. Michael had warned her that the police were keeping a close eye on him. She imagined him to be a well-built man, with a rough brutish look the type displayed in films. Tess was pleasantly surprised. He *was* a big man, but a real softie. To see his huge hands gently cradling his little baby and kissing him, was a joy to see. He had just come home from the Cardiac Clinic and had been told that he must lose weight. The consultant wanted to see some weight loss, next time he saw him, at his annual check-up.

His wife, an attractive girl no more than five foot and slim despite having recently given birth, was not the image of a gangster's moll that Tess had conjured up in her mind. She smiled to herself; she knew Michael would say, that she had been watching too many gangster films.

'My husband eats such huge meals. It's not going to be easy to restrict his food.'

'I could get you a diet sheet from the dietician if it would help.'

She sighed. 'I suppose we could try, couldn't we Billy?' she said, giving him an adoring look.

Tess picked up a diet sheet from the local hospital. But before Bill had a chance to try the diet, he had been re-arrested and imprisoned for theft. When he came out of prison a year later, on a diet of prison food, he found his appointment for the Cardiac Clinic had arrived.

'My word, you have worked hard. You have lost five stone in one year. That is absolutely brilliant.' The consultant shook his head in disbelief.

'I have no idea how you have managed to do it. But whatever it is that you are doing, all I'm going to say to you Bill is this… Keep it up!'

Chapter Fifteen

Michael rang Tess at work.

'Darling, the papers have arrived.'

'Do they look complicated?'

'Not really. We can sit down tonight and go through them together.'

'It's exciting isn't it?'

'Now you know what I told you dear. Don't get excited just yet. It could take several months. Our application has to be assessed, then it goes before an adoption panel. The leaflet says it takes approximately six to eight months.'

They filled in the assessment form together.

'Any past convictions?'

'Now let me see. Ah sure wasn't there a chocolate bar I stole from Mrs Kelly's shop when I was six. I was fed up waiting for her to serve me. So I just took it.'

'That's really serious. Nearly as bad as when I took a man's clothes off the beach and put them under someone else's towel. I watched him, like a maniac, he was tearing around the beach looking for them.'

'Now be serious Michael, what type of fostering would ye say we had been doing?'

'Tick that one. Ours comes under Private Fostering. Although you don't get paid, you made arrangements directly with Lena. Apparently there is still some legislation attached to this. We don't have to be assessed or approved, but they do have to check on Jade's welfare.'

'Ah, that's why they went to the school then the other day and asked to see her. Must be after I'd phoned up and asked for the adoption forms.'

'I think that's all we need to do. I'll post it, on my way into the 'nick' tonight.'

She hugged her husband. 'Wouldn't it be grand if we could keep her?'

'Don't get your hopes up love, there are a few hoops we have to jump through first.'

The following morning, a woman called in to ask for a home visit. She had some concerns about her neighbour's child. Tess called in to see her, on her way home.

'It's Lucy, I caught her putting her hands down my little boy's trousers.'

'How old is Lucy and ye'r little boy?'

'Lucy is six and my boy is three. Something is going on in that house. At the Working Men's Club last night, her dad was in, drunk as usual. My hubby and the other men heard him say, *'My little girl said to me, make love to me daddy.'*

'My husband and the other men in the club couldn't stop talking about it. They were all shocked. They all thought that no child of that age would say that would they?'

'No definitely not. I will contact the authorities, they will be wanting to speak to ye and ye'r husband, as well as Lucy and her family.'

Tess knew this was sexual precociousness. The little girl was much too young to be interested in sex. She lacked the hormones of puberty, that would stimulate an interest. It might indicate a history of sexual abuse.

It was several months before Tess heard from the social worker. Both police and social worker had interviewed the family without success. Each time they called, the father insisted on being present. Lucy would look at her father and wouldn't say a word. Now that the little girl was having problems wetting the bed, the social worker wondered if the health visitor could go in and advise the mother, and to try to get the evidence they needed. Tess confirmed the same as the social worker. The father wouldn't leave the room and leave the child alone with her mother. She thought she might try a discreet psychological approach.

'Would ye like to draw me a picture, while I talk to yer mummy?'

She gave the little girl a scribbling pad and some coloured pencils. Tess started to give advice to the mother about getting Lucy to double urinate before going to bed. And the possibility of getting a special alarm system to wake the child, soon as she started to wet the bed.

'I've drawn a picture of you,' the child said, handing her the drawing.

'Thank ye Lucy, I'll have to take that home won't I, put it on the wall.'

She folded it over and put it in her briefcase. Once home, she was shocked to see what the little girl had drawn. This was no match stick person, that a child of her age would probably have drawn. It was as though Tess had sat in a life study art class. It was a drawing of a naked woman complete with nipples and pubic hair. She placed it back in her briefcase to file in her notes.

The following week, when she returned, once again she gave the little girl the pad and pencils.

'How about drawing a picture of Lucy today?'

A quick glance at the drawing and she swiftly put it in her briefcase. Given to a child psychologist, here was the evidence they needed. Lucy had drawn another naked picture. This time of herself. Directed to her genital area, was a large bright red sword. Tess arrived home feeling hopeful that now the abuse could be dealt with.

'Sorry Tess. 'It's bad news.'

'Why? What's happened Michael?'

'No don't tell me. No, not again.'

'I'm afraid so. She's done it again. When I dropped Jade off. I told her our solicitor had got everything ready for the adoption. She had only to sign the papers.'

'What did she say?'

'No! I've changed my mind, I'm not going to sign them. And don't ask me again.'

'It's so unfair Michael, she doesn't want Jade and she doesn't want anyone else to have her either.'

'Tess, it's the third time she done this. I think it's because she knows she would lose all her benefits as a single parent.'

'I think ye are right. We'll just have to carry on as before. Lena's never interested in anything to do with her daughter. Yet she won't sign the papers.'

'Never mind Tess, we have each other and we still have Jade part-time.

Chapter Sixteen

'The Registrar has been asking for you.'

'Oh no, not again Lyn. I bet it's the Ali family.'

'I had better go out again and see them. Can you put the chairs out for me? I've got my new group, Mothers of Hyperactive Children this afternoon.'

Lyn raised her eyebrows and looked at Tess in astonishment at her proposed new group.

'Mrs Ali, yer baby has to be registered within six weeks?'

'I know. I have been given the alphabet letter 'A' from the Imam.'

'Oh great. So what will ye be calling the baby?'

'I've sent the letter 'A' home to my mother-in-law.'

'Have ye heard back?'

'Not yet.'

This naming of the baby had been an ongoing saga for some time. Tess was hopeful that by now Mrs Ali would have heard back from her mother-in-law.

'Has yer mother-in-law been in touch?'

'Yes, I've heard from her.'

'Oh good, so what name are ye going to call yer little boy?'

'She wants me to call him Abdul.'

'I see Abdul.' Tess started to write the name in the baby's notes.

'I'm **not** calling him Abdul.'

'What do ye mean?'

'I'm **not** having that old-fashioned name.'

Tess sighed. 'I have had the registrar on the phone. I have to tell ye, ye have five days left to name the baby, before it becomes a criminal offence.'

'Well, they can lock me up. I'm still not going to call him Abdul. Anyway I've sent it back.'

Back in the office she mentioned the Ai family to Lyn. 'She's hopeless, what can I do?'

'I'd give her three more days, then call in again. She's British-born, more westernised. She's not going to be bossed about by her mother-in-law in Pakistan.'

Tess's new group, *Mothers' Hyperactive Group*, by using that name, it had not occurred to her that the mothers couldn't leave their hyperactive children with friends or relatives. Judging by the state they left the clinic, they couldn't leave them with anyone, unless they took out additional insurance. It was a disaster.

One boy wanted to be a monkey and wasted no time in swinging on the curtains. The fittings gave way. Curtains... rod... child. All in one tangled bundle landed on the floor with a crash. The child, wrapped up like an Egyptian mummy in the heavy drapes, was unharmed.

Whilst this was happening, another child had taken the jug of water, put there for the speaker, and poured it all over the floor. The other children seized the opportunity to use the floor as a skating rink. It was hopeless. The mothers sat motionless. No doubt they were so used to this 'human zoo' behaviour it was 'normal' for them.

Exhaustion was written into their body language as the mothers filed out of the clinic. Whilst all the excitement was going on in the room, one boy had disappeared out into the corridor. Undisturbed, he'd had a field day, he had quietly dismantled the radiator. It was in bits. So was Tess. She felt like lying down in a darkened room to recover.

'I've only had them for one afternoon, Lyn. Those poor mothers have got them all the time. I could probably manage one at a time, but not a whole group of destructive delinquents.'

'Whilst you were in there, a mum rang up to say she couldn't make the group this week. Will you be having another one next week?'

'What! Over my dead body. Oh and Lyn, saying that, don't invite any of them to my funeral.'

Three days later, Tess was able to put the registrar out of his misery. The Ali family settled on the name for their son and called him Aalim. She was told it meant wise, a man of learning.

Round the corner lived the Khan family.

'I think it is wonderful that you come and call on us like this. You don't wait to come when my children are sick, you come before. Then you tell my wife how to keep our children healthy. In my country a doctor or nurse call, they hold out hand for money. You don't do that. You come for free.'

She hadn't the heart to say that he had actually paid for her visit. He had paid in his National Insurance contributions, through his job as a bus driver. Both he and his brother worked on the buses. Mr Khan had to interpret everything, his wife didn't possess any English and he was reluctant for her to learn.

'It's best she doesn't get muddled up with a different language. I need it for my job. Although it mean I have to do lots of running about. Take this one to dentist. Go speak to teacher about that, and so on. When we bring someone to marry our children, my wife must speak their language. We go back to Pakistan one day. So not worth her learning the language here.'

It all sounded feasible, until she overhead the two brothers' conversation in the adjoining room.

'You going to nightclub when we finish tonight?'

'Yes it's singles night.'

'I know, I have Mo's divorce papers to show manager when we go in.'

'What's with you?'

'I have papers they say I'm single.'

'We should have good time. Plenty of women. Some jiggy-jig tonight.'

His wife moved her head in the direction of the raucous laughter, nodded and smiled. The reason her husband didn't want his wife to learn English was clear. It enabled the brothers to talk freely on any subject in their wives' presence, without a clue to their conversation.

On one occasion in a similar household, she plainly heard the husband calling his wife a big, fat, lazy slob in English. His wife just smiled sweetly, unaware of his verbal abuse.

The two Ahmed brother were different. They were happy for their wives to go to English language classes. It saved them having to accompany their wives to the school or doctor.

'It meant always having to take time off from work. It is good now they can explain the situation for themselves. Once a year, my brother and I give our wives a break from the children. We hire a minibus and take our children and their friends on a trip somewhere for the day.'

'Each year,' his brother smiled, 'we say never again don't we?'

'It can't be worse than last year, we took them to a Navy Day at Portsmouth.'

'Fourteen kids,' interrupted Majid, his younger brother.

'Yes. For a start one of the boys let off a stink bomb in the mini-bus. It was terrible. We were glad to get off the bus. As soon as we got there, the children all wanted ice-creams. They had to eat them before they were allowed on the ships. The little ones made a terrible mess all down their clothes.'

'What about that little girl?' said the brother. 'That one that wanted to go to the toilet? We couldn't go in with her. We had to wait outside. She came out with her knickers wrapped round her ankles. It was so embarrassing.'

'Majid, how about the boy who was always getting lost?'

'Oh yes… that loud haler. It would announce, *'We have a little boy here in a blue jumper and blue trousers. He says his name is Khalid.'* We would have to run over to the lost children's hut. Then an hour later, the loud haler would go *again!*' *'We have this little boy Khalid again, would someone PLEASE come and collect him.'*

'It was exhausting. Then when we got back, the mothers were not pleased were they? They thought we were supposed to give them a break. Now they would have to do all the washing. Not just their clothes. The children's faces and hair needed washing. They were smothered in chocolate and ice-cream.'

'Kids, eh? Never again.'

The younger brother shook his head. 'No, never again.'

Chapter Seventeen

'Mrs King. How long have you been with us?'

'Ten years.'

'It's about time we sent some of you on a refresher course. Four of you will go for a week to Chester College. It will not be a holiday camp. I will expect you all to come back full of new ideas.'

They arrived in one car and quickly settled into dormitory life. It transported them back to their student nurse days and they were soon reminiscing. Tess saw what she thought was a familiar face, wheeling her luggage and about to go into the next room.

'It's Yin isn't it?'

The Singaporean girl looked puzzled.

'We did our midwifery together. Ye don't recognise me without my nun's habit?'

'Sister Bridget? No, is it?'

'Just Tess now.'

Yin came over and hugged her. 'You here for refresher? You also health visitor?'

'Yin, it's grand to see ye.'

'We will talk of old times.'

'Let's go and get a coffee in the dining-room.'

'Yes. I unpack things later.'

They chatted excitedly. Tess knew what Yin's burning question would be. Why had she left the order?

'Tell me why you not a nun?'

'I wanted my freedom. I no longer felt happy in the convent. Please don't say anything to the girls that came with me. I have never told anyone, except my husband of course.'

'You married? How nice.'

'Yes, I married a police officer.'

'So instead of convent, he will keep you in order instead.'

'We are very happy. How about ye?'

'Oh yes. You remember Doctor Davies, that one telling me off? He went into general practice. I met him again when he was trainee. We went out a few times together. Later we marry.'

'Did yer mother approve?'

'Not at first. She was unhappy, I was marrying a white man. When she learned he was a doctor, she was very happy.'

'Any children Yin?'

'Not yet.' She started to laugh. 'I know you thinking about different coloured babies.'

They reminisced about an incident when they were both student midwives.

The Midwifery Sister had asked them both to go and fetch a baby from the neo-natal ward. The midwife pointed out the baby to take down to the ward. Both of them were shocked. They checked the name tab.

'Are you sure this is right baby?'

'Yes, of course it is. Hurry up, that's the one.'

The student midwives looked at each other in disbelief. The parents were both white and the child was black.

'I'm not giving her that baby, you do it Sister Bridget.'

The mother looked up and remarked, 'Oh! He doesn't look a bit like me, does he?' The father showed no sign of surprise.

Together the two student midwives, went in the office and found the mother's notes.

'Look Yin, it says the mother's grandfather came from Jamaica.'

'So baby's great grandfather was black. Not possible. Don't believe it.'

'Yin, let's go to the hospital library at lunch, have a look at a book on genetics.'

They spent an hour pouring over the book and eventually found that it was possible.

'Well I never, here it is. It is possible it says, to miss a generation.'

'If I took home white baby, my mother would kill me.'

'What would happen today Yin, now that ye are married to a white man, if ye had a white baby?'

Yin smiled. 'I'd be delighted.' She drained her cup. 'I'd better go up and unpack.'

Tess was pleased to have met up again with Yin. Glad too that she didn't open up old wounds, probing further as to why she had left the convent.

Back in the dining room for tea, Tess and Yin sat with their respective groups. The four of them in Tess's group, could not help over-hearing an excited conversation at a nearby table.

'They are fantastic. You can eat any amount of food and you won't put on any weight.'

'Is it a drink or pills?'

'Herbal pills. They really work. They are really effective.'

Unable to resist something that would enable her to eat as much as she liked without putting on an ounce, Shirley, one of the girls went over to the next table.

'We couldn't help over-hearing about slimming pills. What are they called?'

'Speedy Slim.'

'Where did you get them from?'

'You can get them down the main street at a health shop.'

They wasted no time and hurried out of the dining room.

'Come on girls,' called Shirley. 'Let's leg it. It's nearly five, they could shut soon.'

They chased down the street and found the health shop. Denise grabbed the bottle of pills.

'We could share the bottle between us. Then buy our own when we get home.'

'Quick Tess, you did some pharmacy, what's in them?'

'I'm afraid I will have to hurry you. We are about to close up,' came a voice from the till.

She quickly scanned the formula. Most of the ingredients were herbal and seemed innocuous. Bladder wrack, rhubarb extract, ginger…She was out of time and unable to read the final contents. The fact that she was unable to read to the end of the formula, was to prove a bitter pill for the girls to take. Within twenty minutes almost to the second, after eating a meal, the pills activated. As the four took breakfast together, within twenty minutes, of digesting the meal, one by one in the classroom, their hands shot up, to be relieved from the class. They dashed out to be relieved not only of their breakfast, but of the most offensive, earth shattering, breaking of wind.

'I know one thing,' Pat remarked, 'I'm not going to the toilet on my dormitory floor. I'm going on someone else's.'

It was true they could eat whatever they liked. True they didn't put on any weight, but the side effects were drastic. The Southend group of four, excusing themselves from class after every meal en masse, continued throughout the week.

One evening, they crossed over the border into North Wales and went into a pub, where a quiz was taking place.

All four of them found they had individual knowledge. Denise was clued up on sport. She knew the name of the goal-keeper in a particular football match, which person bowled out which player in cricket, how many runs, athletics, swimming, the Olympics, names of baseball teams in America. The other three were astounded at her knowledge. Pat must have spent hours watching TV or going to films. Shirley must have read most of the books in the library. When it came to Tess, she couldn't be faulted in theology or questions on the Bible. Between them they whispered the answers to the team sitting at a nearby table. To the team's surprise they won the quiz. Their prize was a bottle of wine and a basket of fruit.

'This is the first time we have won, when are you coming again?' one man asked. Another joined in. 'We want you all on our team.'

They were so pleased they insisted that the four girls had the basket of fruit. Minutes from the college, they decided to eat a couple of pieces of fruit each. By the time they had parked the car in the car park, they were all desperate for the toilet.

'What else was in those pills Tess?' asked Shirley.

Reluctantly she told them. 'Cascara Sagrada. What you might call a dynamic purgative.'

They could hardly walk. 'Pinch your bum cheeks together girls.' said Pat. 'Don't laugh, it's fatal to laugh.'

Of course that was lighting the touch paper. Difficult not to laugh watching their colleagues waddling across the car park.

'With luck we may make it.' said Denise.

'You speak for yourself,' said Shirley, 'My luck's run out...or at least something has.'

Chapter Eighteen

After Chester, the four girls were not keen to continue on their slimming plan. Instead, they concentrated on promoting health education. They were given a stall to highlight their 'No Smoking' campaign. Tess was keen to bring the skeleton. So she collected it from the Health Education department. It certainly drew attention from the moment she picked up 'Jimmy' until she arrived at the stall. The skeleton was able to be hooked onto a stand. This she found difficult to manoeuvre into her small car. In the end she had to sit the skeleton upright in the front passenger seat. As you can imagine there was a good deal of swerving, and near misses by other drivers, once they had noticed the skeletal passenger.

Driving was similar to the attention created on the road in the vicinity of Southend Airport. As the aircraft flew unnervingly low coming in to land, unwitting drivers to the area, such as holidaymakers in the summer, would precariously slow down. This meant local drivers often found themselves having to break sharply. Unfamiliar drivers were convinced that the aircraft was about to land on top of their car. All this to a background of screeching brakes, swearing and shaking of fists by the natives.

Now even the local drivers were slowing down, unable to believe their eyes on seeing a skeleton sitting in a car.

Once out of the car she had to carry 'Jimmy' through a busy thoroughfare. Then the public banter began. One man came out of a men's tailoring shop.

'Hey, does he want to be measured for a suit?'

A woman shouted out, 'Poor thing, what have you done, starving him like that?'

At the stall, the skeleton was a crowd puller. Along with all the other equipment.

'I don't smoke, 'e's the one what smokes.'

The mother grabbed her teenage son by the collar and veered him towards her. ''ere test 'im.'

Sure enough, when he blew into the apparatus, the carbon monoxide reading was high.

'There you are. I told yer.' The boy seemed unimpressed. 'Now let me do it.'

To her dismay, the machine still registered a small percentage of carbon monoxide in her lungs. With that, she turned round and thumped her son with her handbag.

'See what you've done. That's all your fault. I gave up fags sixteen years ago, when I was 'aving you. You're not smoking in the 'ouse. Any fags indoors, I'll shove 'em down the bog.'

The teenager thought it was amusing.

Others took the matter seriously. Another piece of equipment used was Smoking Ginny. The doll had a test tube under her skirt. A lighted cigarette was placed in her mouth and a small hand pump would keep it alight. At the end of her *smoke*; the test tube was shown to the crowd. Thick black tar had accumulated in the tube, after just one cigarette, an indication of what was happening in their lungs.

After a morning of demonstrations, several people had signed up to Tess's Smoking Cessation Course. The women were more concerned with their appearance. Being told that their clothes and hair reeked of cigarette smoke, often prompted them to give up smoking. One woman made a firm decision to give up, when her friend would not allow her to give her new-born baby a cuddle, because she was a smoker.

The men were more interested in how much money they could save. A calculation would be made from the age that the man started smoking. Some were as young as twelve having started with a packet of woodbines, shared between the lads behind the school bicycle shed. When they added up the annual expenditure at the current price, multiplied by the number of years of smoking, the figures went into thousands. Many realised that they could have had that deposit for their own house or taken an exotic honeymoon in the Seychelles, somewhere with palm trees and golden sands, instead of a rainy week in Skegness.

Studying their behaviour, they all agreed that they would not go into a shop and purchase sufficient cigarettes to last them the month. It would be too much of a reminder as to just how much they were spending every month. All literally going up in smoke. With the only thing to show for it, a husky voice and hacking cough. In order not to be faced with the reality of how much they were spending, they would only shop for cigarettes on a daily or twice-weekly habit, except when going abroad when they would bring back their 200 duty frees. Did they last as long as they had hoped? No, not really, they remarked. In fact they found that they smoked even more after they had returned from their holiday.

'Relaxing on holiday and not restricted by work, I had notched up more cigarettes than usual. Then once home there seemed an endless supply of duty frees,' said someone.

'Easy come — easy go,' said another.

A new product had come on the market, in the form of nicotine chewing gum. Many found they had become hooked on that instead. One woman showed how addictive nicotine could be, in that she had gradually reduced the amount and almost eliminated the gum.

'I just have a tiny piece the size of a pin head. I stick it in my tooth and when I get the urge, I lick it!'

An agricultural director experienced intolerable withdrawal symptoms. He found it extremely difficult to concentrate after five days without a cigarette. He had to bluff his way through the mire, and get his deputy to sign documents on his behalf. One evening it reached a peak. He stopped his car and rang his wife.

'Darling, can you tell me where am I'm supposed to be going this evening?'

'You are supposed to be going to the No Smoking Group.'

He admitted that had this not been the turning point and his concentration had deteriorated further, he would have gone back to smoking.

Tess used the buddy system. All their names went into the hat and they were each given a person to contact when their resolve had started to weaken. Their buddy would talk them through what they had achieved and try to keep them on the right track. The buddy for the company director was a likeable young man, a farm labourer. He explained in confidence that he was illiterate.

His buddy suggested that if he took a literacy course twice a week at a local evening class, he would give him a step up the ladder with a job in his company. The lad dutifully attended the literacy course and the director kept his promise.

When two single, bed-sit mums came into clinic, Tess thought about trying to get them out of their one room to meet other mothers.

'Don't ye go to the Mums and Toddlers group around the corner?'

'No, we don't go to those sort of things.'

'We went once. They're all a stuck up lot. Going on and on about their new kitchens.'

'Older kids going to posh private schools.'

Both young girls had been brought up in care. Now with children of their own, their children were all on the child protection register.

One of them, Anne, told Tess what had happened after they had both left 'care' at sixteen.

'There was eleven of us, what left care together. We decided to have a reunion the next year. When we met up, ten of us was pregnant.'

Tess could understand this. The girls had been deprived of love. They sought it with the first boy that showed them any affection.

'Have you ever been able to contact your own mothers?'

Anne pointed at her friend, 'ers is in prison isn't she?'

'And yours?'

'Yeah, I was only two when I went 'in care.' I did try to find my mum when I left care. It took me ages to find her. I had this lovely idea my mum would be pretty and hold out her arms and make a fuss of me. It weren't like that. She sat there smoking a fag, surrounded by loads of scruffy, snotty-nosed kids.

'Who are you?' she said.

'I've been told you are my mum.'

'What's yer name?'

'Anne.'

'Anne? Oh yeah, I got shot of you to care years ago. Don't ask me who yer Dad is 'cos I ain't got a clue. What yer want now?'

'Nothing.'

'She were 'orrible weren't she Annie?'

'Yeah. I walked out. I didn't even say goodbye.'

'Why don't we set up our own Mum and Toddler group, just for bed-sit mums?'

'Yeah.'

'Cool.'

'I'll try and get the premises. Ye get the girls.'

A few weeks later, a group of young mums and their kids hurried into a toy-filled room. A friendly lady, a Quaker, volunteered to play with the somewhat unruly children.

As a health visitor, Tess was not allowed to run a group, without having an input of Health Education. On this occasion, she decided she would give a short talk on contraception. She was joined that morning by a male social worker. He'd heard about the group and thought he would look in and see what it was all about.

'Ye need to know girls, that if the doctor puts ye on antibiotics, this can affect the pill.'

A girl called out, 'In what way Miss?'

'It could cause the birth pill to be ineffective, in other words it won't work.'

There was a sudden crash. A chair had fallen on the floor. The social worker had leapt off and was seen making a dash for the door. He later explained that they had five young children and his wife had just seen the doctor that morning and he had put her on antibiotics.

Chapter Nineteen

The Paediatrician has suggested that a health visitor might find it useful to sit in, on one of his consultations in outpatients clinic. Tess was unfamiliar with the hospital outpatients, so she asked a nurse standing in the corridor, reading a notice board, where to find Dr Edwards' room?

'You are standing by it.'

'Thanks.' She knocked on the door.

'Come in.'

One doctor sat behind a desk, flanked by two junior doctors. She thought it odd that the doctors were not wearing white coats.

'Your name please?'

'Mrs King.'

The doctor glanced down his list of patients.

She interrupted, 'I'm a health visitor.'

In a patronising manner, he said, 'Oh I see, we are a health visitor are we?'

Then in a stage whisper to the other doctors, 'She thinks she's a health visitor.'

'What do ye mean, I *think* I'm a health visitor? I *am* a health visitor.'

'I understand Mrs King,' he tried to pacify her. 'Is that's who you are today?'

'I don't think ye *do* understand? Who are *ye*?'

'I am Dr Edwards.'

'A Paediatrician?'

'No dear, Psychiatrist.'

Hardly had the words left his lips, when he remembered that there was another Edwards in the clinic that afternoon, Martin Edwards Paediatrician.

'Oh! I'm am really sorry, you are in the wrong room.'

'Obviously.'

'Dr Martin Edwards, has his office down the other corridor!'

Tess thought it would be a long time before he lived that mistake down. Especially in front of two junior doctors. She imagined that joke would resonate for some time amongst their colleagues.

The Paediatrician's, first patient was already in the room. Tess quickly introduced herself.

'This is Mrs Croft with her daughter Christina. How old is Christina now?'

'Eight, Doctor.'

'Last time we met, I prescribed some new medication for your daughter's persistent diarrhoea. Has it had any effect?'

'No doctor, it's still very bad.'

'I am wondering if this could be an environmental problem. I'll arrange for the health visitor to call. Meanwhile don't stop the medication.'

Once the mother and child had left the room, he spoke to Tess.

'I think this is Münchausen's syndrome by proxy. You may have come across this before, where a parent in order to draw attention to themselves, will sometimes fake an illness in their child. The difficulty is trying to prove it. I've had that child on the children's ward a couple of times, with dramatic improvement.'

Despite looking as though they had just had their annual bath night, Tess instantly recognised the next mother and child. It was Babs with Wayne. Wayne had on his wedding outfit that he would grow into, in several years' time. Babs wore a man's tracksuit. An athletic running track was not something Babs had ever ventured to. She found it an effort to climb out of her caravan and walk ten paces to the nearest bus stop.

Tess could have easily diagnosed Wayne's problem as environmental; washing hands after the toilet would have been a start.

She listened to the consultant go through all the usual questions on diet. One visit to them at their caravan would have answered many of his questions. She could see how the patient's health visitor, could prove a fund of information at a paediatric clinic. Christina Croft was also on Tess's patch. She made a note to follow-up Christina's case.

Back at the office, Lyn found the psychiatrist scenario highly amusing. Fortunately, she was familiar with the Croft family.

'As long as I can remember, that child has had chronic diarrhoea; trying to find the evidence is going to be difficult.'

Thanks to Lyn, it proved not to be as difficult, as they had first thought. Walking through a Chemist shop one lunch time, she had a stroke of luck. She spotted Christina with her mother and heard Christina call out to her mother and point to something on the shelf. Lyn followed the child's pointed finger.

'Look mummy, there's those pills I have to take.'

'I have your answer for Dr Edwards. What do you think she pointed to? Senokot tablets! Can you believe it? All this time she had been giving that poor kid laxatives.'

The following week, Lyn and Tess were on a child abuse course. The course was for health visitors, social workers, GP's and community physicians.

'Children find it very difficult to tell someone, when they have been abused,' commenced the lecturer, 'especially with sexual abuse, when the perpetrator, has insisted that it's their little secret. That they mustn't tell anyone, or terrible things could happen. I would like you all to write on your paper, a secret that you have never told anyone before.'

They all started to write something on the paper and quickly folded it up.

'Now turn to a stranger next to you and exchange your secrets. Do not unfold the paper. Find a very safe place to keep that secret, in your handbag or wallet.'

The lecturer continued to say how prevalent child sexual abuse was.

'You may not believe it, but sitting in this room today, there are fifty people. One in four of you will, as a child, have been sexually abused.'

Most looked amazed at this.

'Should anyone wish to discuss this with me, I am very willing to listen and advise you, either in the lunch break or at the end of the day. If so, please leave a note on my desk.'

They all filed out to have lunch in the canteen. On coming back early in the class room, Lyn and a couple of others, saw the GP that Tess had given her secret to, take a paper from his pocket, unfold it and start to read. Lyn and several others rounded on him.

'What the hell do you think you are doing?'

'That is someone's secret.'

'You wouldn't want us to read yours would you?' Lyn tried to snatch it from him.

'Just a minute. Stop! I didn't get a chance to read my correspondence this morning. I am not reading anyone's secret.'

Tess missed the drama, but thought it was interesting to learn how protective people were of her secret. Looking out of the window she saw two figures walking in the grounds, one of whom was the speaker. On her desk were a dozen folded notes.

Chapter Twenty

1983

'Hi Tess, you home darling?'

'In the kitchen.'

'Where's Jade?'

'Ssh! Would you believe, doing her homework at last, without any nagging.'

She had reached that difficult age of fourteen, when everything seemed a chore.

'What sort of day have you had?'

'Crazy day. Can you believe it, some thieves actually broke into our station and stole four uniforms? The media will give us a bloody nose on this one.'

'Could it be serious?'

'I'd say. Until we catch them, how will the public know if it is a genuine police officer or one of the thieves?'

'Uncle Michael, can you help me with my maths homework?' A voice called out from the sitting room.

'I'm in the kitchen. Just let me have a cup of tea, and I'll come in and give you a hand.'

'I had to take her to the optician this morning, she's having glasses for strabismus.'

'What does that mean in English?'

'A squint.'

'Oh not too bad then, can be corrected.'

'Hope so.'

'I heard that. I don't want to wear glasses and be called four eyes.'

'Go on off with you. I'm coming in now to help you with your homework.'

They both agreed that glasses could be another reason to bully her. Tess had already been up the school regarding bullying. She also made it her business to attend all the school functions: sports day, plays, parents evenings.

The tide had changed, Jade was now able to stay with them permanently. Not just for weekends and school holidays. Although Lena didn't want her child to be adopted, she decided she didn't want her back home either. She had always pulled out at the last minute when it came to adoption; that was money orientated. She would lose her benefits. This time she was becoming agitated that she might be getting into further trouble with the law. Her daughter was showing signs of puberty and already a couple of punters had tried to take advantage of this. Lena was no doubt concerned that if Jade told Michael, she would swiftly be arrested for running an underage brothel. Therefore it was best that her daughter was out of the flat completely. She didn't want to risk any interference with the law. She was more worried about her business and losing her regular punters. Lena didn't let on why she didn't want her back, except to repeat that she hated the sight of her. Jade had mentioned to Tess what had been happening, she drew her own conclusions.

As Tess drove to work, a yellow car cut her up at the traffic lights. She narrowly missed hitting it and had to swerve sharply to get into the right lane. Waiting at the red light there came a loud tap on the passenger window. She looked up to see a uniformed policeman and immediately turned to see if she could see a police car. There wasn't one. Mindful of the stolen uniforms, she tried to ignore him. He banged again and made a hand signal for her to wind down the window. She refused. The traffic lights changed and she drove on, with the policeman in hot pursuit. He managed to get her to pull her car over to the side. He banged on the window again. Nervously, she opened the window a little. In a flash, he had put his hand in and found the means to wind down the window, opened the door and jumped in. Tess trembled as he sat himself down in the passenger seat and started to interrogate her.

'What the hell do you think you were playing at? Why didn't you open your window back there when I asked you to?'

'I wasn't sure if ye were a genuine policeman or not?'

'What do you mean?'

'With those stolen uniforms that I heard about on the radio. I turned round and didn't see a police vehicle.'

She hoped it *had* been broadcast on local radio. She didn't want to mention that it was her husband that had told her, and get him into trouble.

'That is precisely why we drive around in unmarked vehicles, to catch idiots like you on the road. I saw you swerve recklessly at the traffic lights. What's the stopping distance at forty miles per hour?'

'Ye saw the yellow car then, that cut me up as well?'

'What! What yellow car?'

'The yellow Ford car.'

He hesitated. It was obvious that he had not observed what had really taken place. He had just seen her car zigzag at the traffic lights.

'Ye have no right to jump in here and intimidate me.'

She took a leaf out of Alison's book and asked for his number to report him. She was angry. It unnerved her for the rest of the morning. She couldn't wait to get home and see if Michael knew him.

It was nine o'clock. Her husband was late. She didn't worry too much. He would ring her if he had got caught up in something or had been asked to stay on. By midnight she was in bed, he had not come home. In the early hours of the morning she went down stairs to see if he had come in and fallen asleep in the chair.

Unable to sleep, she made herself a cup of warm milk. Anxiety crept in. He was bound to call soon. She heard the door rattle and dashed to the front door. It was nothing, just the wind rattling the letter box. After breakfast, she hurried Jade off to school.

Ah, well 'tis no good fretting, she thought. Then aloud, 'He'll contact me when he can.'

The day passed and now Tess was getting really worried. A message on the answerphone sent her into a panic.

'Don't try to contact me; I'm not coming home.'

What did it mean? Her first thought was had he left her? She couldn't rest. Was he in some kind of danger? Could he be in trouble? She couldn't wait any longer to find out. She drove to the police station.

'Is Sergeant King on duty?'

'Hold on love, I'll check for you.'

The police officer on the desk came back five minutes later.

'No. He's not working.'

'Where is he then? He's not come home.'

'All I can only tell you is, that for the time being he has decided to stay with a colleague.'

'Where, which colleague?'

'I am not permitted to tell you that?'

'I am his wife. I would like to speak to yer superior.'

'There is nothing more to be said. The message I have given you, *is* from my superior. Go home. He will get in contact with as soon as he can.'

She explained the little she knew to her manager and was given time off from work. Advised, to go home and wait a few days to see what developed. Her manager reasoned that if they had not had a row, it was unlikely to be a domestic situation, more likely to be a police issue. Especially, as the police did not seem to be unduly concerned about Michael's absence. She took little comfort from her manager's summing up of the situation, but was glad she had been given permission for her to have a few days off. Had he left her? Was the colleague he was staying with female? They work long hours. Her husband is handsome, funny, friendly. They are often thrown into the company of flirtatious police women.

She decided to call on a neighbour, a woman married to a police officer, that she had briefly met. She lived in one of the Home Office houses nearby.

'Here, have a coffee. I'm sorry I can't help you. I can't say I've had this situation myself. Well, not being absent for as long as this without an explanation. Like you say, my husband usually rings me too, if he is held up. Try not to worry, if I hear anything I'll let you know. My husband may have heard something.'

Tess gave her their telephone number. Later that day the phone rang. She dashed to pick up the receiver. Her neighbour spoke so quietly, she had to strain to hear what she was saying.

'All my husband would say,' she whispered, 'was that he heard that there had been a fight, something to do with drugs. He thought your husband was involved. If I hear any more I'll let you know.'

It was to be several days before Michael phoned, to say he was coming home.

'Oh Michael, whatever happened to ye? I've been so worried. I thought ye had left me?'

He hugged her. 'I was frightened to come home. I walked into a fight that was taking place between two drug barons. I got stuck in the middle. Then one of them bit me in the face.'

He pointed to a nasty gash on his cheek.

'Did ye have to go to hospital?'

'Yes. I had to have it sorted out.'

'But why couldn't ye come home? I was worried sick?'

'I was worried sick too. They reckoned the guy that bit me, had this AIDS, everyone is talking about.'

'Mary Mother of God, are ye all right?'

'Yes, I'm fine.' He hugged and tousled her hair. 'Yes darling, I got the all clear today. I didn't want to come home until I'd got the results. Or I could have passed the infection on to you or Jade. So I stayed at Jack's place; he lives on his own. We were both involved in the fight, he got a cut on his leg and that had to be checked out too.'

Tess was aware the British public were beginning to wake up and pay more attention to AIDS. It followed a panic, when it was discovered that several haemophiliacs had contracted AIDS through contaminated blood transfusions.

'Ye crazy, lovely man. I was so worried. I thought ye had left me for another woman.'

'Now who's crazy. As if I would leave my lovely little colleen?'

Chapter Twenty One

'I've only been here a week. It's already driving me crazy.'

'I agree, those steps are terribly dangerous.'

'How am I supposed to get out of this dump to go shopping? First I have to take the buggy down all those steps. Then I have to go back up again. Fetch the baby. Carry her down the steps. By that time, if I'm lucky and no one's nicked my buggy, I can go shopping. The boiler's packed up. I've no hot water. No heating. How am I supposed to bring up a baby in this pig hole?'

'I know Sheena, it's not a good place. When I get back to the office, I shall be ringing the housing officer David Bird, to see what he can do to get ye moved out of there.'

Sheena was right. She had to negotiate about thirty steep, stone, steps from the top flat. If she tripped holding the baby, it could be disastrous. It was not a suitable place to bring up a baby. This was not the first time she had been in touch with David Bird, about this flat. As soon as he managed to get Tess's client moved, another mother and baby would move in and the problem would start all over again.

There had been a variety of residents in this particular flat. On one occasion it had been a flat of 'ill repute' as David Bird called it. Even after he had evicted the woman, men still called and pestered the innocent tenant.

'I can't understand it, I keep having men calling here asking for Gloria.'

Tess reassured her that they would soon realise that Gloria had moved elsewhere. Even she was solicited on leaving the flat, with a man asking 'are you open for business?'

Before that, there were two sisters sharing. They would not have hesitated to take a baby buggy and flog it.

'I can show you how to nick stuff, no problem,' she promptly gave Tess a demonstration. She rolled up a newspaper, put it in her bag. Then with her hand over the top of the newspaper she would swiftly funnel the goods into the bag.

'Or you could wear a cape, very popular now. They're great for hiding stuff.'

'I'll be bearing that in mind. Although I don't think I'll be wearing *my* cape in future, when I go into a store. I'm not wanting to raise any suspicion, not when I'm married to a policeman.'

'Oh blimey, we shouldn't have told her all that should we. She might tell her old man?'

By the next week, the sisters had gone. She saw one of them in Tesco. She was pregnant again. Or was she? Was that bump a baby, or another load of stolen goods?

'Tess King, not that flat again. No sooner I put someone in, the following week you are wanting them out. In goes the next person and guess who is on the phone to Housing…?

'I know, but ye are a very kind and understanding person. This young girl is having real problems. Poor girl, she is up and down all those stone steps with a young baby. First it's down the steps with the buggy, then up again to carry the baby down. The baby starts screaming. She stops to change its nappy. Off again to carry the baby down the steps. By the time she reaches the street, she's lucky the buggy is still there. By now Mr Bird, she must surely be asking herself, '*Is my journey really necessary?*'

'Okay Tess, I get the message. I will once again, see what I can do.'

'Ye're a grand man, so ye are.'

Janine and Peter lived on a crowded housing estate with their little girl of three years. Janine mentioned that she had to drag her three year old daughter, past one particular shop that had a large poster of a monster in their window, advertising a horror movie.

'I have to cross over the road. Otherwise she is kicking and screaming.'

Apart from this, all seemed well. That is until one morning when Tess called. The kitchen door was ajar. The mother had always told Tess, 'If the door is open, come straight in.'

'Janine?' No reply.

She walked in. There was no one in the kitchen. Muffled sounds were coming from the bedroom. In case she was getting dressed, Tess opened the door a fraction and put her head around the door and peeped in. What confronted her was beyond belief.

The father was in bed with his little girl and was sexually assaulting her. The girl leapt out of bed, wearing the attire more suited to a call girl. She wore a laced-up black and red basque-type corset. Her little legs were encased in black stockings with suspenders and black leather boots. The father had rolled over to the opposite side of the bed and hadn't realised his daughter had slipped out of the bed. Tess was horrified. She had witnessed a father involved in a sexual act with his young daughter. He was unaware that he had been caught in bed with his daughter in the actual act of sexually abusing her. He was now asleep.

Tess knew not to question or disturb him. She wanted the social worker and police to interrogate him. This was a situation where he was oblivious that he had been observed. Had he spoken at length with the health visitor, he could have easily refused to say anything further. Stating that he had already told the health visitor everything. This would have prejudiced the police from obtaining a statement. It would have been Tess's word against his. It was imperative that the police could question him first, unhindered. She rang the authorities.

When the police and social worker arrived, they went into the bedroom. He was lying naked in bed. He was told to get dressed and the reason why they were there. He walked in the sitting room, smiling and focussed on Tess.

'You don't believe what the police and social worker are saying about me do you? You know me? Do I look the sort of man that would do that to my own child?'

Tess was silent. In her head, she wanted him to look like one of those horrible looking men seen on a police 'Wanted' notice board. No, he was handsome, with an innocent-looking face. Not at all as she had imagined a paedophile would look. But there was no denying, what she had witnessed. She learned his wife had walked out on him the previous week. Before she left him, he had probably hung his dressing gown on the hook on the bedroom door; hiding what was now prominently displayed. The poster. The *same* poster that had always terrified the little girl.

Chapter Twenty Two

Tess sat with her manager on a bench in the County Court waiting area. Their conversation was interrupted by a man's voice asking, 'Can I sit here?' She looked up to find the perpetrator staring at her. It was difficult to believe that he was able to mingle alongside, or threaten a witness.

'You *are* on *my* side aren't you?'

'No, I am on the side of the child.'

He scowled and walked away.

The barrister for the prosecution fired his questions non-stop. At one point Tess was able to put an end to his questions.

'I am sorry I am unable to answer that.'

'Why not? Why can't you answer the question?'

'Because I am not a paediatrician.'

The judge gave the barrister a fierce look and he concluded his questioning.

After the defence lawyer had finished, Tess mistakenly thought with a sigh, that she could leave the witness box. She had forgotten it was now the turn of the Guardian ad Litem, the spokesperson on behalf of the child. The day seemed endless. After they left the court, waiting at the traffic lights, the father banged on the car window.

'It's all your fault, my child is going to be adopted. Wait 'till I get hold of you.'

'You will not be going on that estate for some time,' said her manager.

Her manager was adamant that when she gave Tess, permission to go there, she would not be allowed to go alone. Because of her problem case load, that would not be the only court case. There would be numerous attendances at case conferences and several court appearances. It didn't matter how many times Tess had to go to court on behalf of a victim, once the prosecution barrister started to question her, she always felt that *she* was the one on trial.

A lawyer once told her not to worry about it. 'Remember the court listens constantly to lies day after day. When a social worker or health visitor takes the stand, their honesty is unmistakable and so refreshing, it radiates like a beam of light illuminating the court.'

Driving back to the office following another case conference, Tess recalled the first time she had seen health visitors in their offices. It was a mistake to think they had an easy life. As she approached a junction, the lights were already green in her favour. A car was waiting to turn right at the lights. Without warning the waiting car, turned right, crashing into the side of her car. Tess's car crumpled and caved in. The other car, spun over and landed on its roof. Tess flitted in and out of consciousness. When she could open her eyes it was into a blue, flickering haze. A cacophony of sirens could be heard in the distance. Then her whole body started to hurt and shake. The shaking was the vibration of the fire service equipment, used to cut her out of the crushed metal, that once resembled a vehicle.

She didn't remember emerging from the shattered car. Or the ambulance journey to hospital where she stayed a few days, with a couple of broken ribs and a knee injury.

Having momentarily seen the car turn over before she blacked out, she was anxious to know what had happened to its occupant. The night sister had told her that no one else was admitted at the same time. That did not reassure her, in fact it did the opposite. By three o'clock in the morning, she was convinced the driver must be in the morgue?

Before dawn, she asked the night sister to check for her. On seeing that the patient was getting over anxious, she returned with some news. The woman driving, had sustained a minor injury to her face. She was treated in the Casualty Department, but not admitted, as she was getting married the next day. It explained why she had lost concentration.

Tess's car was taken by chance to her regular garage. The men at the garage could not believe anyone could have got out of the car alive. One mechanic rang the hospital and was pleased to learn that Tess was recovering. 'Please tell her she must NOT come and see the car.

An ambulance driver was an unexpected visitor at the hospital.

'All your personal papers were strewn all over the road. I could see they were marked confidential. I swiftly scooped them up and left them with your manager at the clinic.'

It had not occurred to her, what had become of her belongings.

Her manager visited with some accident forms to be signed as it was a leased car.

'It asks Mrs King, what were you doing at the point of impact? What should I put here?' Tess sighed. 'How about… praying?'

Michael had seen the crushed car. He too, implored her not to view it. Which of course made her all the more determined to go round and see it.

Once home, Michael went to give her a big hug.

'Ouch! No. Don't!'

Both he and visiting colleagues and family had forgotten about her broken ribs.

'I think I ought to wear a placard around my neck saying, *please don't hug me*!'

'I was so worried about you. You have no idea. Lenny, one of my colleagues attended. He came back and told me about it. I dashed over to the hospital as soon as he told me. You were unconscious. Then when I saw the car at the garage, I was shocked. It looked like one that had been through a crushing machine. I was scared I was going to lose you.'

He held her hand and gently kissed her on her forehead.

'I was scared too, the last thing I saw was the car turn over. I thought I had killed someone. That poor girl, fancy getting married the next day, with a facial injury.'

Whilst convalescing, and with a new car, she got Michael to accompany her as she drove repeatedly over the same area of the accident.

'No not again surely.'

'Yes Michael. I need to feel confident. I mustn't lose my nerve.'

Back at work, several non-urgent messages awaited her. The phone rang.

'Good morning Tess, David Bird here. Whatever happened to you? This phone has been silent for days. I read about your accident in the local paper, I've been waiting for you to contact me. I was quite expecting you to ring me from your hospital bed!'

Chapter Twenty Three

The health workers had been astonished at the sixteen year old mother.

'You can't feed a small baby Chinese food from a takeaway.'

'He doesn't want milk, he needs food now. He's always hungry.'

'What about his nappies?'

'He's got diarrhoea at the moment.'

'I'm not surprised.'

'I change him, he's nice and clean. He drives me up the wall. He knows when I get ready to go out and deliberately fills his nappy!'

After a case conference, the child was placed on the child protection register. A special foster mother was placed to work in the home with Jenny. She would help her to feed, bath and change the baby.

After four years there was a great improvement. Jenny was more mature, confident and sensible. She had learned a lot from her motherly helper. Now that she had another baby, a discreet, watchful eye was needed.

It had taken months for Tess to win over the confidence of Jenny. She was suspicious of anyone in authority.

'How are ye getting on?'

'Fine. The little one is doing great.'

The older child, now four, was squatted on the floor, absorbed in watching the children's programme *Danger Mouse* on television.

'Is that a bruise on his arm?'

Instead of making excuses, his mother was completely honest.

'Yeah, he was hitting the baby, so I hit his arm with my wooden spoon. Not hard, just a tap really.'

'The problem is, when he sees ye hitting him, he will think it is all right to hit ye, or the baby. In his mind that is the right thing to do. He will copy the behaviour.'

'What's the best thing to do then?'

'What I would call 'time out.' Remove him from the room and put him in his bedroom. Tell him he can come down and watch TV when he says he is sorry.'

'Does that work?'

'Usually. Ye have to start as ye intend to go on.'

'Yes, that's what Mrs Guthrie used to say, when she used to come to the house.'

'I noticed ye haven't got a stair-gate. Would ye like one? I have one in the car.'

'Oh thanks. I wanted to get one, but haven't got the money.'

Tess went to the boot of her car and stood the stair-gate in the hall.

'I'll see ye next week. Ye have my number if ye want to see me before then.'

When she got back to the office, she pondered over the situation of the bruise on the little boy's arm. Should she tell the social worker? The relationship was working so well, she didn't really want the social worker to intervene at this stage, over a small mark on the boy's arm. Yet common sense had to prevail. She rang their office.

'It is only a small mark. She made no excuses, she told me straight away why she did it. Because he hit the baby. She was extremely co-operative, quite unlike the Jenny we were used to, who would normally have flared up and told us where to go.'

'Yes I understand.'

'I don't want anyone going in there with hobnail boots, the matter is sorted really.'

'All right, I won't go in on this occasion as you are keeping tabs on her.'

'Thanks.'

Hardly had she replaced the receiver when the phone rang. It was Jenny's social worker.

'Sorry Tess, my manager is sending in Karl, another social worker.'

'Oh, when? I'd like to go in with him'

'Now. In fact I think he has just left.'

She chased out the door in an attempt to reach Jenny in time. She needed to explain why she had reported it and that she wasn't *expecting* anyone to go out from Social Services. Without an explanation, it could destroy the tentative relationship that she had been trying to build up with her. It was too late. She arrived at the same time as the social worker, although she did manage to dash in front of him to be first in the house.

'Hi, you're back soon,' came a cheery voice from the kitchen. 'Have you forgotten something?'

There wasn't any time for an explanation. Karl wasted no time and did the unforgivable. Instead of sitting down to calm the situation, he stood stern-faced, arms folded.

'I understand you have been hitting your child.'

Jenny was furious. So was Tess.

She turned on Tess. 'You bitch! You bloody squealer. I trusted you. You didn't tell me you were going to snitch on me to them sods,' she pointed at Karl. 'Get out …GET OUT,' she shrieked.

They left the kitchen and hurried into the passage way.

'Here, take your bloody stair-gate.'

Tess felt a searing pain in her back, where the heavy gate landed and she collapsed to the floor. Did the social worker come to her assistance? Did he hell. He had already legged it out of the front door and was driving back to his office. A few weeks later, she learned that Karl no longer worked at the same office. He had been moved from the area and possibly suspended.

There was no way now that the relationship with Jenny could be repaired by either branch of professionals.

When Tess first qualified as a health visitor, she found there were occasions at case conferences, when she hoped a very neglected child would be taken into care. She found it difficult to comprehend how social services could not see the problem glaring at them. They would thumb through their rule book, to find it did not permit the child to be removed. Other measures would have to be taken instead: such as a foster mother to go in, appointment with a child psychologist, daily social work visits or to go to a family day centre.

After a while Tess noticed what happened when a child *was* taken away from the family home and put into care. It wouldn't stop there; the first thing the mother would do, would be to become pregnant and have another child. It proved to be better to work with the mother and baby number one, than repeatedly take each child into care.

At one time in some instances, as many as six or seven children from the one family would had been taken into care, as the parents produced each replacement child.

Tess came across many of the life stories of how the parents had been beaten and neglected without any intervention, it begged the question as to why they were left to suffer and not helped out of the abyss they called home? Contrary to public opinion, Tess found that all child abuse doesn't takes place in poverty-stricken homes, many cases have come to light over the years where child abuse has taken place in wealthy families.

One wealthy family lived in a large manor house, with a maid and butler. Following anonymous calls of suspected abuse, due to their position in society, they were able to deflect the numerous visits from professionals that came knocking on their door. It was easy to believe the glib explanations for the child's absence.

'She has gone to stay with her aunt in Spain.'

'Her grandmother has her. She is staying with her in Paris.'

Yet all the time Bettina, was chained to a radiator in the attic. Bowls on the floor–fed like a dog. Left in despair that so many visits were being made. Yet no one insisted on coming in the house to look for her. Eventually the police obtained a warrant to search the place, and Bettina was removed and placed with a foster family. But not before nearly fifty *no entry visits* had taken place.

When Bettina left care, she was so anxious to find love, she fell for the first boy that showed any flicker of interest. In no time she was pregnant. She was determined to keep the baby; desperate for someone to love her. In her mind, she thought the baby would automatically do that. The council gave her a flat; but not having had a decent role model, found it difficult to cope. She hadn't reasoned with having to contend with an enormous amount of repressed anger, that could suddenly rise to the surface. A great deal of support and advice was given to her and the baby.

Tess and Bettina got on well. They had set up a system of coping mechanisms. From time to time the phone would ring in the office and a voice would say, 'Please come quickly.'

Tess knew immediately who it was. She would drop everything and make her way as quickly as she could to Bettina's flat. Inevitably the baby would be screaming and the mother would be in an extremely anxious state. Tess would take over.

'Have ye a feed made up? Bring it here with a jug of hot water.'

She would then take the baby and start to feed it.

'Now go and make yerself a cup of tea and have a lie down.'

Within a short while, mum and baby would have calmed down and Tess could leave... until the next time. Considering her dreadful upbringing, over time Bettina began to cope very well.

Tess found that most teenage mums, with parental support, coming from sizeable families, were quite remarkable. They had learned confidence dealing with younger siblings and with mum's latest baby. They just got on with it. Older mums in their thirties, would often panic with their first child. The babies would sense their mother's stress and often have infantile colic. Yet babies of teenage mums rarely did. Their mums took everything in their stride. A teacher told Tess, prior to having her first baby at the age of thirty-four,

'Huh, what's one baby? I'm used to controlling a class of thirty infants.'

Her confidence soon vanished, once she had the baby waking up every two hours to be fed.

Another, a pregnant general practitioner, incredibly asked Tess,

'Can you please forget I'm a GP. Tell me all you know!'

Chapter Twenty Four

Damien had been placed on the child protection register, following a series of cigarette burns found on his body. When Tess called she received a curt response.

'It's no good coming here. He's not here. He's in the nursery.'

She called in the nursery to check on his condition.

'He's fine now. We haven't seen any marks on him. Dad seems to be taking charge and giving mum a break.'

She looked at the dark-skinned, curly-haired boy playing happily with the other children.

The following week she called on the mother again.

'I told you last week, he's not here.'

'I know, I thought I'd come and see ye.'

'Come and see me? Oh… come in then.'

Karen lived in a council house, which she kept spotless. She seemed unable to relax and continued cleaning the already clean kitchen surfaces, whilst waiting for the kettle to boil. She gave Tess a cup of tea and sat down.

'That's a surprise, nobody usually wants to see *me*?'

Karen was a tall attractive girl in her early twenties. Her gleaming dark hair was tied back in a ponytail. She was pleased that someone had taken an interest in her.

'Never knew me mum. Put in a care home, when I was a baby. Met Terry. He was the first one to show he cared about me. He's a good man. Bit older than me, but that don't matter does it?'

Tess shook her head in agreement. 'No of course not.'

'I suppose you are going to see Damien now at the nursery?'

'No, not this time Karen, I have just called to see yerself.'

She grinned. 'Oh really, thanks.'

'I'll call again next week, if that's convenient?'

'Oh yes. Fine, thanks.'

As she left and walked down the pathway, Karen called out,

'I'll have the kettle on for you.' They both waved goodbye.

The following week Karen was in a foul mood, swearing and banging saucepans about in the kitchen.

'Are ye okay? I'll make the tea if ye like?'

'I'm pissed off. Terry has dumped all his clothes on the floor. Wait 'till he gets home. I've already done a whole pile of washing, now look, I've found some more.'

'Calm down Karen.' Tess filled the kettle and made the tea.

'Oh shit! *Now I've run out of biscuits!*' She spat the words out in a temper.

Karen's anger was spiralling.

'How often do ye get wound up like this?'

'Dunno. Sometimes I get so angry I feel like throwing a brick at the back wall.'

'When was the last time ye felt like this?'

'You mean when I burned that fag on Damien? I haven't done that again. But I do get angry every so often, it seems to build up.'

'How often?'

'The last time, I s'pose about a month ago. It happens about every four weeks, then I calm down.'

'Ye could have PMT Karen.'

'What's that?'

'Pre-menstrual tension. To do with ye hormones about five to ten days before ye have yer period. It can affect yer mood on a regular basis. Make ye irritable, anxious, headache that sort of thing.'

'I had a stinking headache this morning. Wait a minute, I'll look on the calendar. Oh yeah, I get the 'curse' in about six days.'

'Would ye like me to make a doctor's appointment for ye?'

'Can do.'

'I'll come with ye if ye like?'

'Would you?'

'Yes.'

'Okay.'

Tess took Karen to the doctor. She explained her menstrual cycle and bouts of anger. The doctor prescribed some medication.

Visiting over the next few months, it became obvious that PMT had caused her anger problem. From that day on, Karen did not lay a finger on Damien. A few months later he was taken off the child protection register. Karen never looked back. Terry, was very supportive and as soon as the little boy was in full-time school, she was able to take a part-time job in a supermarket. She was delighted to be able to help out financially, and it gave Karen her independence.

It was nearing Christmas, and the health visitors at Tess's clinic decided they would put on a one act play. It would be shown at their Christmas party.

To Tess's amusement, she had been cast in the role of a 'good time girl.' Lyn had lent her a very short skirt and some long dangly earrings.

'This skirt is a joke Lyn. It's no bigger than a scarf. Have ye ever worn it? It only just about covers me bum.'

'What are you complaining about? It doesn't need to fit you, as long as it fits the part.'

The group assembled at lunch break for a dress rehearsal. The skirt was so tight, Tess could just about put one leg in front of the other and shuffle.

'Oh yes,' called out the 'director', 'I must say Tess, you look very seductive.'

The door of the clinic opened and a flustered man walked in.

'Whose is that little white car outside?'

Tess looked puzzled. 'It's mine.'

'Well can you shift it? I need to get my van in there with the deliveries. Just park it outside the gate in the main road. You can drive it back in when I've finished unloading.'

Tess tottered to the door and left the building in high heels, heavy make-up, and a skirt the size of a handkerchief. Her outfit left nothing to the imagination. Once in the car, she drove outside onto the main road. Due to the Christmas rush with shopping in town, there was a build-up of traffic. To her dismay, she was confronted by the traffic police and the car was waved on. Every time she tried to park, there was either a sign with NO PARKING, or double yellow lines. Eventually she managed to find a parking spot down the bottom of a tree-lined road with its proliferation of large Tudor-style houses. She was a good half mile from the clinic, when the realisation hit her. That half mile had to be attempted, dressed as David Bird would say, as a woman of easy virtue.

It wasn't long before she was stopped on her way back to the clinic. In fact she was stopped a couple of times. The first was a mother with a young daughter, aged about seven years.

'Disgusting. Fancy coming down our street dressed like that. This is a respectable area.'

Another, a young man, wasted no time in chatting her up and asking her if she was free for business? She tried, but couldn't hurry. The road seemed interminably long. When she reached the clinic, she was greeted at the door by a reception committee and gales of laughter. Tears streamed down Lyn's face.

'It's all right for ye lot. Sure it wasn't funny. I was even propositioned.'

That made them laugh all the more. Looking at all their amused faces, she couldn't help smiling and blushing at her embarrassment.

Chapter Twenty Five

One of the saddest calls she had to make, was to the parents whose child had suddenly died. He had died of a cot death. It was hard to believe that the lively smiling baby she had only seen a few weeks before, had gone.

Tess knew, sudden infant death syndrome (S.I.D.S.) could happen around two to six months and under two years. This baby was eighteen months. She also knew it could be genetic, or that about 48 hours before, the baby would have had an upper respiratory viral infection. According to mum, the baby had been a bit snuffly. In fact they had all recently had colds, especially the older girl aged ten.

'I am just numb. I can't cry. It doesn't seem real.'

There was little Tess could do, except provide a listening ear and suggest bereavement counselling, or supportive organisations.

The following week when she called she was shocked to learn how the neighbours had reacted. She had hoped that friends and neighbours, would have rallied round to comfort a grieving mother. On the contrary, they had shunned her.

'I can't believe it. Mandy across the road. She had her baby the same time as me, she deliberately ignored me. She even crossed over the other side of the road with her buggy; wouldn't even speak to me.'

'That's terrible, Katie. I think people are very frightened. They're worried it could affect their child. She may think it could be infectious.'

'But we were friends. We used to go to Mum and Toddlers together.'

'I suspect that Mandy is lost for words. One minute ye were both happily pushing yer buggies together and comparing notes about yer babies. Now she doesn't know what to say to ye. The babies were the link between ye. Now that link has been broken.

'I feel so alone. I've been in touch with one of those organisations you gave me. I am having a visit tomorrow, from someone who lost her own baby like me.'

'Katie, only a person that has been in the same position, can truly understand what ye are going through.'

'I keep thinking it was something I did, or should have done? Did she cry out in the night and I didn't hear her?'

Tess hugged Katie and tried to reassure her.

'There was nothing ye could have done. How is yer husband coping?'

'I'm worried Tess, he hasn't shed a tear. But I know he's grieving in his own way. He's bottling up his emotions as he always does. He always says that I do the emotional and that he does the practical. He's had to go back to work, so that helps I suppose.'

Tess felt so helpless. But there was nothing she could do to ease Katie's enormous grief and pain. She wouldn't dream of quoting those well-meaning platitudes that people always trot out.

You'll get over it. Have another baby. Time is a great healer.

She found herself shedding a few tears with Katie. At one time she would have held back her feelings. Over the years, she found she couldn't help but let a tear or two streak down her cheeks, especially when it involved children. Together there was unashamed weeping. When this happened, some clients would later remark how it had helped them realise that someone really cared.

As she left the house, she recalled the incidents of when a child died when she worked on the children's ward, how everyone had tears running down their cheeks, nursing staff, doctors, even the domestic staff and cleaners, especially the cleaners.

When confronted with several emotional incidents during one day, a child's death, an abused child, it would be easy to think around every corner was some disaster. Where were the normal families? Tess would then take off to visit someone in a non-problematical family for a developmental check.

She always looked forward to going home to her foster child. Although unable to adopt her, it didn't matter anymore. To go home to a happy contented child, that she had managed permanently to rescue from a house of horrors, made up for everything she had encountered during the day. Despite Jade's dreadful background, she had grown into a normal healthy teenager. The school had got used to Tess standing in loco parentis. Any event, whether it was a play, a sports day, or a parents evening, either Tess or Michael, or both would be there.

The latest excitement was a school trip to France for five days. Jade spoke of nothing else.

'I'll be able to use some of the French we learned at school, won't I Mum?'

The word Mum was a revelation. Until now, she had only called her aunty. This was the first time she had called her mum. Tess held her breath and thought, if only it were true. Her heart skipped a beat at the sound of the name, but she didn't correct her.

'Ye will. Would ye like to have a little practice this evening?'

'Do I have to eat snails there? They eat them don't they?'

'Not if ye don't want them. But I don't think they are the same as garden snails.'

'What other funny things do they eat?'

'Here's Michael,' she hesitated to say uncle, 'Ask him. He went to France to play football.'

'Did you Dad?'

Tess noticed he gulped at his new title.

'Yes darling. I went with our local police team. We played against Calais Gendarmerie.'

'What did you eat Dad?' Jade grinned, pleased that Michael hadn't contradicted his new name.

'Oh, snails, frogs legs all that sort of thing.'

'Ugh! I won't eat that garden stuff.'

'You eat lettuce, that's out of the garden.'

'That's different, we don't eat the caterpillars we find on them, do we?'

'No, because they are hairy, like the spider that would wriggle and jiggle inside you.'

She leapt up and pummelled Michael on the chest in fun. They laughed together.

'Calm down ye two. I'd better start cooking some frogs legs for our meal.'

Jade was so excited, the following day she brought home a form to sign, consent for the school trip to France. Later that evening, Tess showed Michael the form.

'Mm. Parental or guardian consent.' He gave her a worried look.

'Can we say we are her guardians Michael?'

'Nope 'fraid not. We are *not* her Legal Guardians. That has to go to the Family Proceedings Court at the request of the parent or social services.' He sighed, 'Once again Lena has to sign papers.'

'What can we do?'

'Try and get Lena to sign. I'll try if you like tomorrow.'

'She doesn't care if he she disappoints her and she can't go.'

'I know. I'll do my diplomatic best.'

The following evening when she got home, she knew the verdict. Jade was curled up on her bed sobbing.

'Dad told me Lena won't sign the paper, for me to go to France. I hate her, I HATE her.'

'Oh darlin,' I'm so sorry. We will take ye somewhere special instead.'

'I want to go to France. I promised Lois my friend, we would sit together on the coach. It's not fair, It's not FAIR, Lois is going.'

'I know darlin'. Life isn't always fair. No one can go through their life on this earth, without finding at some time, that something is unfair. Life can be full of disappointments. That is how we learn to grow strong.'

'I can't believe she would be so rotten. I know she hates me. Now that's proved it.'

'Don't cry. Ye will go to France one day, not with the school. We will take ye one day. Meanwhile we will think of something different for the weekend. A fun adventure place to go.'

Jade cheered up a little at the thought of a fun trip, rather than an educational one.

'Kids seem to like me now Mum. At one time kids would ask the teacher if they could sit somewhere else. They didn't want to sit near me. They don't seem to mind now. That's how I got Lois as a special friend.'

Now that she always had clean clothes on and doesn't smell, thought Tess. Michael came in the bedroom.

'Has she told you?'

'Yes.'

They left the bedroom and went down stairs.

'We should have known how she would react. Anytime there is a paper to sign, Lena always backs out. I've told her *we* will take her somewhere, an adventure place.'

'I've got an idea darling, one of my colleagues has just come back from Butlins at Bognor Regis. There was a big pool, a funfair, entertainment. His family had a great time. He reckoned some people just go for a weekend.'

'That sounds grand, Michael.'

'I'll organise it then. I'll nip up and tell her.'

'What do you think Jade?'

She leapt off the bed and flung her arms around Michael. 'I love you… Dad.'

Chapter Twenty Six

1983

The school nurse called in at the baby clinic looking for Tess.

'Hello, I spoke to Leonard Yeo this morning, he's an eight year old boy. His mum is one of your clients.'

'That's right. I saw his mum the other day. She's pregnant. Although not very happy at the prospect.'

'According to the boy, he overheard his Mum tell his Dad, that if they make her have the baby, she's going to kill it. She's a strange woman. I noticed she was more concerned at the state of her son's trousers, than his leg wound.'

'I'll go and see her this afternoon.'

The woman was out when Tess called, so she knocked on a neighbour's door.

'I'm looking for Bernadette Yeo? I'm her health visitor. Does she go to work?'

'Work? She has a small job round the corner. She's a compulsive cleaner.'

'What do ye mean?'

'Non-stop cleaning. When she's finished her own, which takes her all morning to reach perfection, she's off to clean a lady's house. Have you been in there?'

'Yes.'

'See all the notices on the walls then, did you?'

'I didn't read them.'

'They're all instructions for her son and husband. Different cleaning jobs that must be done every day. Another one in the bathroom, says they've got to clean down all the walls after a bath. Would you like to come in and wait a minute? She'll be back about three.'

The neighbour gave Tess a cup of tea.

'Are ye friendly with Mrs Yeo?'

'Just neighbourly. I think her husband works at the tax office.

'How long have ye known her?'

'Mm, couple of years. She lived in Spain for some time, with her husband and little boy. She had a Spanish nanny for him. She told me once, she never wanted any children. Poor kid, he couldn't speak a word of English at first. She reckoned she never spoke to him. Left all the conversation to the nanny. Ah, there she is, going in the gate.'

'I'll give her time to get sorted and then I'll call on her. Thank ye for the tea.'

'You won't tell her what we have been talking about?'

'No of course not. What ye have discussed, is in confidence.'

'Bernie, can I come in?'

'Yes. Wipe your feet. What's wrong? You heard from the hospital?'

'No. Why?'

'I'm having an abortion?'

'The hospital will only terminate a pregnancy Bernie, if there are medical grounds.'

'They're going to terminate on mental grounds.'

'Why is that?'

'I've told them, if they don't give me an abortion, I'll abort it myself. If I can't pull it off and it's born, then I'll have to kill it.'

'Bernie, that would be murder. If ye do that, ye'll end up in prison.'

'That's what the doctor at the hospital told me. In the end I made him believe me. He's going to abort the foetus on Monday.'

'Would ye not consider having the baby and let it go for adoption? There are plenty of women desperate to have a baby.'

'My husband asked me about that. No, I couldn't bear to get fatter and fatter and go through all that pain again. No, my mind's made up. I'm going in hospital Sunday night. I'll be in theatre Monday morning, then I can forget the whole thing. He's going to sterilise me at the same time.'

There was no reasoning with her. She was resolute to destroy the child in her womb. If she felt that strongly, it was best that she was going to be sterilised, thought Tess. It shocked her that she had this positive reaction about sterilisation and realised just how far both of them as Catholics, had rejected their faith. Bernadette would be seen as committing a mortal sin by the church. The teachings would say, 'To kill the embryo and cause the child to die is murder, a mortal sin.' Thomas Aquinas had written, *it was done with the full knowledge of the grave and sinful nature of the act.*

How hypocritical, she thought. We hear about priests violating the bodies of children in their care. Yet they are given sanctuary. Their crimes for years are hidden from the police and the public. Did that monk that raped me, or that Abbot, still remain in the Mother Church? Bernie had some mental health issues. For whatever reason she seemed to be eaten up with anger and revenge. Tess pulled herself up sharply. She would *not* go there. Her life had changed radically with a wonderful husband and 'daughter' lent to them, whom they both loved dearly.

She tried not to think how their lives would change, once Jade became an adult, got married and left home. Already the young lads were beginning to show an interest in her and she was flattered by their attention.

On Saturday, Jade was off to the bowling alley with Lois and her brother Matthew.

'He gave me a small box of chocolate sweets the other day. I think he likes me Mum.'

As she approached the front gate, dad did a sly peep out the window.

'Quick, it's the big romance. He has just given her a peck on the cheek.'

'I shouldn't worry darlin', it's the sort of thing a four-year-old would do.'

'Have you no romance in your soul girl? This is boy meets girl. Hearts and flowers stuff.'

'Away wid ye, sure she's no age at all.'

She came bounding in. Her face flushed with excitement.

'Had a good time dear?'

'Brill. I didn't win, but it was good fun. Matt bought me a coke. I told him I had my own pocket money, but he insisted.'

'That was nice of him.'

'Yes, I think I quite like him.'

'What, because he gives you sweets and buys you a coke?' chimed in Michael, listening in the next room. 'We are going to have to watch this young lady. Methinks I feel romance in the air.' He grinned and teased her by singing, *'Love is the greatest thing, the old but yet the latest thing.'*

'Oh! stop it Dad, we are just friends. Like me and Lois.'

Michael and Tess smiled at each other. We are just friends aren't we Tess? They were soon giving each other long, lingering kisses.'

'Ugh! That's gross. Do you two have to? I feel sick.'

Chapter Twenty Seven

'It's Matthew at the door. Come in. She won't be long.'

'Mum, can you come up here a minute?'

'Take a seat Matthew.'

Tess disappeared upstairs to the bedroom.

'Mum, can you zip me up at the back please?'

'There ye are. Ye look lovely dear. A little less lipstick I think,' she handed her a tissue. 'That's it, ye'll be fine. Do ye know which cinema it is?'

'No, but Matt does.'

'Don't be late. Ye've school in the morning.'

'We won't.'

Knowing that Matthew was waiting, she hurried downstairs, grabbed her coat and they were gone.

'I hope they'll be all right Michael?'

'Of course they will. He seems a nice enough lad. I've seen enough of the others to be able to pick out the decent ones.'

Matthew was tall with fair hair. He was wearing jeans and a T-shirt blazoned with, No One Understands My Generation.

'I've seen his mum a little dumpy lady, always in a hurry.'

As Tess would say, the pair were *doing a strong line*.

At sixteen Matthew, was two years older. His mother had hoped he would stay on at school and go on to university. He lost interest when his father left them a year ago.

'Mum, it makes sense for me to leave school, get a job and then I can help you pay for food and stuff.'

It did make sense at the time. His mother was grateful for any help she could get, especially as her husband had vanished. She had been unable to trace him, which enabled him to avoid paying any child maintenance money. Rumour had it he had gone off with a woman with two children. For some time their relationship had hit a rocky patch. He had been coming home from the pub, in the early hours of the morning and sleeping on the sofa. One night he failed to return home and hadn't been seen since. Lois and Matthew were greatly upset too. They loved their father.

The teachers noticed a lack of concentration especially with Matthew. It soon started to affect his school work. Jade had noticed it too. He would make arrangements to meet her, then forget.

One time she waited outside the library. When it started to rain she decided to wait inside. Matthew had a day off from work at a Tesco supermarket and she had half-term holiday.

She waited for two hours and started to walk home. In a corner down an alleyway, she saw him, huddled together with a group of other lads. He was crouching down. Two of the boys were fighting; the others laughing at their antics.

She was angry. She had wasted a whole morning waiting for him. He didn't care about her, he was too keen on being with his mates.

The next time at his mum's house, he began to act out of character. He didn't seem to be able to relax. He lost the thread of their conversation.

He jumped up, 'You'd better go home now.'

'It's only six o'clock, I thought we were going to watch that film?'

'No. I'm not interested.'

'It looks as though you're not interested in me either.'

'Not really. Could do with a change. A different girl. One that's more fun and adventurous.'

She stormed out and slammed the door, just as his mum was about to come in.

'What's upset her?'

'Dunno. She wanted to watch a film. I didn't. She always wants her own way.'

'Ah well then Matt, you are probably better off without her.'

Michael found her crying in the kitchen.

'What's the matter?'

'Matt's the matter.'

'Oh dear, you two had words?'

'Dad, that's the problem, he won't speak to me. He's gone all moody and snappy.'

'I expect he's still feeling upset about losing his dad.'

'That's not it,' she snivelled. 'He doesn't want me anymore.'

Michael put his arm around her. 'I'm sure that's not true, not when I've seen you two together.'

'Dad, you haven't seen him lately, not since he left school. He's gone off me. Probably going with someone from work. Anyway he's told me we're finished.'

'I know it's hard to take darling, when that happens. It's not much good if you don't feel the same about each other. It's best to go your separate ways. But when it's your first love, I know, it seems like the end of the world.'

'But I love him Dad,' she started to cry uncontrollably.

'Come on now. This will all blow over in a few days and you'll be back together again. Strange things happen, when that old devil love comes on the scene. Take my sister; when we were kids, she would say she couldn't stand my friend

Jim who lived next-door. Hated him. Left home to work in London. Came back a couple of years later. The next thing I heard, they were going out together and getting engaged. They eventually got married. You know Uncle Jim? Well he used to be my old school mate, now he's my brother-in-law. Here drink this.'

'What is it?'

'Drinking chocolate. Cheer up. What say you mum and me, we go to the bowling alley this evening. On the way home we could stop off at a fast food restaurant? Blackened tears from secretly applied mascara, streamed down her flushed cheeks. He handed her a tissue.

'Go on, have a hot bath. You'll feel better afterwards. Don't let mum see you upset when she comes in. You know what she's like. She'll be knocking on his door demanding answers.'

Michael and Tess both appreciated that for Jade, having come from a loveless home, the loss of her first love, was more traumatic. They did their best to cheer her up and get her to focus on other activities.

A few days later, Michael rushed in at six o'clock carrying a white, paper-wrapped parcel. No need for anyone to ask what was in it? The delicious aroma of fish and chips quickly wafted throughout the house.

'Where's Jade?'

'In her bedroom. She had some homework to do. I'll warm some plates.'

He hurried up stairs. 'Can you be ready by a quarter to seven?'

'Yes. Why?'

'I would like to take you somewhere that starts at seven.'

After she'd had a quick bath and changed into some casual clothes, they sat down for their meal.

'This is all very mysterious Michael?'

'I'll tell you about it later dear.'

'Ready Jade? Come on then.'

She jumped in the car. They arrived at a large well-lit community hall. Music and young people laughing and joking, brightened up the damp evening air.

'What's happening here Dad?'

'You, my love, are happening. You are about to join one of the best youth clubs around. I've spoken to the senior youth worker. They are expecting you. Here, take this. Here's some money to join and for refreshments. I'll pick you up later.'

Her face broadened into a huge grin.

'Go on. Go on in and enjoy yourself. You'd better like it. I've gone to a lot of trouble today to sort it.'

'Thanks Dad.'

She gave him a quick hug and hurried into the hall. As the door opened, bright lights and eighties disco music spilled out on to the normally quiet neighbourhood.

Chapter Twenty Eight

'Ye were going to tell me darlin' why the rush to get Jade into a youth club?'

'Did you know she was still trying to get back with Matthew?'

'Yes, she keeps phoning him. Leaving him messages.'

'I heard one of his messages. She doesn't know that. One of the places he suggested to meet tonight, was where a gang of druggies hang out.'

'Holy Mary, ye don't think he's started taking drugs do ye?'

'Could be. Can't be sure. I didn't want to say anything to either of you, but I saw him the other day, with this gang. He could have been smoking a spliff. I was off duty, on my way home. Two of my colleagues were dealing with it at the time. Without stopping and searching him myself, I couldn't be sure. I was desperate to sort something out for her. I did a run around of all the youth clubs I know. The most popular one had a waiting list and it was also the only one meeting tonight. I had a word with Keith, the youth leader who runs it. Managed to twist his arm. I promised to give a short talk one evening to the youngsters. I wanted to get her in straight away.'

'Why the rush?'

You know what teenagers are like. Try to stop them doing something, they look for another way around it. She could have sneaked out to meet him.'

'What about Matthew?'

'We'll be looking into this new gang. They call themselves the Chasing Tigers. Stupid name. Asking for trouble. It's a play on Chasing the Dragon. They may only be using weed, or it could be worse.' He looked at his watch. 'I'll have a quick cuppa then I must think about getting back to this youth club.'

The youngsters began crowding the pavement, laughing, joking. There was plenty of happy banter, all without drugs or alcohol. Several cars drew up to take them home. Michael's eyes searched the crowd.

'Hi Dad,' Jade began to weave her way through the group.

'Bye Jadie,' called out a couple of lads.

'See you next week,' called another.

'How did it go?'

'Great Dad, I loved it. There was a disco and there were several little rooms leading off from the main hall where you could do all sorts of things. There was table tennis, a small gym, pool table and in the kitchen they were baking cheese scones.'

Michael grinned and put his hand out.

'Sorry, I ate one and gave the other to one of the boys. After the individual activities we all went in the hall for the disco. I recognised quite a few of the kids from school.'

She chatted all the way home, highly elated at having found some new friends.

'Go on in then and tell mum all about it.'

They were both delighted that she had found a new interest and new friends. Over the next few weeks, thoughts of Matthew faded into the background.

'I was right about Matthew. I can tell you now, because it's in the evening paper. I've just seen our girl reading the paper in the sitting room, so she'll soon know all about it.'

The headlines: **Teenage Drug Gang Busted**. Chasing Tigers chased off the street. It gave the names of two boys of eighteen. Others were aged sixteen. Three caught in possession of large quantities of cannabis and two with cocaine. One is to be charged with dealing class A drugs.

'Hey Mum, Matthew's been caught taking drugs.'

'Yes we were just talking about it. They are up in court on Monday.'

'Do you think that was why Matthew was nasty with me? He used to be so nice.'

'Could be, cannabis can alter someone's personality, can't it Tess?'

'Yes. The brain keeps developing into the twenties. So the effects can bring about changes in the brain.'

'What do they feel like when they take it?'

'When they first try it, some don't feel anything, others feel more relaxed or 'high.'

'So it's not that bad then is it?'

'Yes it is. It's addictive. Some become depressed, anxious, problems with their memory. It's unpredictable. They lose motivation.'

'It was only the other day I saw his mum,' said Tess. 'She stopped and had a quick chat. Apparently he used to be keen on playing football.'

'Yes he did.' Jade put the newspaper down and looked up. 'He wanted to be a professional footballer.'

'The way he's going, the only football he'll be playing, will be in a Youth Custody Centre.'

'I heard on the radio,' said Tess, 'they'd all been involved in burglary and were found carrying offensive weapons. I feel really sorry for his mum and yer friend Lois.'

'Lois will probably tell me all about it tomorrow.'

'I see Matthew was given a custodial sentence, I think you had a lucky escape, Jade. The court took a serious view of the burglary and that he was found threatening an elderly gentleman with a knife. These youngsters think burglary is a victimless crime' said Michael. 'They think the insurance will pay for another television, or they will get money to replace their jewellery. That old man, Jade, is in a bad way. He can't sleep. His nerves are shattered. Even though Matthew isn't out on the street, that poor old chap is frightened to go out. Anyway you don't need the likes of Matthew. Since this past year, you've been going to the youth club and made some new friends there haven't you?'

'Yes, especially Stefan, we get on great. I haven't given Matt a thought, not since Stef and I became an item. Last week after the cinema, we went back to his place. His mum and dad are really nice. He goes to the convent school, so I would never have met him if I hadn't gone to the youth club. I'm glad you made me go.'

'What I've seen of him, he seems a decent enough lad.'

'Oh Dad, he's so different from Matt. I think he's cool. He's adopted, you know, doesn't know his real mum and dad. He said it doesn't bother him. His adoptive mum and dad are lovely…nearly as lovely as you and dad.'

'Well thank ye darlin'. It's a good thing ye found someone ye really like.'

'That's true, otherwise like Matthew, you could have ended up sewing mailbags!'

Jade was reluctant to give away her true feelings of love for Stefan. Despite the fact they had been going together for some time. She knew her dad would only tease her and she would have to suffer a lecture from mum. So she quickly changed the subject.

'The youth club are putting on a comedy play later on. It should be fun.'

'We'll have to go darlin'.'

'Yes we certainly will. I'm doing my pep talk there next week. Listen Jade, I don't want any hecklers.'

'Oh Dad, have I got to listen? I think I've heard everything possible about drugs these last few weeks.'

'You could find it interesting. My boss has allowed me to take along the tray of sample drugs found on the street. I shall be mostly talking this time on cocaine. One of the local pubs is rife with it. Even the owner was found using.'

'What does it look like?'

'It's usually sold on the street as a white powder. Those street dealers put all sorts in it; cornflour, sugar, even talcum powder. When they talk about crack, that's the noise it makes when the mixture is smoked.'

'Is that the same as snow? Jason's dad was on snow.'

Michael chuckled. 'He was probably skiing in the alps.'

'Dad, don't be silly, seriously, he was saying if his dad wasn't on snow, he wouldn't have hit his mum. Those men at Lena's, used to talk about snow or flake, they weren't talking about the weather.'

'Take no notice. He was only teasing.'

'I think you had a lucky escape, young lady. If you had gone off and met Matthew, as he asked you to, you could have found yourself being dragged into the gang and ended up being arrested with Matthew that night.'

'How did you know about that?'

'Ah ha,' he tapped the side of his nose, 'that's what detectives do, sniff out all the places where these gangs meet.'

'But how did you know I was going to go?'

'I didn't, but I wasn't prepared to wait around and find out. That's why I got you into that youth club pretty sharp.'

Later when Jade was in bed. Tess and Michael discussed her latest romance.

'This lad, she seems keen on him. He obviously thinks something of her to take her home to meet his folks and did you notice that chain she was wearing?'

'Wasn't it the Celtic knot my sister Maura gave her?'

'If you look closely it's very similar, with one exception, I noticed inside the knot is a tiny Claddagh floating heart. My mother being Irish, used to have one. It has a special meaning doesn't it? You would know what that means Tess, wouldn't you?'

'Sure I do. It means love, loyalty and friendship. Saints preserve us, she's only sixteen. Here we go again!' exclaimed Tess.

Chapter Twenty Nine

The Senior Manager called a meeting of health visitors.

'In future you are *not* to address women according to their marital status. When speaking or enquiring of a client, where possible refer to their first name. Not Mrs, Miss or Ms, there are many unmarried women today, with no intentions of entering matrimony. They can be capable, confident and caring parents without a legal piece of paper. We should not make distinctions.'

The staff murmured agreement.

Emma Brown was Tess's first call. Every new-born child is visited on the tenth day, unless the midwife is still in attendance. She was about to do a new-birth visit on behalf of a colleague who was on holiday. She remembered the pep talk from her manager, no titles first name only. She knocked at the door. A man in his late twenties opened the door.

'I'm the health visitor, I've come to see Emma.'

'Oh, come in. We are in a bit of a muddle, I'm busy decorating at the moment. Doing up the sitting room.'

Odd, she thought, usually the last minute job is to wallpaper the nursery. He showed her into the wall-stripped room and offered a lone wooden chair. She looked around and couldn't see any congratulation cards on the mantelpiece or window-ledge. Where were the usual trappings of a baby in the house? Baby clothes or nappies on the sofa? Nor was there any sound of a baby. For one dreadful moment, she wondered whether the baby had not survived. Until Emma came in the room, smiling. Like most recently-delivered mothers, she noted she had not yet returned to her normal body contours.

'Emma, this is the health visitor.'

'Hello, would you like some tea, I've just made some.'

'Thank ye very much. I'm gasping, we had a very dry lecture this morning.'

Emma returned with a mug of tea. Looking at the notes, Tess, knowing that the Registrar called on the maternity ward twice a week, noticed the baby had already been registered.

'I see ye have called the baby Christopher.'

Her husband looked shocked. 'What! She hasn't had the baby yet!'

Trying to cover her embarrassment, she bluffed her reason for the visit and said,

'Oh well then, I suppose I'd better do an ante-natal visit instead.'

So much for not using the client's title thought Tess. Who is this woman? *Will the real Emma Brown please stand up!*

The prospective father leaned over to look at her file. He realised it was a mistaken identity.

'Let me see the address.' He paused. 'Ah now, this says Emma Brown 21 Station Terrace. My wife is Emma Newson. We live at 21 Station Close. In other words you are in the wrong house, mate.'

'Oh I'm dreadfully sorry. I apologise. I've only ever made that mistake once, and that was really awful. The worst thing was, I happened to be tucking into the woman's home-made cakes before I discovered it was the wrong house.'

Emma with a far-away expression remarked, 'We don't have any cake in the house do we Derek?' As though cake was a necessary requirement for the health visitor.

'Thank ye for the tea. I'll be catching up with ye both at a later date. Hope all goes well.'

With a sigh and a blush, she waved the couple goodbye. Had I been able to say Mrs Brown, she mused, I would not have got a foot in the door. The mistake would have been corrected by her husband.

'Emma Brown?' This time, she was greeted warmly by an older woman.

'I'm Emma's mum, do come in.'

Emma entered carrying the baby.

'So this is Christopher,' said Tess this time with confidence.

'I suppose you heard about my unusual delivery then?'

'No, what happened?'

'You tell her Mum.'

'The idea was for me to take my daughter to the hospital once she went into labour. Being farming folk, we have a Range Rover. I thought it would have been more comfortable for Emma to lay on the back seat.'

'Yes, that was how we planned it didn't we Mum?'

'We know the saying about *best laid plans* and all that. I had the call about three in the morning. Woke my husband and told him I was on my way. Jumped in the car. Doing well until the police stopped me for speeding. I explained what was happening. They took no notice. The police officer was not in a hurry. He was more like a tortoise on heat. Had I got my driving licence? Was the car insured? Whose name is on it? I was sweating. The more I panicked, the more I suppose I was giving out the wrong signals. It looked as though I had something to hide. They opened up the boot and scratched around. By the time I reached the house, I was too late, Emma and Ricky had taken off in an ambulance.'

'Not quite as straight forward as that though, was it Mum?'

'No, you tell the health visitor what happened next.'

'My waters had already broken. Pains were coming fast and furious. Ricky reckoned that we couldn't wait any longer, that we'd have to go in our car. That was supposed to be plan B. As we walked down the pathway, the baby's head was coming through. I'm moaning in pain. Trying hard not to wake the neighbours. Ricky actually caught the baby, it was delivered on the pathway in the front garden. He carried the baby, still attached to the umbilical cord, and I waddled indoors. The ambulance man came and cut the cord. I didn't see any reason to go to hospital. But he was insistent on account of any infection. Cheeky devil he said.'

'People are supposed to plant seeds in the garden – not babies!'

'What does it say on the birth certificate as his place of birth then, Emma?' asked Tess.

'Here, I'll show you.' She went over to a cabinet and took out the certificate, which stated: *Born in the vicinity of 21 Station Terrace.*

They both found it amusing at Tess's faux pas of going to the wrong house, when the woman hadn't even had the baby.

Her next visit was to a wealthy Indian family. It was such a contrast to most new birth visits. The door was opened by a woman in her forties, dressed in a colourful sari. She smiled her welcome and beckoned her in with, 'She's upstairs.'

As she ascended the huge, white, spiral-staircase she could see into the large bedroom. The mother could hardly be seen for bedclothes. Her head peered out from under the thick, sumptuous, bedcovers.

This family were observing the traditional forty-day lying in confinement, which they named Jaappa in Hindi. Tess recalled in Hindu culture, it was often considered a time of impurity, because of the normal processes of childbirth. During this period the mother is looked after by her own mother or a mother figure. She is released from undertaking any household tasks or religious rites. Sex is forbidden. Although Tess had met the father, he was not staying in the same house. She had learned that he would have a ritual bath first, in order to purify himself, before he could visit his wife.

Tess remembered when she did her midwifery, that before a mother could observe Jaappa and leave the birthing room, she first had to be bathed and massaged with oils.

When the new mother was being helped to the toilet, by her own mother, she noticed that they had decorated the young mother's legs with henna art. This was supposed to deter her from getting up. In a way Tess wished a brief version of this confinement, could be the norm for some poor women she had met. Many would be up and on their feet the next day. Up and about doing the washing and other chores, as well as feeding and tending to the baby, without any help from family or friends. Although some forthright mothers, would no doubt shun the idea, as the utmost in laziness.

This mother as a consequence, was relaxed, without a single problem with breast feeding. She was rested and able to produce plenty of milk to feed the baby, and bond with him. The whole scene was one of tranquillity and of a restful sanctuary.

Chapter Thirty

1987

'Tess, you remember Matthew?'

'That was some time ago, Jade's been going with Stefan, let me see… two years? It's lucky she got out of that romance in time. What's happened to him? Don't tell me he's been arrested for possession of heroin this time?'

'Worse, he was found in a shopping centre stairwell. You know, where you come down the steps to the exit. Several people say they saw him. As usual, they say they didn't want to get involved, they just walked on. No one asked him if he was all right, he was flat on his back with a syringe at his side, so they just left him. The cleaner found him in the morning. Nothing she could do, she called an ambulance. He was pronounced dead on arrival at the hospital.'

'Oh, how awful, his poor mother. If only one person who'd walked by had just sent for an ambulance, he may have survived. No one gave a thought that this boy was someone's son.'

'Exactly, that's what the doctor said at the hospital.'

'That's terrible Michael.'

'Another waste of a life, I can't get used to these young kids ending their lives like that.'

'What a sad end. When ye think back to what a fine lad he was, when we first met him. Jade was so smitten too. At least she didn't get embroiled in all that. That boy she's with Stefan now, he's a grand lad, seems very sensible.'

'She's coming in now, *you* going to tell her Tess, or shall I?'

'No good keeping it from her, she'll only hear about it from Lois, or read it in the paper.'

'Hi Mum, Stef's calling for me earlier tonight.'

'Just a minute, your mum has something to tell you.'

'Your dad has just been telling me about Matthew.'

'What about him?'

'Something dreadful has happened to him.'

'I know, Lois told me. He overdosed on heroin. He'd been in rehab trying to come off; but after two days, he discharged himself.'

'No it's worse than that…he's dead.'

'What! How?'

'He was found this morning. Taken to hospital but it was too late.'

'Oh my God, it's that Tiger Gang's fault. I didn't see Lois today. She will already know. Why the hell do boys join gangs?'

'Not all gangs are involved in criminal activity. People hear the word gang these days and tend to think the worst; it's not illegal to join a gang. It's illegal to be involved in drugs or use knives. If you were to walk out of here carrying that kitchen knife, you could be arrested. Or anything that could be considered an offensive weapon.'

'Yes Dad, I know. But some people, tell me they take a small knife out with them to protect themselves.'

'It's no good someone saying they take it out with them for protection. In the eyes of the law, it means that person intends to use it. If they are caught carrying a knife that person could be arrested.'

'You haven't answered my question Dad; why do boys join gangs?'

'There are lots of reasons, often to feel protected from other rival gangs in the area. Could be to make money, some young people think it's a glamorous life; they like to have power over other people.'

'Why do you think Matt joined?'

'Family reasons may have triggered it off. He loved his dad, his dad abandoned him for someone else with children. He could have been looking for a male role model, the leader of the gang took his place. He looked up to him, admired him; here was someone that the gang members respected. There are many reasons.'

'Oh, gosh, is that the time? Stef will be here in twenty minutes. He's taking me somewhere special he said, for my birthday. He told me not to eat before I left. I think he's going to take me to a posh restaurant, like he did last year.'

'Or a burger bar on the sea front,' joked Michael.

Jade frowned and poked the tip of her tongue out at him. Michael grinned.

'Ye'd better hurry up. Ye know how long ye take to get ready.'

She scampered up the stairs and was soon racing to the front door.

'Have ye seen that enormous boxed card in her bedroom, that Stefan sent her?'

'No, I'll have a peep in a minute.'

'Ye were going to try and call in and see Adam today, did ye find time? Didn't ye say he had a new flat?'

'I didn't get time today. Why don't we both go after dinner this evening?'

'Yes, why not. It's a while since I saw him. How do ye think he's doing?'

'He seems a lot more stable on those new drugs the hospital gave him. He should feel a lot safer too in Supported Housing. The warden or psychiatric nurse, go in every day. They check how is. Make sure he's taking his pills. Check if he has any problems. Mind you, I can't see him ever being able to do a job of work.'

'As long as he is settled and feels happy. That is all ye should wish for.'

Later Michael clattered down the stairs two at a time and joined Tess in the kitchen.

Breathless he remarked, 'Crikey, that's one super-duper card up here. Did you read what he wrote in it? Crikey, it sounds pretty serious.'

'That's what I thought. Don't forget she eighteen on Monday. Her college course finishes in July.'

'You know what that means darling?'

'What?'

'No more bended knees at Lena's, for her permission for anything. Not ever again.'

He drew her close to him. They embraced each other. Michael whispered in her ear.

'Did we promise to go and see Adam tonight?'

'I think it was just a suggestion,' she smiled.

'Come on let's cuddle up on the sofa.'

Later Tess joined Michael in the bedroom. After they had made love, he leaned over and opened his bedside cabinet and took out an blue oblong velvet box.

'Your hint has paid off darling.'

'What do ye mean?'

'Those little subtle hints about how long we have been married. I was going to give this to you on our anniversary next week, with my card. But if the two love birds can celebrate early, so can we.'

She slowly opened the box to reveal a beautiful gold watch.

'That is lovely.' Oh Michael, I do love ye.'

'I know, just because I buy you presents from time to time.'

'No silly.' Giving him a mock thump on the chest. 'Ye mean everything to me.'

Chapter Thirty One

'Mum, Dad, look what Stef gave me?'

On her left hand, sparkling on her third finger, was a small solitaire, diamond ring. They both looked startled. 'Does this mean what I think it means?'

'We're engaged Dad.' She was flushed with excitement.

'It's beautiful darlin'. But ye do know what it means don't ye? Ye have both made a commitment to each other. It is a firm promise?'

'Yes of course I know. After the meal, we sat on a bench on the seafront and Stef started to tell me about a job in his father's business. He spoke about getting enough money, to buy a little place and get married.'

'I said to him, what do you mean, get married? Then he said, this is what I mean and he brought out a little box with this ring in it. He asked me would I marry him? He didn't go down on one knee or anything like that. Anyway, I said yes, I'd love to. He said he was going to ask me in the restaurant, but lost his nerve.'

Michael winked at his wife, remembering *his* marriage proposal in the restaurant.

'Hold on, don't you think we should meet Stefan's parents first, see what they think?'

'We could invite them round for dinner?'

'Good idea Tess.'

They were both astounded by the news.

'Darlin,' would ye like to phone them tomorrow and fix a day.'

'Okay Mum.'

Tess and Michael lay in bed talking over the events of the day, until the early hours.

'Have we got everything Michael? Can ye sort out the wines? I'm hopeless at that.'

'Relax it's all organised. Better nip upstairs and get ready they'll be here in a minute.'

Michael opened the door to Stefan and his parents. Stefan was very polite. He immediately shook hands. His colouring was opposite to his father. Stefan was handsome, blond and fair- skinned with a freckled nose. Much thinner and smaller in stature than his father. Felix by contrast, was tall, big built and lightly tanned. He wore a distinctive oatmeal coloured suit complimenting his thick black hair, sprinkled grey at the temples. Michael directed them into the sitting room.

'I'm Felix,' they shook hands. 'This is my wife Jeanette.'

His wife had on a smart, navy-blue dress and jacket, discovered in the petite section of a well-known local store. Her wavy brown hair was worn with a fringe.

'I would like to thank you for inviting us, it was very kind.'

The detective in Michael, thought he could hear in Felix, a slight Mediterranean accent.

'Our pleasure Felix. Tess, my wife, will be down in a minute. Can I get you both a drink?'

Having heard voices, Jade swiftly negotiated the stairs to greet Stefan with a kiss and say hello to his parents.

'Ah, here's my wife. Tess, this is Felix and…'

'No, it can't be, it's Jeanette isn't it?'

'You two know each other?'

Jeanette looked puzzled. 'I know your voice and your face.'

'Ye knew me when I was Sister Bridget, a midwife. It's Tess now.'

'That's it, I knew the voice. Felix, you remember Sister Bridget don't you? I can't believe it. You're the last person I thought, would leave holy orders.' They hugged each other.

'Darlin', I met Felix and Jeanette, must be what... eighteen, years ago? When Stefan was just a we 'an, fast asleep in a drawer.'

They grinned. 'Yes that day was chaotic. I was so glad you decided to call in.'

They found their minds flashed back to that special day. Little did they know then, how their paths would cross in such a remarkable way.

Tess was intrigued, that the two children not living with their birth mothers, should be brought together; almost as though they had been drawn by magnetism. Was it a need for both to find common ground and an identity? Coming from backgrounds where they had both been unwanted by their mothers at birth; did they sense this in each other?

'How did you feel Jeanette, when your son broke the news of their engagement?'

'I don't think it was quite the shock for us Tess, that you had. We knew, didn't we Felix, the week before.'

'Well yes. He needed to draw out a large sum from his savings. More than I thought he would need, for a meal in a restaurant. So I ask him, what is all this money for? We couldn't argue. You see we understood. We married young. On Jeanette's eighteenth birthday.'

'It was different for us, Felix, said Michael. You knew Tess when she was a nun. She'd left the order, when I met her. We met and married when we were both in our forties.

I was divorced with two grown up sons. So yes, it was a bit of a shock to learn about the engagement.'

'We'll soon get used to it,' said Tess, glancing at the romantic couple touching hands, snatching the occasional kiss. They only had eyes for each other all evening. Since meeting Stefan, Tess noticed how much happier Jade had been.

'I need to tell you. My son, next week joins my Travel Agency. He will have secure future.'

'Jade finishes at the College of Further Education in a few months, said Tess. She has been promised a job in her friend's salon as a beautician. So they have both taken steps towards having a career.'

She hoped to persuade Michael that the young couple were moving in the right direction. Observing them, she felt they were meant for each other. Once again they discussed the situation well into the night.

'They are only getting engaged. Some couples are engaged for ages.'

'If only I could believe that. Once she has had her eighteenth birthday if they decide to get married, there is nothing we can do about it Tess. Lena can't put a stop to it. You seem to forget we have only *borrowed* Jade.'

'I know that. And I know how fond ye are of her and concerned for her welfare. I know she isn't legally ours on paper. But I couldn't love her anymore, than if I had nurtured her in my own womb and given birth to her myself. But we still have to be realistic. The greatest gift *we* have given her, is love and some roots. She knows where her loving family is. Now we have to give her some *wings*. We must allow her to fly and claim her independence.'

Chapter Thirty Two

'How far is it to Adam's new flat?'

'Not far. I think he would be pleased if we took him out to lunch today.'

'How is he at eating these days?'

'Better. I do believe he is beginning to put on weight at last. He's improved tremendously since he allowed the psychiatric team to help him.'

'I shall never forget the day ye took that phone call. To fetch him from Birmingham.'

'No, nor me. Believe me, that's a day I shan't forget in a hurry…'

1974

Michael and Tess tried unsuccessfully, to find Adam, to let him know they were getting married. At twenty one, once Adam had graduated from university, his father assumed he was settled. He'd applied and been accepted for a history teacher's post. He was looking forward to teaching at a London Further Education College in September. Melody, his girlfriend, had secured a teacher's post in a junior school in Surrey. They both looked to have very promising careers. Following their graduation, without telling their family, they suddenly took off to India to join a religious sect. The cult was controlling, demanding up to fifteen hours of meditation a day coupled with long periods of fasting. When they *were* allowed to eat, they were given very small portions of strictly vegan food. Forbidden to have sex or look at their own naked bodies.

Both families had no idea where they had disappeared to. They presumed they had decided to take a gap year and would then re-apply for teaching posts. It wasn't until two years later, that Adam contacted his father.

'Dad, can you come and fetch me?'

'Where are you?'

'Birmingham.'

On arrival at his destination, Michael was shocked to see his squalid living conditions. He was living in a boarded-up shop with several other people. Michael hardly recognised his son. Having always been so meticulous, his father was shocked to see his torn and filthy clothes. He was in rags. His shoes were missing and in their place he had torn rags wrapped around his feet. Usually clean shaven, he had a long unkempt beard. Water and electricity had been disconnected; Adam hadn't washed for months. The telephone was ripped out and an overwhelming stench of urine and alcohol permeated throughout the building. His son had been sleeping on a stone floor, in a filthy, torn sleeping-bag.

The whole area was covered in cans, bottles and empty food containers.

'How long have you been here?'

'Don't know?'

'Where's Melody?'

He shook his head. 'Home please.'

'Okay. Get in the car.'

Once in the car, Adam curled himself up into the foetal position and was practically mute throughout the long journey back to Essex.

Nearer home his father asked, 'How long since you last ate something?'

He thought for a few moments. 'Don't know?'

'As soon as we get home Adam, we'll sort you out. First a bath, then something to eat.'

Tess was shocked at the sight of Adam. She could barely recognise that this was the same person that a few days after Alex's twenty first birthday, they had waved him off to London from Southend station. He was filthy. His hair and beard matted and encrusted with dirt. She didn't want Jade to see Adam in this unkempt state, she was at school when all this happened, due to arrive home shortly with a neighbour. At five, she was easily frightened of men. Especially ones as rough and scruffy looking as some of the men that frequented Lena's place.

She quickly took Adam upstairs and ran the water for a bath. His clothes were stuck solid. Gently she tried to remove them. Eventually they had to be cut off. When it came to his underclothes he refused to let her touch them.

'It's all right Adam, ye forget I'm a nurse.'

He clawed at his clothes and shook his head. Adamant that no one was going to see his naked body, not even himself. To Tess's surprise, he stepped into the bath, complete with his underwear on. He appeared sometime later, dressed in some of his dad's clean clothes and slippers. His beard and hair dripping water.

'Just a minute son,' his father took him back into the spare bedroom. Offered him a towel to dry his hair with. Then took him into the dining room, to join the others for the evening meal. He looked at his plate of beef casserole. Slowly with his fingers he removed all the meat, put it onto his side plate. Picking up the plate of vegetables, he left the table and disappeared into the spare room. Michael rose to follow him.

'I should leave him alone dear, he's not at all well. We should get the doctor to see him tomorrow.'

'Tess, do you think that's a good idea? Should we let him take his time, not rush him to see a doctor. We have no idea what has happened?'

'He's seriously ill Michael, both physically and mentally.'

They discussed the situation and both felt given time and gentle handling, maybe they could help him back to normal health, initially without medical intervention. Just large doses of T.L.C.

Over the next few days they were startled by his strange behaviour. He refused to allow them to give him his food. Only *he* could handle his own food. They were very concerned and decided to contact his girlfriend's parents. Their daughter was teaching at a private school.

Michael and Tess arranged to meet up with Melody and her mother. Gradually, they were able to fill in some of the huge gaps. Melody had stayed with him in India. Over time she could see he was beginning to deteriorate.

'His memory was failing. I wanted to bring him back to London. At first he was adamant that he wanted to stay in India. I was frightened to leave him there.'

'*You* were beginning to have some lapses in *your* memory too, weren't you dear?'

'Yes Mother, I put it down to the long periods of meditation. I was scared that if I didn't leave, I'd go the same way as Adam. In the end I managed to get him to change his mind. I was able to bring him back to London. As we were coming out of the station, he disappeared into the crowd and was gone. I spent hours searching for him. I later found out, he had been picked up by the police and put into a homeless hostel. He was unable to tell them who he was or whether he had any family. Then one day he vanished.'

'What made you both decide to go to India?' asked Michael.

'When we were at university, Adam had been experiencing a great deal of stress and anxiety. He was smoking a lot of cannabis, thinking that would help. A counsellor suggested he might try meditation to help him to relax. He found a commune with a religious teacher in India. I thought we could go for a couple of months. He was becoming suicidal. He was so vulnerable, I didn't want to leave him on his own. We thought we would both come back revitalised, ready to take up our teaching posts. Adam spoke about it offering him *peace to his troubled soul*.'

When they left, Tess felt Melody was holding something back. A feeling that she hadn't told them everything. They both seemed on edge. With all the anxiety Adam had caused his father, she put it out of her mind and didn't mention it.

It was true, Adam's memory was extremely poor. Over time, they had to painstakingly piece together his past years. He couldn't remember going to university and was vague about applying for a job. He didn't know what sort of job. Most of the time he had no idea what his father was talking about. The many hours in India, spent in meditation and fasting had appeared to have damaged his brain. At a time when he was already having problems, it seemed to have exacerbated the situation.

One Saturday morning when they got up, Adam had gone. His back pack which he would never be parted from, had gone with him. Tess quickly dressed and wandered out in the street looking for him. Being early morning and barely light, the street was deserted.

'He could have left very early and had a head start.'

'I'll keep a lookout for him Tess, during the day, when I'm driving around.'

Two days later, he had a call from a fellow police officer. Adam had been found sleeping inside a tumble-down shed, on a remote strip of waste land. Back home, bathed and with clean clothes again, he was unsettled. Reluctant to talk. From time to time he was apt to disappear. To their embarrassment, neighbours by now, were on the alert to any sightings of him. He was harmless enough, but Tess and Michael, were concerned about his mental health. They tried many times to get him to see a psychiatrist. He always refused. They were informed he had to be willing to see a psychiatrist. Unless he was a danger to himself or others, they couldn't make him seek treatment.

Watching television one evening, an historian was talking of ancient Egypt. To their astonishment Adam said,

'I think I would like to learn ancient history?'

This was a sad moment for his father, as his son had a degree in Ancient History and Egyptology. His appointment at the college before going to India, was to teach history, at degree level.

One morning, Tess, was told by a neighbour's son, that Adam had been seen at the local college of further education. He had arrived one morning, produced a pen and note book, sat himself at the back of the classroom and took notes. They found he would sit quietly and didn't disturb the students, so they allowed him to sit there. He became a frequent 'student' at the college. He was quiet and gentle. Never asked any questions. Never disrupted the class. They allowed him to become a permanent fixture at the college.

Suddenly, his behaviour changed. In the kitchen and without warning, he attacked Tess.

'You are not my mother! What are you doing here?'

He'd picked up a knife and stabbed Tess in the arm. Hearing the disturbance, Michael rushed in and rugby tackled him to the floor. He wrestled him into his bedroom, locked the door and called an ambulance. The psychiatric team and ambulance arrived and Adam was sectioned and admitted to a psychiatric hospital. They were upset that he had been sectioned, but pleased that at last Adam would receive treatment. Once in hospital he had various blood tests, a skull x-ray and explored his mental condition. The doctors felt that hours and hours of non-stop meditation, involved in emptying his mind of all thoughts had taken its toll and destroyed a large amount of his memory. They also took into consideration his regular drug use at college. Information was beginning to surface at this time, regarding extensive use of cannabis, how it had been found to cause schizoid tendencies.

It would be many weeks before he could be discharged; when it was arranged for him to go into a protected housing complex and attend a psychiatric day centre. Slowly he made small steps towards recovery. He recognised and spoke freely with his father and stepmother and eventually to Jade. All this happened when Adam was a young man in his twenties. He was a different person now. Happy, talkative and kind, having just moved into a special flat. Twice a week, a psychiatric nurse called to check on his condition and that he was taking his medication. An on-site housekeeper at this village-type housing complex, was there to keep an eye on him. She made sure that he was eating properly and taking his pills. She would also collect up his laundry and do his ironing for him. There was a canteen where he could have a meal and mix socially with others, if he wished to. Today he would be taken out for a meal, to his favourite eatery. A vegan establishment? No, not anymore. His favourite now – a fish and chip restaurant, followed by a dairy ice-cream.

Chapter Thirty Three

'Hello, can you call round and see my baby? He's not at all well. He's swelling up.'

'Have ye called the doctor?'

'Yes, she's a stand-in doctor. My own doctor is off. She says she can't come out.'

'I'll be with ye in five minutes.'

It was half past five, Tess was about to leave the office. She made her way to the housing estate. It was serious. The boy hadn't passed urine all day and his body was beginning to become oedematous.

'Which doctor did ye call?'

'I had to ring the emergency number. A lady doctor is covering my doctor's practice.'

Tess rang the number and was connected to the doctor.

'I can't come out, if I do, I would have to bring my own baby in the car.'

'What do ye mean? Ye are on call aren't ye?'

'Yes, but my husband has just had to dash out to an emergency meeting.'

'Okay, then, the mountain is coming to Mohammed. Where do ye live?'

'Get the baby ready Mother, we are going to take him to see the doctor.'

'What do you mean?'

'I have her address. Would ye believe it, if she had to visit ye, she would have had to bring her own six-week-old baby in the car as well? So we are off to her home address.'

The large detached house was along an unmade road, the signs of which indicated not only had it been raining, but a herd of cows had stumbled along recently, leaving their calling cards. Tess stepped out of the car onto a muddy bank. The mother holding her baby, stepped into something even less welcome. As promised the door was left ajar. They stepped into a palatial hall, fitted throughout, with – yes, you've guessed it – a plush, cream-coloured carpet.

'Come through,' a woman's voice called from across the hall. 'I'm in my office.'

They looked down at their shoes. Tess looked at the mother and grinned. They hurried across the hall into the doctor's office, leaving evidence of their highly visible, highly smelly, footprints. The doctor gave the baby a thorough examination, took his temperature and some blood.

'His temperature has come down slightly. I am going to give him an injection and some medication for you to give him. You must take the baby to see his own doctor, first thing in the morning. If you have any further concerns before that, you must ring for an ambulance.'

The mother was pleased to have been able to see a doctor, have some treatment and the baby checked over.

The doctor may have been pleased to see them go, not so pleased with the mess they had left behind on her previously pristine carpet.

In the morning, the anxious locum doctor had already spoken to the GP of her concerns. The child not having passed any urine overnight, the GP initially intended to admit the child to hospital. That is, until he mentioned the word *hospital*, when like magic the baby promptly peed all over the doctor's couch.

That morning Tess had to visit a new family having moved into the area. She could see this was no ordinary family. The parents were dressed in 'gothic style'. The walls were black and she noticed the mother had painted one fingernail black. They had a five-year-old boy who was at school. The baby girl she had come to see, was eighteen months old and Tess was there to carry out a developmental check. The toddler, with red rimmed eyes was in a pram.

'Hello sweetie.' Tess bent over the buggy. The child made no response; she neither smiled nor moved.

The atmosphere was heavy, within the gloomy house. Despite approaching midday, the curtains were still closed. Father stood in the corner, with a disinterested expression on his face. He wore a see-through net-type top, to show off his tattoos. Copies of which, could no doubt be found in a horror comic. His long leather boots rattled with the attached chains. Both parents had numerous piercings through the nose, lips and ears. The mother wore a piece of jewellery, a silver serpent, wrapped around one ear. So far Tess had not seen a flicker of affection from the parents to each other, or to the child. They appeared as robotic as ghouls, with run down batteries. The mother had on a long black dress slit above the knee. On the full length of the bodice, was an appliquéd, studded crucifix. Looking at it, sent a shiver down Tess's spine. She too had once worn a large crucifix on *her* chest.

Reluctantly the mother took the child out of the pram. The child sat motionless on the sofa and looked with curiosity at the developmental toys that Tess produced. The child had no idea what to do with them. She was not surprised, as there was no sign of any toys in the house. Alarm bells rang loud and clear.

'Has she any words?'

'A few.'

'What are they?'

'Can't remember?'

'I have found some developmental delay with yer child. I think it best for ye to bring her to clinic, to see the Community Physician. He's at the clinic twice a week.'

Tess wrote the information on a card and gave it to her. The fact that her child was not developing at the normal rate, did not seem to worry either her or her husband. The atmosphere was so oppressive that Tess was relieved to be out of the house, into the sunlight and fresh air. Tess couldn't see the mother making an effort to bring her child to the clinic.

She called in at the Social Services offices. The social worker was also concerned at the child's environment. Shortly after, Michael told Tess in confidence, that they went into the house to look for drugs. Along with drugs, they made a startling discovery in a shed at the back of the house. They found a small rectangular table with skulls, a chalice, bell and candles. Behind the altar was an image of a goat pentagram. All indicative of *Satanic Worship. But it was the photographs of the five-year old son that were most disturbing. The boy had been stripped naked. He looked as though he had been drugged, held high and dedicated to Satan. Other pictures were kept for evidence of child abuse. Both children were placed in care of the local authority.

*Modern Goths, would not be involved in Satanism.

Chapter Thirty Four

Routine hearing tests on babies, were the prerogative of health visitors, having been trained by audiologists. On this occasion Julie, the baby's mother, seemed very anxious. Tess had visited her before she had the baby and found her to be a very friendly person, coping with a major hearing loss. Her two children of six and eight were both hearing children. As she observed them they seemed typical mischievous children of that age group. Although they were not very helpful to their mother; they kept talking with their hands over their mouths. Although children often do, this was different. This was so that their mother could not lip-read what they were saying. They would say something and then snigger. Most mothers would take little notice when their young children laughed and had little secrets amongst themselves. They would know that it would usually be something trivial. To Julie, it felt as though they were taunting her. She felt hurt and saw it differently. She felt continuously shut out from their world. The hearing test of her third child was crucial.

Julie sat the child on her lap, whilst sounds were made from different directions. The child was observed making swift responses to the sounds. Tess and Lyn both smiled at the mother and, enabling her to lip-read, mouthed the words that her child's hearing was perfect. To the health visitors' surprise, Julie burst into tears. They took this to mean tears of relief. They both smiled back at her. She produced a little notebook and wrote:

You don't understand. I cannot communicate with her!

It was clear, her children needed to be taught how to sign and lip-read. Julie was put in touch with an organisation that would help her children to do this. They hoped this would relieve the frustration and anger that the mother felt.

Later that day Tess was asked to visit a family whose five-year-old twins also caused communication problems for their family. The twins would only communicate with each other, by use of their invented language. This twin talk, or cryptophasia, was very frustrating for the parents and teachers. There also seemed to be some form of telepathy going on between them. As well as with their parents, they did not communicate with their peers at school either. The education authority, decided to separate the sisters and they were sent to different schools. Slowly they began to speak to their teachers and other pupils. Over time, they dropped their twin speak and spoke normally.

In many homes, Tess would be offered a cup of tea, which depending on the home conditions she would accept. She found it was always wise to wash one's hands in the kitchen first, before anyone could come up with the suggestion. A swift hygiene inspection was often useful. A week's collection of crockery in the sink did not bode well. The same would apply when desperate to use the toilet. Tess had quickly learned that visits interspersed with comfort visits, needed to be planned strategically. Some scruffy areas, could give rise to the requirement of exercising the water retention of a camel. Yet to survive all disasters and catastrophes, it is well documented that it is vital that the British imbibe frequent infusions of tea. This common beverage in the community took a variety of forms. From perfumed to floating rose leaves. Teas of many shades from light beige to ebony. At one time, taps covered with muslin in Southend, were definitely a no no! This was a sign that the water board had mentioned that dreaded word…**weevils** in the tap water. *Quite harmless* came the official notification from the Water Board. Did that reassure people? Mm…so it was all right then, for anyone who didn't mind a mouthful of worms in one's tea. People were advised to catch them in muslin, wrapped around the taps.

After a hectic day, Tess hurried home, there were many arrangements to be made. The engagement was going to be very brief. Stefan had announced that they would be getting married within three months.

Michael was exasperated. 'Didn't I say that's what they would do? Just what I thought would happen. Well, at least she is spared from having to go crawling to Lena for her consent.'

At one time Stefan was curious about Lena. He asked if he could meet her.

'Sorry Stef, you really wouldn't want to meet Lena. I haven't seen her myself for years.'

She felt too ashamed to take anyone there. Now that she had lived with Michael and Tess and seen how 'normal tidy people' take care of their homes, Jade realised that Lena's home was a disgrace – degrading – a dump.

As soon as she had started to call Tess and Michael, Mum and Dad, she had tried to block out her real mother from her mind. Lena had never asked to see her. Lena's only interest, was in the financial benefit she received as a single parent. After the drug-dealer had threatened to set the flat alight, she managed to get the council to move her to a different district. After the drug incident, Tess and Michael feared for Jade's safety. They would not have stopped her seeing her mother, if she really wanted to. Michael had always made it clear that he could accompany her.

Despite Lena living in a more respectable area, Jade had not made any move to go and see her, that is…until now. Now that she was getting married, her thoughts started to turn in that direction. She wondered if Lena's attitude towards her might change, after all, she was no longer a child.

'Do you think I should invite Lena to the wedding Mum?'

Tess's heart sank. That after all this time, she would ask her this question? It was an unfair question. How could she wholeheartedly let her do this, when her mother was an alcoholic and drug addict. What sort of behaviour could anyone expect from her, either in church or at the reception? Yet she knew this wasn't her decision to make.

'That is entirely up to ye darlin'. The only thing I would say before ye make any decision to invite her to the wedding, go and visit yer mother first. Come back – sleep on it – then make up yer mind.'

'Thanks Mum, I'll go round there on Saturday. But I'm not taking Stef with me.'

Chapter Thirty Five

'It's crazy, Lena would ruin everything.'

'I know that darlin'. I've told her to go and see her first, before making any decision.'

Michael gave a deep sigh. 'I can't believe it after all this time. But you're right it is not our decision to make.'

'If she goes over there, sees the way she behaves, she'll realise that Lena could spoil everything on their special day.'

'But you know what Lena can be like. Abusive and violent. Just imagine if she started puking up in the church or at the hotel.'

'Oh don't be saying that Michael, I can't bear the thought of it. We have to wait and see.'

'When is she going?'

'Saturday morning.'

'Oh yes. It would be Saturday wouldn't it? When I'm being fitted for my suit. Any other day and I could have gone with her.'

Jade was nervous and hoped that Lena would be alone. Her mind was made up, if she heard a man's voice she wouldn't go in. Having pressed the lift button to the block of flats, it chugged and rattled its way to the fourth floor. She had the coat on her fiancé had bought her for Christmas. It was crimson and black with a black peter-pan fur collar. It showed off her neat figure to its best advantage and brightened up the depressing, drab surroundings. At the last minute, she nearly decided not to go in, and was about to step back in the lift, when someone on the ground floor pressed the button. The doors clanged shut. The lift descended without her.

She took in a deep breath and knocked firmly on the paint-chipped door. A wizened looking woman, with flame-dyed hair opened the door.

'Yeah, what yer want?'

'I'm Jade.'

The woman looked puzzled at the attractive teenager.

'Well I suppose you'd better come in.'

If she imagined the place would look a mess, she was not disappointed. How she appreciated the clean and tidy home she had found with her genuine caring family.

She managed to stutter out the words, 'How are you?'

The woman did not reply. She brushed aside a pile of clothes that had hidden a chair. Pulled it over for her to sit on.

'What yer doin 'ere? Shouldn't yer be at school?'

'It's Saturday. I've finished with school anyway. I work in a hair salon with a beautician.'

'Ooh, that's posh. A bootishen are yer? Good money?'

'Not yet. I'm only a trainee.'

'What yer come 'ere for? See if I was entertaining?'

'I'm getting married.'

'Married? Whatever for? Wait a minute. Don't think I'm goin' to give yer per…per…mish… mishon to marry, 'cos I ain't.'

'You don't have to. I'm eighteen, I don't need permission.'

'Oh… I see. That's a crafty move. Fed up living with that snooty, la de da, pair are yer?'

'No.'

She knew it was useless to talk to her about her love for Stefan. Lena didn't know what love was? She found herself beginning to feel sorry for her. How could she express love, if she had never received it?

'Don't think I'll be comin' to your weddin' 'cos I won't. Sittin' wiv all them posh toffs.'

Jade realised that this could be her last chance, to ask about her biological father.

'Who was my father?' she blurted out.

'Huh! Bit late asking about that aren't you? If yer must know, it was when I came out of prison. I was raped. I don't remember who 'e was. Could be anyone.'

The word *raped* rang discordantly in her ears. She felt sick to realise that she was the product of rape. No wonder Lena had always hated her.

'Satisfied now? Where yer getting married?'

'We're getting married at the Catholic Church, not far from where I live. The reception's at the big hotel on the corner.'

There seemed no point in going into any more details. She realised it would not be the happy occasion they wished for, if her mother put in an appearance.

'When's the 'appy day?' she said sarcastically.

'Two weeks today.'

'All arranged is it?'

She reached across the can-littered table and grabbed a half empty bottle of *Teacher's* whisky; glugged the remainder and slammed the empty bottle on the table.

'I'm going now. I've lots to do.'

There were no farewells. Lena eyes were already closed, she had slumped in her chair. Jade made for the door. The horrible news of her conception and her father, compounded her feelings of despair. Once outside, tears streamed down her face. It was not the happy reunion, she had dreamed of.

Once home, she couldn't speak, she ran upstairs to her bedroom. Tess knew not to ask how it went? Instead, she made her some tea and took it up to her.

'Oh Mum, it was horrible. I'm never going there again. She's no different. I asked her to tell me who my birth father was?' She started to cry. 'It made me feel sick. Did *you* know?'

Tess nodded, 'Yes, but I never wanted ye to find out. That information I would have taken to my grave.'

She put her arm around her and hugged her. Jade laid her head on Tess's shoulder and burst into tears.

'Come on dear, ye must put all that happened this morning, out of yer head. Ye have so much to do. Loads of things to organise. Some I can do, some ye can do, and some we can do together. This guest list seems to be growing by the minute. In a fortnight's time, darlin,' ye will be walking down the aisle. Then it will be *my* turn to cry.'

They heard the key turn in the door. Tess went downstairs into the kitchen.

'I've sorted my suit out it will be ready in ten days. How did the girl get on?'

'She didn't. She was in terrible state when she came home. She's in her room.' He moved towards the stairs. 'Leave her dear, for a little while.'

'How the guest list going?'

'Well, the invitations went out ages ago, but Jade keeps thinking of someone else. From school, from youth club and so on.'

'The only friends I've invited, are a couple of lads from the station. What are the numbers at the moment? I have to give the hotel numbers by Monday.'

'I haven't added them up lately. With Stefan's list, about a hundred I should think. Do ye think Adam will be alright?'

'Hope so. He's not happy in crowded places. He'll be fine in church, he's used to going to Mass now. And he'll be okay once he's seated at the reception. It's when people start milling around, talking loud to make themselves heard, that's when he might panic. I'll keep an eye on him and whisk him into a quiet corner.

Chapter Thirty Six

'What about her wedding dress?' asked Lyn.

'I haven't a clue yet. I was pleased when Jeanette, offered to take Jade up to London's Oxford Street. I am not terribly good at fashion. I'm more for comfort and something practical, which apparently when it comes to wedding dresses, is last on the list. It's style and fashion I'm told, that is most essential. She chose a dress that had to be altered. It supposed to be ready on Monday along with the bridesmaids' dresses.'

'Who is she having as bridesmaids?'

'Her friend Lois, a girl from youth club and Alex's two little girls are coming down from Scotland.'

Even now, Lyn did not know how Tess had 'acquired' Jade, she had never asked. No doubt she assumed that she was part of Michael's family before he and Tess married.

'Michael's retired now from the force, so he's been helping Felix in one of his local travel agencies.'

'So the happy couple will be off on an exotic honeymoon destination then?'

'Yes, after the wedding, Felix has paid for them to stay at a luxury hotel in Barbados.'

'Wow! That's the right sort of father-in-law to have. That sounds lovely. I see you're taking all next week off Tess. No doubt you'll be dashing about, trying to fit everything in?'

'I can imagine everyone else will be dashing about Lyn, like demented spalpeens. I am hoping to be able to follow what a Saint once said, *to do everything quietly and in a calm spirit.*'

The morning of the wedding was neither quiet nor calm. Tess was yelling at the top of her voice, 'Mary Mother of God, will ye be after getting a move on the cars will be here in a minute!'

'I'm coming. I'm coming.'

'Like hell she is Tess, that woman is still up there messing about with her hair. You heard what your mum said, HURRY UP! Unless you want to leave poor Stefan at the altar.

'I've said I'm coming, Dad.'

'Phew! I don't remember it being like this when Alex got married?'

'That's because for men, it's only a shower – a shave – a suit.'

'That reminds me, can you fix my tie?'

Meanwhile back at the Rondo household, the scene was no different.

'Stefan, I shan't be telling you again, GET OUT OF BED!' roared Felix. I give you two minutes. After that, I will be coming up there to pull you out feet first.'

'Okay, okay, keep it cool man.'

Miraculously the bride and groom just managed to get to the church on time. Already the church was full of whispering women and muttering men. The driver had to take the bridesmaids around the church three times, to give the groom time to take his place at the altar. The bride arrived on the arm of Michael, to the sound of the organ playing Wagner's Bridal Chorus, and took her place next to her future husband. The usual low whispers of dress–lovely–beautiful, filtered around the church.

A little old lady in a grey mac and black wellington boots carrying a shopping bag full of groceries, scurried down the aisle. She knelt alongside the bride and groom at the altar. Being a Catholic Church, it was open to the public. To the old lady it was the same as any normal day. Fortunately for the young couple, they only had eyes for each other. As they knelt at the polished wooden rail, oblivious to their uninvited stranger. Amongst all the finery of a wedding taking place, it looked absurd. The couple stood facing each other.

'Jade, do you take Stefan to be your lawful wedded husband…?'

The congregation was silent, anxious to hear her reply in the affirmative.

'Oh I don't know?' came the reply.

A simultaneous gasp came from the congregation. They must have thought it only happened in films. The priest asked the question again. There was complete silence. People held their breath. Strained their ears to hear her reply. Stefan was visibly trembling.

'I'm not sure,' she said.

The congregation stared at her in amazement.

'Ladies and gentlemen,' said the priest, 'I'm sure this is just wedding nerves.'

The priest whispered something to the couple. Together with the best man, they followed him into an adjoining room. The congregation buzzed with indignation and unanswered questions.

'What will happen to the reception?' asked someone.

'Will I get my present back?' a small boy asked his mother.

Ten minutes later they returned smiling. The vows were taken. The bride and groom kissed. After the Eucharist, the congregation sang with relief, *Love Divine All Loves Excelling*.

The young couple slowly made their way down the aisle with the bridesmaids. Confetti thrown. Photos taken. All may be forgiven, but a wedding never to be forgotten.

Back at the reception, the meal was being brought to the tables and the chattering began. Once the tables were cleared, the best man, speech in hand, gave an hilarious résumé of Stefan's life and then how he met Jade.

'Stef found her, crawling under a table-tennis table. Searching under there for a non-existent Ping-Pong ball, which had already been recovered. He hauled her out. They started chatting. They suddenly walked away, completely forgot all about the table tennis game they were supposed to be playing. I discovered them later, snogging in the cloakrooms. Game set and match I call it. And no better match, than Stef and Jade. Raise your glasses please.'

After the final congratulations and chinks of glasses, the guests dispersed from the dining room, to the lounge bar in the hotel.

Before flying out the next morning, for two weeks in Barbados, Michael had booked the newly-weds into the honeymoon suite, for one night at the hotel.

'Adam come with me.' Michael, took him to find a quiet spot away from the crowds. 'There's another small bar in this room.' He settled his son on a comfortable sofa and brought him a soft drink.

'Let me know when you want to leave, I'll take you home.'

He reckoned on returning within the hour. Meanwhile, he needed to check that all arrangements were going to plan.

Later when he went to fetch Adam, he had to go through into the main lounge bar. He was shocked at what greeted him.

'Michael. Michael how are you darling?'

He was furious to find Lena swaying and swearing at the bar. She had on a tight, black, above the knee skirt, with white leather thigh boots. She was flirting with the barman and a commercial traveller. Once again plying her trade. When she called out his name, several heads turned. He was fuming, especially as he had just seen Felix, collecting a tray of drinks from the counter. Once Felix had disappeared, he went over to her.

'What the hell are you doing here?'

'It's my daughter's wedding.'

'You were *not* invited.'

'So I need to have an invit…invit…ashhion do I? Tough. Get stuffed.'

She was beginning to cause a commotion. Jade walked in, looking for her dad.

'What's going on Dad?'

'Dad is it, huh?' He's not your dad.' She swayed precariously. Then leaned over to a nearby table and took a bottle of wine from a startled couple sitting there.

'Aren't you s'pose to look 'appy? You don't look 'appy'

'What are *you* doing here?'

'Is that the way to talk to yer mummy? Yer bitch!'

Michael launched in with, 'How *dare* you talk to her like that!' He managed to hold on to a swaying arm to prevent her from falling. In a split second, with the other arm she had swung the bottle in his direction. It missed and crashed down on Jade's head. Glass, blood and wine splattered and her skull shattered. Instantly she fell to the ground unconscious, amidst gasps from wedding and hotel guests. Michael cradled her in his arms and called over a police colleague to summon an ambulance.

Within seconds, hearing the commotion, Stefan arrived and took over. Two of Michaels police colleagues, guests at the wedding, dragged Lena out of the hotel, into a waiting police car. Lena was later charged with causing grievous bodily harm.

The Ambulance staff, placed the severely, injured patient on a stretcher, bleeding and unconscious. She lay motionless in her wedding dress drenched in wine and blood. Stefan was distraught. He accompanied her in the ambulance to the local hospital. Tess was crying. Jeanette tried to comfort her.

'Tess,' Michael called over to her. 'I'd better take Adam home first. Then we can go to the hospital.'

'Don't worry Michael, Felix and I can take Tess to the hospital. You take your son home and join us later.'

The elder son Alex, gathered up his twin daughters. They were still showing off their bridesmaids' dresses, twirling around in the ballroom. Before leaving Michael called Alex over.

'Alex, you and your family can stay here at the hotel tonight. I had already booked the suite for Jade and Stefan, you may as well stay here instead.'

A hushed atmosphere of disbelief, descended on the hotel. How had this happy occasion, turned so swiftly into one of such tragedy and disaster?

Chapter Thirty Seven

Adam was asleep when Michael reached him in the small bar. The soft drink was still on the table.

'Adam, wake up. Have your drink. We're going home now.'

'Is the wedding over?'

'Yes son, it's definitely over.'

After he had driven Adam home, he drove straight to the hospital.

'How is she darling?'

'She's in intensive care. We are not allowed in yet. They've put her on a life support machine. I had a word with the nurse. She's still in a coma. Obviously Stefan will be allowed in first, as next of kin.'

'Don't say it like that, next of kin, it sounds sort of final doesn't it?'

The sister appeared with a clipboard. 'Mr Rondo?'

He leaped up from his chair near the entrance to the intensive care unit.

'Yes.'

'You can go in to see your wife. But only for a few minutes.'

He hugged his mum and went in. Within the space of a few hours, before their eyes, they had watched a young teenager develop into a young man.

'I'm sorry,' the Sister spoke to the rest of the family and friends waiting. 'Only one in today. You can phone up later. Close relatives only. You may be able to go in and see her tomorrow.'

Tess tearfully hugged Jeanette and Felix before they left. They drove home in silence.

Days sitting at her bedside turned to weeks. It was to be six weeks later when Jade opened her eyes and whispered a name. That person was already at her side. He squeezed her right hand; no response. He squeezed the other to feel a limp pressure.

She'd had a subarachnoid haemorrhage. It had left her partially paralysed down her left side.

'She said my name Mum, she recognised me.'

'That's good. It's the first step, dear.' They hugged each other. 'Jade's mum told me, it will be a long journey for her to get back to somewhere near normal health, after a stroke.'

'I always thought a stroke was for old people?'

'Any age apparently.'

'Mum, I have to go and speak with Sister in her office this afternoon. She is going to discuss Jade's condition with me, now that she has begun to regain consciousness. I'll tell you all about it later.'

'Mr Rondo, what happened to your wife when her skull was fractured, is that blood leaked out and this caused a clot on the brain. The doctors hoped that the clot would disperse, but every stroke is unique.'

'Please Sister, I need to know everything.'

'Well… if the blood flow cannot reach a particular part of the brain, the part of the body that it causes to function, can be impaired. One side of the brain enables the other side to function. If the left side of the brain is affected, the right side of the body can be paralysed. It can also cause some memory loss or visual problems. If the left side of the body is paralysed, then it is the right part of the brain affected. This can also cause some memory or language loss, speech can also be lost. If the stroke is in the brain stem, then both sides can be affected.'

'Thank you Sister.'

He joined his mum at the bedside.

'Mum, Sister explained everything to me. I was scared to ask her, but do you think she will ever walk again?'

'Of course she will, she is a very determined young lady.'

'I wish I had your confidence,' Felix remarked, later that day.

Gradually as the weeks turned to months, each week they noticed some improvement. Felix continued to pay the mortgage on the couple's new flat. Stefan had stopped working. He was spending every day at the hospital.

'I can't see them moving into that flat, Jeanette. It's ready to move into. How will she manage those stairs?'

'We can't predict how she will be in the future dear. We must trust that God will give her strength and heal her. I have been saying a Novena to Our Lady of Perpetual Help.'

'Jeanette, you think that saying a Novena will never fail? Your wish *has* to be granted. God can't always be at our beck and call.'

Their conversation was interrupted by the telephone ringing.

'It's Stefan, from the hospital,' she whispered to her husband.

'Yes. I can hear you.'

'She's started talking Mum.'

'Oh thank God.'

'But Mum, I don't think she remembers the wedding? She doesn't seem to know we were married?'

'Don't worry about that love, her memory is bound to be a bit disjointed for a while. At least if she doesn't remember the attack, that must be a good thing. As long as she is still talking to you. She knows you, that's the main thing.'

'Ask him how she's doing in physio?'

'Your dad is asking how is she getting on with the physiotherapy?'

'Great. They have her walking between two parallel bars. She's doing well.'

'We'll be up the hospital later. See you both then.'

They met up with Tess and Michael at the hospital, who were also pleased with her progress.

'Stef, my mum brought in two rings, she says they are both mine? Have *you* seen them before?' said Jade.

'Yes, babe, one is your engagement ring. The other one your wedding ring.'

'I don't remember them. What do they mean? Are we engaged?'

'We're married babe, don't you remember?'

She shook her head and laughed. 'Don't be silly! How can we be married? We're too young aren't we?'

'We're both eighteen.'

'Really? Oh! We can get married then. I don't remember any of it.'

'Babe, you will need to take my word for it. Here, I have some photos of our wedding.'

She looked at them, puzzled that she was unable to recall any preparation – the wedding dress, the church…nothing.

Tess and Michael came into the room and heard the tail end of the conversation.

'Never mind darlin'. When ye are able to go home and feel well, ye could always have a renewal of vows. It can be just like a wedding. Ye two men have a chat with Jade. I'm just going to see Sister in her office.'

'Yes Mrs King, it's been a long haul, but as you can see, she is doing very well. We will be looking to discharge her in around two weeks' time. We will be arranging for district nurses to call and a community physiotherapist. She'll be fine. Her walking has improved dramatically this week. With help, she is able to manage the stairs too. Two more weeks we'll have her skipping out of the hospital.'

'Ye've done a wonderful job Sister.'

'Couldn't have done it without your daughter's determination. She only had a ten per cent chance when she was brought in. She has a strong will power and is always so cheerful. A lovely girl, she's a credit to you.'

It was the first time that Tess had felt appreciation from a stranger. The memory of the time she was thrust in her arms, came flooding back. All the love care and attention she had given to her over the years, trying to give her a normal childhood, it was worth all the anxiety, sacrifice and effort. It was a miracle how she had found the determination to break away from her dysfunctional home. Unhindered, left with Lena, what sort of life would she have had? One of poverty and neglect. She could have ended up the same as Lena, working in the sex industry, an alcoholic and on drugs. Jade had shown her devotion and appreciation for everything that she and Michael had done for her. They had been recompensed by her love, a thousand fold.

Chapter Thirty Eight

Lena was sentenced to four years for causing grievous bodily harm to her daughter. The Judge also took into account her previous convictions of theft and aggravated burglary and sent her to a women's prison in Essex.

Many of the women there, had left behind young children and teenagers. Some because of their crimes, had their children taken away from them. Others were being looked after by relatives. Nevertheless, once they were incarcerated, the majority of the mothers began to miss them. Those that worked on an outside working party, would often gravitate towards any of the civilian staff's children, that lived in the houses and happened to be playing outside in the grounds. If they saw a small child fall over, they would rush to be the first to pick the child up and comfort it. Only trusted prisoners soon to be discharged, were allowed on an outside working party. The rest were enclosed in the high-walled security prison.

Moors murderer Myra Hindley, was once at Bullwood Hall for a short period, before being transferred to Holloway Prison in London.

A few days after Lena had been at the prison, she was ushered into the recreation room. Two prisoners made their way to where Lena was standing. Whilst one girl distracted the prison officer, the other two pounced on her and pushed her against the wall.

'Let's punch the granny out of her,' said one prisoner.'

One kicked her in the stomach, the other punched her in the face.

'Just a little present from your daughter.'

'A little gift, to welcome you to Bullwood Hall.'

The three mothers were appalled at what she had done to her daughter, especially on her wedding day. They were determined to dole out their own justice. Once they had done that, they scarpered to the other side of the room. Picked up their table tennis bats and carried on with their game.

The prison officer found Lena sitting on the floor, her face covered in blood.

'What happened to you then?'

Lena knew better than to mark someone's card. Not unless she wanted worse punishment.

'Bloody stupid. I tripped and fell against the wall.'

'We'd better let the nurse look at it then and clean you up.'

She raised the alarm for another officer to go to the recreation room and Lena was taken to the medical room. The three offenders laughed triumphantly at being able to get away with the attack.

Yvonne, one of the gang of three, commented,

'She looks a right slag, doesn't she?'

'I've seen her before,' said Wendy. 'Haven't you Vera?'

'Yeah weren't she up before the beak, when we was?'

'Yeah for AB,' said Vera.

'What was it for?'

'Aggravated Burglary.'

'Yeah, I know that, but what did she do?'

'She was the one what threatened to burn the old geezer with a hot iron? I forget what she got for it?'

'Oh yeah, I remember now.'

The two girls who set about Lena, continued their game of table tennis unperturbed.

The nurse sent Lena for an X-ray which revealed a fractured nose. When the gang heard via prison whispers, the outcome they found it most amusing. A few days later in the canteen. One of the girls went over to Lena.

'Oh dear your nose is all twisted. Looks like it's been busted. They say your face is your fortune too, don't they? Still, it won't trouble your punters, your fortune isn't your face, is it?'

Lena pretended not to notice. She put her head down and carried on eating. She found it difficult to stay out of trouble when a couple of the prisoners already knew she had form. It meant having to watch her back all the time.

As in male prisons, many of the prisoners missed having sex. They would turn to what they could find amongst other prisoners. Several advances were made to Lena. At night, girls would shout out of their barred windows to their 'girlfriends' in nearby cells. The night air was filled with woman calling out to their mates or girlfriends.

'Good night Lena. Love you darling.'

She returned the message, 'Love you Maggie.'

'Gemma, do you still love me?' came another voice.

On and on the cat calling continued into the night air, until all had decided to turn in for the night. Lena may have joined in and called out of her window about love, yet she was incapable of love. She had only ever loved one thing in her life, her childhood kitten, Minnie. Once she was taken into care, her father did as he had threatened and drowned it. Until she was taken from her home, Minnie had been the focus of her love, it deflected her fear of being abused by her father and his friends. Since then, it was as though any feelings of affection had long been extinguished by her abusive family.

Her father, a well-known, respectable business man in the city, was expected to love and protect her; be her role model. Instead, he had left her physically and mentally damaged. The destructive misery he had left her with, had turned to revenge, especially when she had her own daughter. Her body had been so violated, she had no respect for it. She presumed that if men wanted her body now, they would have to pay for it. Alcohol and drugs helped her to blank out the past. She craved them more than ever, now that she was back in prison. But she didn't have any suitable contacts to obtain them for her. She would have needed to give something in return.

Maggie cheered her up one day, with talk of an escape attempt. Maggie had been more than just friendly with Lena, they were in a relationship. She told her that she had a friend on the outside *who was connected*, to help them escape. Lena was immediately interested.

'We can make a break one Sunday morning. There are fewer staff on then. Pretend to go to church, slip out the side door. My mate Ruth and me, we had a plan. It was all worked out. Then they sprang a surprise that she was going to be released earlier than she thought. Before she left, she told me she could still help me. When the time was right, she would leave a small parcel, this side of the barbed wired wall.'

'What's in it?' 'You know, wire cutters, thick gloves, that sort of thing. When we were outside in the fields on supervised work, we managed over several weeks to make a ladder?'

'How? What of?'

'It took ages to nick the stuff and smuggle it outside. The ladder is made of broom handles tied together with ropes. We hid it in the grounds. Covered it over with branches in the woods. We tested it. It's okay. Strong enough for a couple of little-uns like us.'

Lena certainly qualified as being a little-un. Since her admission to Bullwood Hall and not having access to alcohol for so long, she had begun to lose weight. That and the devious antics of the gang of three. One of them worked in the kitchens. This meant Lena had to be wary of what she ate, as it could easily have been doctored by Yvonne. As a consequence, her weight had dropped to seven stone.

Lena was excited at the prospect of escaping, although she didn't know where they would run to without being discovered? Maggie had it all planned.

'I have a gaff where we can hide out for a while, it's in London. My cousin's place.'

'Won't he mind?'

'He can't stop us. He's banged up for two years. No one's living there.'

Her plan began to look foolproof. They both started to ask for permission to go to church.

'Church?' The officer was surprised at their requests. 'Since when did you become religious, Maggie?'

'I just wondered what it was all about Ma'am? Some of the girls here have turned their lives around haven't they?'

'That's true, I'm not sure it would work for you two. Worth a try I suppose.'

Lena used a different excuse. 'Ma'am, I thought I might be able to find some peace in religion. I'd like to try the church here first.'

It was agreed that they could go the following Sunday. Their plan was beginning to take shape. Saturday night they both had difficulty in sleeping. They kept going over in their mind the plan that they had set for themselves. Their feelings were tinged with fear and excitement. Sunday morning when they both got up, the adrenalin began to flow.

Chapter Thirty Nine

Jade was coming home. It was a huge responsibility on her husband's shoulders, to care for his disabled wife at such a young age. Both sets of parents could see he was anxious as to how he was going to cope. He needn't have worried, friends and relatives soon set up a rota of care to help with shopping, cleaning and laundry. He hadn't counted on the involvement of so many helping hands and he was delighted. They hoped their pitching in to help, would eventually enable him to return to work.

Whilst Jade was in hospital, the occupational therapy department had arranged for a hand rail to be installed outside the flat; with a gradient area to the side of the entrance steps. Another bar had been fixed to the indoor staircase. Initially it was thought a bed would have to be brought into the sitting-room. The patient, vehemently rejected this, especially as she found she was now able to walk, albeit with assistance.

The other side effects were headaches and memory loss. Huge chunks of memory seemed to have disappeared down a black hole. Any preparations for and participation in the actual wedding ceremony, had been lost. She had to accept at face value on looking at the photos and wedding certificate, that she was in fact married.

Fortunately she didn't have any recollection of Lena's attack. Despite everything that had happened, she was stoic and motivated to get back to normal health as soon as possible.

'What you doing, gorgeous?'

'I'm cleaning the indoor windows with my weak right hand. I thought if I'm supposed to exercise it, I might just as well do something useful.'

'Be careful, pet, I'll do the top ones, don't try stretching up there. Has my mum been in?'

'Yes, she stayed a while and prepared the vegetables for dinner. Who's Aunty Maura? She's been in.'

'That's your mum's sister.'

'My Aunt Sheila is coming down from London next weekend. You'll probably see her.'

'I didn't know we had all these relatives. Do you have a sister?'

'No, it's just me.'

'Then who was the girl that called in this morning. I've forgotten her name. She said I was her best friend. When I couldn't remember her, she started to cry. She told me I used to go out with her brother for a while. Who was that? I don't remember. Oh God, is it always going to be like this? It's as though my mind is in a black fog. Now and again the fog clears a bit. Not entirely. Just enough to remember little pieces.' Silent tears trickled down her cheeks.

'You remember me babe, don't you? It doesn't matter about some boy you used to go out with, it's not necessary to struggle to remember. You know what the doctor said, just relax if you can't remember something, don't keep torturing yourself. Doing that, is not going to supply you with the answer. If you clear your mind, relax, it may pop back into your brain when you least expect it. I want to ask you something important. Think carefully babe. Do you remember saying that you love me?' There was a long pause.

'Sorry, I don't remember *saying* it…but I do remember *feeling* it. I feel it deeply now.'

His anxious face relaxed. He was relieved. They kissed each other with unbridled passion.

'Say babe, can you feel the right side of your face, when I kiss it?'

'Yes, I can. It doesn't feel numb anymore.' She began to smile her normal smile, not her lopsided one.

'If you find using your right hand helps you to get it back to normal by cleaning the windows, I had better keep kissing the right side of your face as well then,' he smiled.

He realised, as his mum had suggested, he would have to keep trying to prompt her memory until the pieces of the jigsaw fitted back together again. He decided to put it into practice. He would start at the beginning and ask about her early life? She couldn't remember anything.

'Okay what about your first school?' She shook her head.

'Secondary school?'

'Were *you* there?'

'No, I went to the Convent School didn't I. What school did you go to?'

'Wait, I remember the playground. I can see a teacher's face, but no name comes to mind. That girl that came this morning, she's there. Her name is…Louise?…Lola?…No, Lois. Lois, I've got it. I've got it. Her name is Lois. She was my first friend, when I arrived at the school. Wow! That's an improvement isn't it?'

'Well done. It's gradually coming back. What was the name of the school?'

'Nope, can't remember that.'

'That's enough for one day. Come on angel, come in the kitchen, see what you can do to help. Doesn't matter if you just sit and watch to start with. My dad's a great cook, I've learned a lot from him. I've only to cook the vegetables. Mum brought in a lamb casserole, I just need to warm it up in the oven.'

She was pleased with her small memory steps. She could see the little flickers of light in what was a dark void. She felt with Stefan's help she would eventually recover most of her memory. That night after months of anxious moments and feelings of despair, they were both able to have a relaxing evening and later, to consummate their marriage.

Chapter Forty

Apart from the security lights on the prison, at six thirty in the morning, the place was in darkness. Not a light in one staff house, in the grounds. The modern accommodation clustered together, were family properties for civilians such as engineers, electricians and maintenance staff. The larger houses for the governor and resident doctor.

Ruth, Maggie's friend, left her car on the main road outside, some distance from the long drive up to the prison. As Maggie and Ruth had been on a working party outside, they were both familiar with the layout. Fields spread over a large area containing some cattle with an old cattle trough. Ruth had arranged to hide a package containing food and money just inside the wooded area near to the entrance to the prison. That way, if something happened that they couldn't make contact with her, the women could pick up the package and make their own escape through the wood, which led to a field and onto the main country road. If they tried to make off down the long drive, as soon as it became light, they could easily be seen, by staff driving in for the day shift. Maggie related the tale of a girl's unnoticed escape from a working party, to Lena.

'After she'd walked several miles, she thumbed a lift. She didn't recognise the driver and didn't know he worked at the prison. He remembered her though didn't he, he turned the car round and drove her straight back here.'

In the early hours of the morning, Ruth, with the aid of a torch, found the ladder under some bushes. She carried it onto the small pathway that led to the prison wall. She tied a small package of tools and gloves to the rope. Everything had been painted to blend into the colour of the prison wall, including the attached rope. She threw the rope over the wall and placed the ladder in such a way, that it was partially hidden in the grass next to the wall. This done, she legged it through the wood, across the fields until she reached the main road. She ran to where she had parked her car and whispered *Good luck*, leapt inside and waited.

'Come on Lena,' Maggie whispered, 'quick through this door.'

They had decided on attending the Catholic Mass, as it was held before breakfast at half-past-six. As soon as they arrived in the chapel, they slipped out through a side door. The prison officer was busy checking names. Should she glance in their direction, they hoped it would appear that they had entered the wrong door by mistake, and were assigned to work in the kitchen. If they hadn't been counted, they wouldn't be missed until check-in at breakfast.

As luck would have it, the previous night, Yvonne, nicked a couple of flavouring essence bottles from the kitchen. These could be inhaled and used as a substitute for glue sniffing. In her heightened state of euphoria, she too decided on *her* escape that day. This would serve to divert attention to the kitchen and dining room areas. Yvonne chose to put her plan into action, when the catering officer was distracted, by the routine counting of knives.

In a flash of flesh, Yvonne stripped off, smothered herself in butter and made a run for it; her bundle of clothes tucked under her arm. She knew it would be difficult for the security guards and prison officers to grab hold of her. An ear-splitting alarm sounded. The security guards rushed to the kitchen area.

When Maggie and Lena heard it, they thought they had been spotted. They made a manic rush for the wall, found the rope, quickly removed the package of wire cutters and protective gloves and hauled up the ladder. They propped the ladder firmly against the wall. Maggie climbed up, used the wire cutters to cut a large area free from the top of the wall and tossed the rope back over to the outside. Then it was Lena's turn. With Maggie perched on top of the wall, Lena held the ladder down below, while her friend slithered down the rope to freedom. Lena repeated the procedure and slithered down to join Maggie.

'Run!' came a hoarse whisper from Maggie.

Maggie grabbed Lena's hand and dragged her over to the woods. Ruth quickly found the package, containing food and money, in the same hiding place as the ladder. The woods gave them immediate cover. Having thought the alarm was for them, they ran as fast as they could and kept running until they reached the field and main road.

A little way up the road, Ruth also alerted by the alarm, was waiting for them. They leaped into the waiting vehicle. She drove her red Vauxhall along the rural road, towards the town of Rayleigh. Within a few minutes, she spotted something in her rear mirror.

'Oh shit! I smell bacon. It's the pigs. I'll shake 'em off. I'll shoot up this country lane.'

They waited for some time until Ruth was unable to see them down the end of the lane and assumed they had gone.

'It wasn't a tail up. They weren't flashing their blues.'

'I don't know about you two, but I'm desperate for a pee,' said Lena.'

'Me too,' said Maggie. 'When that alarm went off, I thought I'd wet meself.'

'Be quick then,' said Ruth.

They disappeared up the secluded lane and hid behind some bushes. Just then the police car re-appeared. The pair shaking watched, from behind the shrubbery, as a police officer stood there asking Ruth questions. He then jumped into the passenger seat of the car and they drove off. The two women were stranded, unsure whether Ruth could return to fetch them or not.

'It's not looking good, at least we have the food and money she left us,' said Lena.

'Lena, look over there, it's an old barn. Let's see if we can hide in there for a while.'

'Okay. We might have food, but we've nothing to drink.'

'We won't stay long. We can get a train from the station and get a drink there.'

They crept into the barn unobserved and sat down to eat their sandwiches.

'That feels better.' Lena tossed the wrapper away. 'Just wish we'd had a drink.'

'Hey wait on. Look what I've found in the corner here.'

It was an old beer barrel, with some liquid in the bottom. Between them they managed to prop the barrel up on a wooden box. They raised it to their lips and gulped down the amber liquid.

'Tastes weird.' said Maggie.

'Been here a long time I expect. Can't say I noticed.'

Not surprising, as the liquid barely touched Lena's lips.

'Had enough to drink ladies?'

They turned to see the farmer standing with a pitchfork at the doorway. His farm backed onto the rear of the prison. He reckoned he could smell escaped prisoners a mile off.

Having heard voices in his barn, he first peered through a gap, then rang the police. Told them to expect two guests. He put the gears of his truck into neutral, so that he could silently position his truck to block the exit to the barn. Wielding his pitchfork he ushered the pair outside.

'In the truck ladies, we're going for a little ride.'

It was not the first time he had driven escaped prisoners in his truck. He was beginning to think he should have some form of reward for his trouble. When they arrived at the police station, Ruth's red car parked outside did not bode well. It would not take long for the police to draw their own conclusions. Ruth was remanded into custody, to await a court hearing for assisting and attempting to conceal two escaped prisoners.

'Where did you find them this time George?'

'In my barn. Drinking from that old barrel again.'

The pair stood with the officer, as he was about to unlock the cell doors. They heard George say in a loud voice, 'Yeah many a night when I'm cut short, I've pissed in that old barrel.'

Maggie and Lena turned pale, dashed into their cells and headed towards the sink in the corner.

'You old devil,' said the officer.

'It works every time,' said George with a smug look of satisfaction. It was enough reward for him. He would be rewarded for his cheeky tale for many nights, with laughter and free beers, down his local pub.

The next day Lena and Maggie found themselves back at Bullwood Hall. Their escapade had now added extra time to their original sentence. What happened to Yvonne? She didn't get very far either. The security guard had seen it all before and grabbed a blanket en route. She almost made it. She raced like a nymph across the field, then slipped on a cow pat and went flying. It gave the guards a few seconds to catch up and toss the blanket over her.

Chapter Forty One

'Jade Rondo? To see Mr Dawson? Thank you, through there.'

'Well, well, well. I must say from last year, you look great.'

'Thank you.'

The Neurosurgeon looked at the notes. 'I see it is two years now since your head injury, how are you?'

'Fine, only an occasional headache. Nothing too bad.'

'Walking? Let me see.'

Stefan went to help her up from the chair. She pushed his hand away. She wanted to demonstrate her progress. She walked slowly across the room without a walking aid or stick.

'Brilliant. Your speech is excellent too. No problems there. Finished with the speech therapist?'

'Yes, some time ago.'

After taking her blood pressure, he asked about her memory?

She turned to look at Stefan. 'You'd better tell the doctor. What do *you* think?'

'Her memory is greatly improved doctor. It's improving all the time. At first there was a huge gap. I was really worried because she didn't even remember that we had got married.'

'Now that can't be too bad. You must be one of the few husbands, that didn't get ticked off by your wife for forgetting your anniversary,' he joked.

'Since then doctor, she vaguely remembers buying the wedding dress. So we are getting there.'

'I think you have done extremely well. I'll be honest with you, when you were first admitted, I didn't give much for your chances.'

'We are very grateful, doctor, for all you've done.'

'Not just me, it was the whole team. Well, I think we can discharge you today. If you have any problems and need to see me, do not hesitate to make an appointment.'

'Thank you very much doctor.' Jade smiled and promptly demonstrated that she could walk quite quickly if needed, as she hurried to the door.

A few weeks later, she was getting headaches and bouts of nausea and on one occasion had vomited, so as advised by Mr Dawson, she made an appointment.

Two weeks before her appointment with the neurosurgeon, she received a letter outlining the tests he wanted her to have first. The first was for a skull X-ray, the others for a variety of blood and urine tests.

'Good morning, I didn't expect to see you both back so soon? Only three months ago wasn't it?' She nodded.

After a thorough examination, he addressed them formally with a serious look on his face.

'Mr and Mrs Rondo, I need to tell you something.'

They both looked concerned and listened intently.

'I cannot help you. The condition you have, you will need to be followed up by a different consultant.'

'Why what's wrong with her?' asked Stefan anxiously. 'What's happened?'

'You will need to make an appointment with my colleague John Masters. I wish all my problems were as simple as yours. Don't look so worried, my dear…you are pregnant…you are going to have a baby. Congratulations, to you both.'

They looked at each other, overwhelmed at the news.

'I had no idea?' Her eyes were brimming with tears.

Stefan quickly pressed the tips of his two forefingers to his eyes, to try to prevent crying himself. When they got outside, they hugged and kissed each other.

'It looks as though congratulations are in order?' said the nurse. She was aware of the results before handing the doctor the pathology form.

They couldn't wait to get home to tell their parents. Jeanette and Tess were soon on the phone both highly excited at the news. Felix patted his son on the back. 'Well done son.'

He grinned. 'Good thing the flat has three bedrooms.'

'You must start and decorate one for the nursery,' said his dad.

'Then you can start getting the nursery furniture together. I don't want to see history repeating itself, with a baby in a drawer,' smiled Jeanette.

When Tess heard the news she was overjoyed.

'I am so pleased for ye both. How many weeks?'

'They think about twelve.'

'I can hardly believe it.'

'Nor can I,' she said, patting her tummy. 'I'd lost so much weight when I was ill, I just thought I was beginning to put a bit back on. My periods have been so irregular, I didn't take any notice. Mum, I'm really excited. It will be lovely to have a baby in the place. Stef is thrilled. We can't stop talking about it.'

'Don't go overdoing it. Take it easy, it's only two years since the stroke.'

'Mum, I am being waited on like a princess, Stef won't let me do a thing.'

'Make the most of it then darlin'. Wait until the little one disturbs *his* sleep in the middle of the night. But I'll be able to help ye by the time ye are due, I will have retired by then.'

As soon as Michael arrived home she told him the good news. Later that evening, she also thought she'd mention how Jade's memory was still sketchy.

'I was telling Jade how ye have been invited to talk at her old school about the dangers of cannabis and thought ye would mention what happened to Adam. She had no idea who Adam was? She only had a brief memory of the wedding. Recently, she remembered going to London with Jeanette, to choose the wedding dress and meet Alex's children, who were to be bridesmaids. Then I asked her, did she remember going to see anyone, to ask them to come to the wedding? Of course ye know why I asked her that ?'

'To see if she could remember going to see Lena, and did she?'

'No. No recollection either of anything that happened at the reception.'

'That's a blessing darling.' Tess agreed, that this could indeed be a blessing.

'By the time she has her baby, Lena could be out on early release. Of course she won't be going back to her old flat. That was owned by the council and it would have been re-allocated to someone else.'

'Well darlin' I'd best be getting back. 'Tis alright for these poor retired old folks, working part-time in an office. Some of us are still working flat out.'

'You mean those interfering old dears from the welfare, that still have to work full-time.'

Tess swiped him one with the tea-towel.

'I see, cutting up rough now are we? Go on, get moving or you'll be late.'

The last few months, Tess had been working as a relief health visitor. She quite enjoyed helping her colleagues on different patches. She discovered that some health visitors did indeed have it cushy. One colleague that worked in the more affluent area of Thorpe Bay asked Tess for advice regarding a case of child abuse, explaining that it was the first one she had encountered. A lot of mothers in that area, had it easy with the help of a nanny and domestic help, so they were usually under less stress.

Tess was visiting in the Thorpe Bay area, to a mother with her six-week-old baby. This mother seemed stressed. She opened up to her that she was concerned about her husband; he was about to lose his directorship of a large firm in London. He was spending a lot of time abroad and very little time at home, struggling to keep the business afloat. Her face showed the strain of coping with the baby and house staff on her own. On Tess's second visit that week, the mother had been concerned with the baby having infantile colic and his constant crying.

'I've had the doctor in. He said it wasn't the colic, that he had dislocated his shoulder.'

'How did that happen?'

'He must have done it when he turned over in the night.'

Tess was more concerned now. How could a six-week-old baby turn over on its own? Surely this was not possible? Yet he had been seen by a doctor. Did a red light not come on with the GP? It certainly did with her. As she drove away from the house, she kept saying to herself, a six-week-old baby **cannot** turn over on its own.

Tess knew that all babies were different at reaching their milestones. She also knew that it was not until a baby was about four months old, that it can start to roll from front to back. Most will start at five months. Tess decided to visit the GP involved.

'The mother said the dislocation occurred when the baby rolled over. I took it that she or the nanny had rolled the baby over, to change its nappy or something. This is not a family to suspect any problems surely. She has plenty of help.'

'She told me it was the nanny's night off and the relief nanny was off sick.'

'What are you suggesting?'

'Possible rough handling. Picking the baby up with one arm?'

'But the mother doesn't seem the type to get agitated or lose her temper?'

'She is very stressed.'

'That's the first I've heard about it?'

'Her husband is away a lot. She has just heard he is about to lose his directorship.'

'Oh I see.' He sighed. 'I suppose I have to ring social services do I?'

'I think that would be a good idea, doctor.'

Chapter Forty Two

'It's Jade, she sounded agitated.' Michael handed Tess the phone.

'Okay darlin' keep calm. I'll be there, before ye can say Braxton Hicks.'

'What's that?'

'Never mind. Is Stefan with ye?'

'No, he's not there yet.'

'Right, I'll be there straight away.'

'Is she all right dear?'

'She thinks she's in labour. I'll give ye a ring, when I know what's happening.'

'Come on, just let me feel ye tummy. Let's me see, what are yer, thirty seven weeks?'

'Mm. Ooh ouch!'

'Try and relax darlin'. How often have ye been getting the pains?'

'They come and go, Mum. Sometimes five minutes. Then two minutes. Then they disappear for a while.'

'Have ye had any bleeding?'

'No.'

'Feel sick?'

'No.'

'Slip off the sofa and try walking.'

She slid off the sofa and walked around the room.

'Keep walking. How are the pains now?'

'They seem to have gone.'

'They're probably Braxton Hicks contractions. They're not true labour pains. Otherwise they would be closer together and would increase once ye started walking.'

'What are Braxton Hicks then?'

'Some people say the uterus is having a practice run. That's not quite true, they are contractions that tighten up the uterus, because of the hormone oxytocin. They are not strong enough for labour pains. In labour, ye will have regular contractions about five to ten minutes apart. It will be like severe menstrual cramps. Some bleeding, feeling sick. I'm going to run ye a warm bath. Not too warm, because of the baby. Then it's time ye had something to eat.'

The phone rang. 'Yes dear, she's fine. She not in labour. She's in the bath and I'm making her some toast.'

'I've just had a call, love, from Adam. If I'm not here when you get home, that's where I'll be.'

Stefan arrived home, worried at the phone call *he'd* had.

'She's fine dear, I checked her and the baby, it's kicking away. But baby is not ready yet. The pains are preliminary ones, not strong enough to be labour pains.'

Tess was able to put his mind at rest. She hoped the families could relax now, for the next couple of weeks. When she got home there was a message from Michael on the answer machine.

'Tess, I'm worried about Adam. He doesn't look at all well. He says he's all right, but I don't think so. He's worried that if he goes to the doctor, they will make him go into hospital. I've got him an appointment with his GP for five o'clock tonight. I'll stay with him and take him myself.'

Under protest and gentle persuasion from dad, the doctor was able to examine Adam.

'He has marked tenderness on the right side of his abdomen. It could be appendicitis or one of a number of abdominal conditions. I tend to think he has had this condition for sometime and hasn't told anyone.'

While Adam was getting dressed, they went into an adjoining room.

'I expect you know he has a mental condition,' said Michael.

'Oh yes. He has been writing little notes to me. This week he signed himself William Shakespeare.'

'Oh dear, has he started that again?' said Michael.

'It's not a problem Mr King, he's no problem. He doesn't seem to be depressed, but he's obviously in a lot of pain today. He's usually quite cheerful and chatty isn't he? I know he hates hospitals and he is unlikely to complain of pain, unless it becomes unbearable. So we don't know how long this has been going on? I am going to try and get him into hospital this evening. Are you able to stay with him?'

'Yes. No problem. I'll be staying with him and go with him to the hospital.'

Tess picked up the phone. 'Darling, I'll be late. The doctor is getting Adam admitted this evening. I'll be going with him. I'll get him settled in before I leave.'

He put the phone down and started to pack pyjamas, toiletries and a few other necessary items in Adam's backpack.

'I didn't expect ye back so soon,' said Tess, as she bent down to put a shepherd's pie in the oven.

'They're not taking him to theatre until tomorrow morning. Meanwhile they are doing lots of tests. They told me to ring the hospital in the morning. He looks a funny colour.'

'What sort of funny – grey – white – yellow?'

'Yes, yellow. The whites of his eyes are yellowy.'

'He's jaundiced then.'

The next morning, Michael telephoned the hospital.

'He's had a poor night,' said the Sister. 'The consultant is going to see him on his round this morning.'

'I'm going up there, love. See Adam for myself.'

'Dad, I want to go home?'

'Not yet son, you have to let the doctor see you first.'

The consultant appeared in the office. Sister beckoned Michael in to join them.

'I'm afraid your son's condition is very serious,' said the consultant. 'We have done a biopsy and several tests. I am sorry to have to tell you that sadly, Adam has pancreatic cancer.'

'Isn't there any treatment you can do?'

'Not at the moment. It is unusual to find this disease in a young person. There is little known about this disease and what causes it, whether it's genetic or environmental. Is your son a smoker?'

'He used to smoke heavily at one time, when he was younger. Not recently.'

'We do know that smoking is a factor. I'm afraid apart from palliative medicine and care, I'm sorry, there is very little we can do for him. We can aspirate some of the fluid from the area, that should give him some relief.'

'How long has he got doctor?'

'The fact that he is already jaundiced, means he has probably had this condition for a while. We are probably thinking in terms of weeks, rather than months.'

'I'd like to take him home.'

'Of course. Do you think you could manage him?'

'My wife is a nurse. I'm sure we could cope with him at our place.'

Arrangements were made for an ambulance to take him, to their home. Meanwhile Tess took time off and contacted the Marie Curie Nurses. Together they worked out a care plan. Every care and attention would be given to him.

Two weeks later, Adam, surrounded by his family, passed away peacefully in his father's arms. He was only thirty-six.

Chapter Forty Three

'I thought the priest gave a lovely homily for Adam,' said Tess.

'Did you notice Melody, his former girlfriend? I wanted to ask her to come back to the house, but she disappeared.'

'I did manage to have a quick word dear. She was dreadfully upset. I gave her our number and told her that she would be welcome anytime.'

Michael had not seemed to grieve for Adam. He had set about organising everything to do with his son's death, in a business-like manner. Contacting the funeral director, going to the register office, the church arrangements. He attended to everything methodically. At the church he was dry-eyed and kept a firm grip on his feelings.

A week later, Michael was back at the Travel Office. He took a phone call which triggered off his emotions. He broke down and sobbed. An office colleague brought him a coffee and suggested he went home and took the rest of the day off.

Tess could see he was distraught; she put her arms around him.

'What happened?'

'I don't know. A guy just rang up asking about a booking to India. I was okay until I put the phone down, then I seemed to be overwhelmed with grief for Adam.'

'Michael it's good that ye were able to let go of all that emotion. Ye've bottled it up for so long. Not just the funeral, but right back from the time ye saw him in that awful place in Birmingham.'

'I feel so guilty. I should have been able to do something Tess. I tried to warn him before going to university about being offered drugs. Because it was my day-to-day work in the drug squad, he rounded on me and said, *'All you ever think about Dad, is drugs, drugs, drugs!'*

Michael started to sob. Tess held him close.

'It's not ye're fault darlin'.

'I keep thinking he took drugs out of bravado, to prove to me it wouldn't affect him?'

'No, ye said yerself that all the students away from home tend to try cannabis. They think it can help them relax and have a positive effect on their studies.'

'That's true.'

'I had a phone call today, from Melody; she is going to be in the area this week. She's apparently on a course, staying at a friend's house. She asked if she could call round one evening?'

'What did you say?'

'I said I'd ask ye and ring her back.'

'Tell her any evening she would be most welcome.'

When Melody arrived, there was polite catching up. Conversation as to how her life had moved forward. She had married and had two little girls, both at school. Melody had just been made deputy head of a large junior school, in South East London.

Tess could see that Michael wanted to ask her more pertinent questions about her time with Adam, so she left them together in the sitting room, with the excuse she was going to make some coffee.

'Tell me, was my son taking a lot of drugs at college?'

'Mr King…'

'Please call me Michael.'

'Michael, to be fair we all were. Not a lot, mostly the odd one at parties and weekends.'

'And Adam?'

'You could say he took more than most. On a daily basis. After a while I noticed he was distancing himself from his friends. He told me he'd had the odd one or two at school. It had started with a school outing when he was fourteen. Someone passed around a couple of spliffs in the coach. He said they all tried them. I got to know him at university. After a while I noticed it was affecting his memory and concentration. He didn't always make sensible decisions.'

'What about you? How did it affect you?'

'I found it relaxed me and gave me confidence. But I only smoked it occasionally. Not like Adam on a regular basis.'

'Tell me about India? Why, having secured decent jobs, did you both decide to take off to some religious sect in India?'

'It was after I went with Adam, to see the psychologist on campus. He suggested meditation. Said he had been to this guru in India for six weeks, when he was on his gap year. He found it beneficial for anxiety.'

'So you decided to throw away the opportunity of your teaching posts and go.'

'No, Michael.' She was beginning to feel he was blaming her for his son's death.

'It wasn't quite like that. The posts were not permanent; they were only on a six-month contract and didn't start until the September. Initially, we only planned on going for six weeks. But we both got so wrapped up in the religious teaching and tranquillity, we decided to stay on. I think I mentioned before, we had meditation and fasting. Then there was the abstinence.'

'You mean you were having sex at college, and at this religious place, it was now forbidden?' Melody nodded her head in agreement.

'Tell me the truth Melody, what happened that you both decided to leave?'

There was a long pause before she answered.

'We didn't have a choice Michael. We were thrown out in disgrace.'

Again she hesitated…'I was pregnant with Adam's baby.'

'What! Oh my God! I never knew that! What happened to the baby?'

Tess heard the exclamation and raised voice from Michael. She decided it was an opportune moment, to go in with a tray of coffee, to try and dampen down the tension. Tess slowly poured out the coffee, to give Michael time to calm down. Then she sat down beside them.

'Did you hear that Tess? Melody and Adam left India because she was having his baby.'

'Calm down Michael. These things happen. Ye are only annoyed, because Adam was ill, and ye were kept out of the picture. What did ye do?' asked Tess.

'I was four months pregnant. Feeling unwell. With all that fasting, I didn't know what effect it might have on the baby. I went home to my mother. I had nowhere else to go. Fortunately she was fine about it. I had the baby. She was five weeks premature, a tiny little thing.'

'How old is she now?' asked Michael.

'She's fourteen.' She paused, 'She's nearly as tall as her father, and doing well at school. Would you like to see her? She's coming down to Southend for the weekend, with my mother on Friday.'

Before Michael had a chance to open his mouth, Tess said, 'Yes, we would love to meet her, wouldn't we Michael?'

'Erm…yes. Of course we would. What's her name?'

'Mala.'

'That's pretty Melody, what an unusual name,' said Tess.

'It's the name of an Indian actress and a village in India.'

'Is that why ye chose it?'

'Not really. I took the first letters of Melody – Adam – Love – Always…Mala.'

'That's lovely isn't it Michael?'

'You haven't mentioned your husband?' said Michael.

'I first met Jeremy, when I started as a supply teacher at a school in Peckham. He was deputy head at the time, a studious, confirmed bachelor. Married to the job. I must have found some dormant chemistry between us. We've been married seven years. He took to Mala straight away; she was seven then. Two years later, we had Nicola; she's five.'

It was time for Melody to leave. Michael stood at the front door and hugged her. He felt all the tension leave his body.

'I can't thank you enough for coming. You will never know the relief your visit has brought to me. It would seem Melody, that we were both overcome with guilt at what happened to Adam. The joy of knowing that Adam had a daughter is marvellous news. It's knowing that a little piece of Adam that we both loved,' he fought to hold back the tears, 'will live on…in Mala.'

Chapter Forty Four

'Where are you off to in such a rush?'

Tess was hurriedly leaving the house, just as Michael was coming in. One arm in her coat, and struggling to put it on properly. Michael helped her on with it.

'The baby is on its way. I've contacted Stefan. He's in Manchester, leaving straight away.'

'What's he doing in Manchester?' asked Michael.

'How do I know? Does it matter? As soon as the delivery is imminent, I'll call ye.'

'Bye then, drive carefully.'

On arrival at the flat, Tess realised there was no time to lose. She rang for an ambulance.

'Breathe how ye were shown in ante-natal class.'

'I can't.'

'Yes ye can. Don't push yet.'

Tess swiftly bundled her and her packed bag in the car. At one point Tess thought she was about to deliver in the hospital car park.

'Stay there, I'll dash in the hospital and get a wheelchair.'

She wheeled her swiftly into the maternity wing. The person at the reception area, was patronising. Without looking up, casually said, 'We think we are in labour do we?'

Jade could only respond with a brisk nodding of the head and murmured, 'Mm… mm,' with gritted teeth.

After several hours in labour, pains every minute, an obstetrician was called in. In view of her medical history, he asked for the theatre to be prepared for a Caesarean Section. By the time she was prepped and gowned and ready to go to theatre, Stefan had arrived. Tess was delighted to see him. She gave her daughter a quick kiss goodbye.

'Good bye darlin'. You'll be fine. Stefan, is here now. He will call me when you've had the baby.'

When she arrived home, Jeanette telephoned to say that Jade was on her way to theatre.

They allowed her husband to accompany the stretcher, to the entrance to the anaesthetic room.

Jade slept on, unaware of the drama that had taken place in the theatre. The baby's breathing had stopped. The whole team held *their* breath, until the paediatrician was able to restart the baby's breathing within two extremely long minutes. The Theatre Sister carried the baby out of the theatre.

'Just a quick look daddy. You have a beautiful baby boy.'

The baby was swiftly taken back into the theatre anteroom. Sometime later, a semi-conscious Jade returned to the post-natal ward. Stefan wiped her brow with some wet wipes.

'You're back on the ward babe.' She didn't stir. She slept on.

His parents arrived and sat around the bedside.

'How is she?' asked Jeanette. Has she come round yet?'

'Not properly. She opened her eyes just now and smiled at me.'

'So you have a boy, have you seen him yet?' asked Felix.

'Yes, I saw him briefly outside the theatre. Then I was taken to see him Dad, in the neo-natal ward. Just peered through the glass. I'm sure you will both be able to see him before you go. He's got dark hair, Mum, and blue eyes. But all our family have got brown eyes?'

When he mentioned *all our family having brown eyes*, Jeanette admitted to feeling a warm glow. Apart from Jade, Stefan and Lena, other biologically related family, were unknown.

'I expect they will change later on. I believe most babies have blue eyes.'

'Oh, look, I think she's waking up. You alright, princess?' he said excited.

'What happened?'

'We have a lovely baby boy.'

'I'm not here to have a baby. I'm here because of an accident at the wedding. How can we have a baby already?'

'Oh dear,' said Felix, 'she's all muddled up.'

Jeanette whispered, 'I expect it's the anaesthetic. Don't trouble her son about the baby, let her take her time.'

'She's fallen asleep again,' said Felix. 'It's quite late. The Sister is coming over, I think we had better make a move.'

'It's probably best to let her sleep off the anaesthetic,' said the Sister. 'Why not ring up in the morning? The visiting hours are on the board at the entrance to the ward.'

Stefan kissed Jade on the forehead. She didn't stir.

'Would it be all right for my parents to have a quick look at the baby before they go?'

'Of course, just for a brief look. Nurse, would you take the visitors to see baby Rondo at the neo-natal unit?'

'Isn't he tiny? How much did he weigh son?'

'I forgot to ask.'

The two grandparents arranged between them, when they would visit, so as not to tire Jade. After they had gone, the baby was brought to Jade for feeding. At first this was awkward because of her stitches. The nurses propped her up in a comfortable position. She was bewildered. The midwives kept telling her that it *was* her baby. She found this difficult to accept. The following day, Stefan decided to ask the doctor about his wife's memory loss.

'Usually if there is any confusion and memory loss after a general anaesthetic, the 'fog' tends to clear after two or three days. In your wife's case, she suffered memory loss following her head injury and subsequent stroke. The memory part of the brain was already damaged.'

'When that happened doctor, she lost all memory prior to the injury. She couldn't remember getting married. Slowly she started remembering getting a wedding dress before the wedding. Now she doesn't remember being pregnant or that the baby is ours?'

'I'm not a neurologist, but it would seemed as though the anaesthetic has given her memory a jump start, back to the past. Try not to worry. Give it a couple of months I expect she will start remembering again. If you are still concerned, get her to see her neurologist. I'm sure he can give you the answers you need.'

Stefan *was* worried about her memory problem. Instead of it gradually improving, could it be permanent?

Once home with the baby, they named him Daniel, a name they had previously decided on. Slowly she began to adjust to motherhood. She trusted her husband. If he said it was *their* baby, it was good enough for her.

'Darlin' I'll call back later,' said Tess.

'I thought you would want to stay, knowing the health visitor was calling.'

'No, I don't think so dear. I think I've seen enough health visitors in my lifetime. The conversation you will have is just between you two.'

She knew that there could be some personal questions about sex and contraception. It would not be right, to be listening to intimate details between husband and wife.

Melody kept her promise and brought her daughter Mala, to see Michael.

'Mala. This is your Grandfather.'

The tall, auburn-haired girl walked over to Michael, 'Hello,' she gently held out her hand.

Michael took it in his and to everyone's surprise kissed it. Mala giggled, thought that his reaction was really funny.

After they left, he remarked, 'Don't you think she looks a bit like Adam, Tess?'

'She's certainly got your family's auburn hair.'

'Alex still has the same colour. Mine's beginning to look more like an unravelled *Brillo* pad. Not a scrap of auburn left.'

'Never mind dear, I promised to love ye when ye become old and grey. Or did I say wizened and worn?'

'Hey that's enough. I'll show you who's wizened and worn. Cheeky, come here.'

He hugged her and kissed her tenderly.

'Tess, did I ever say I loved you?'

'Yes, frequently darlin'. Thank God, or ye'd be after doin' yer own cooking and washing.'

'What do you mean? All right, I know I haven't a clue how to operate the washing machine, but what about that chicken pie I made the other day?'

'Oh, so that's what it was? I seem to remember finding a wee bit of meat the size of a postage stamp, amongst all that sauce.'

Michael glared at her. It was one of those looks, that Tess recognised, that said if she knew what was good for her, it was time to make a run for it…

Chapter Forty Five

1990

After three months, the family were delighted to see the progress that both mother and baby had made. Today was to be a celebration of not only the baptism of Daniel, but a blessing on Stefan and Jade's marriage vows. They made arrangements for cars to take the family afterwards, to a special tea at a high-class hotel. One of the godmothers was Lois, who fortunately was a Catholic. This could have caused a dilemma as the other was one was Tess. The priest had told the parents that one of the godparents must be a Catholic. Jeanette and Felix had chosen Tess. They were unaware that Tess and her family in Ireland, had long since denounced the Catholic Faith.

The priest held the baby near the font and, with his hand dipped in the holy water, trickled it over the baby's head. Making the sign of a cross on the baby's forehead, announced his full names.

'Daniel Felix Michael Rondo. In the name of the Father…'

Tess turned to look at Michael. He was smiling broadly. He knew that the baby's second name was Felix; he had no idea they would include his name as well. Afterwards, the two godmothers took turns to hold the baby, whilst the priest pronounced a blessing on the couple. This time it was a very happy occasion for everyone. At the hotel, Michael thanked them for giving his name as well as Felix's to the baby.

'I can't tell you how thrilled I was when the priest read out my name. I had no idea, I am over the moon. Thank you both.' He hugged them. When Jade heard Daniel cry she walked over to her mother.

Stefan said to Michael, 'No I need to thank *you*. If you and your wife hadn't rescued Jade, who knows where she would have been today. I had no idea what her mother was really like until that day. I thought she was exaggerating. I couldn't understand why she wouldn't let me meet her. She has started to remember her mother. It's a very distorted, romantic view. In fact I think what she doesn't know about her biological family, she fills in the gaps herself.'

One year on, Jade decided to take Daniel to the park on her own.

'Good idea; can you remember how to get there?'

'Of course. It's easy from here.'

An hour later, she found the park, not the local one. She had been wandering about for some time before stopping someone, to ask where it was?

She had another intention that day. Now that Daniel was a year old, she wanted to be able to show her birth mother her grandson. She had overheard her dad say that Lena had moved to Westcliff. She manoeuvred the pushchair up the concrete slope to the library.

'Is there any way I could find an address of my mother, in Westcliff?'

The librarian looked puzzled.

'After I got married, we both moved and lost touch.'

'We could try the electoral role. What is her name?'

'Lena Walker.'

She came away with three possible addresses. Then it struck her, she had forgotten what Lena looked like. She put the addresses safely in her pocket and decided to go and see Tess. She thought her mum would be able to give her a description of what Lena looked like.

'Hi Mum, I've brought Daniel to see you.'

'How lovely?'

They went into the kitchen.

'I wondered if you might have a photo of Lena?'

'Not really, why?'

The only picture of Lena that she had seen, was the one on the front page of the local newspaper, when she was sent to prison. Being preoccupied with Adam's illness and the new baby, she had forgotten Michael had said that Lena would soon be out of prison.

'I just wondered what she looked like?'

'She's quite thin, smaller than ye. She hasn't got blonde hair. I think hers was originally short and black. But I have seen it dyed all sorts of different colours.'

Tess wondered what sort of person Lena would be now. Would she have reformed in some way? Become sober, found some remorse for the way she had treated her daughter? Before she went to see Tess, Jade had a blurred picture in her mind. Now it was quite clear. In her mind she could visualise her stature and features. And didn't she wear those big, bangle-like earrings? She tried to conjure up her voice. It was quite loud, high-pitched. All she had to do now, was find her. She had three clues on the piece of paper that the librarian had given her. She called in the post office and bought herself a map of the district. A nagging feeling told her not to tell anyone. Not Mum or Stefan.

She made her way, with Daniel in the pushchair, to the first address. She pushed Daniel up the long pathway. No one was in. She knocked next-door.

'She's at work, love. Gets home about six. Shall I tell her you called?'

'No it's okay, I'll call again.'

The second address was in a block of flats and the lift didn't work. She decided she would have to leave that one, for a day when she didn't have the baby with her. Next week Stefan's mum was going to be babysitting, to enable her to go to the hairdressers. To give herself more time, she thought she might call in on Lena, after going to a hairdresser, that was in her area. She struggled to recall the last time that she would have seen her mother, without success. She must have been at the wedding, she thought. It struck her how odd it was to have two mums, why was that? The psychologist had told her not to try *too* hard to remember. Her memory might come back, if she could try and relax and not get anxious about it.

The third address was a small terraced cottage. Again no one in, so she knocked next door. The door was opened by a curly-haired girl about her own age. She was wearing tortoiseshell, cats-eye glasses.

'Is it Jade? Jade Walker? You remember me, we were in the same class together?'

'I'm sorry. I don't want to appear rude, but I have some memory problems.'

'That's fine. Don't worry. Come in. Bring the baby in.'

'Is this your house? Sorry, I don't know your name?'

'Doreen Baker. Are you sure you don't remember me, we were in the same netball team.'

She shook her head. 'I'm sorry Doreen. I had a bad accident. But my memory is gradually improving. At first I didn't even remember getting married.'

'Gosh, that's awful. Dave and I are getting married next year.'

'I live here with my mum and dad. My dad's disabled, mum's not fit, so I help mum look after him.'

Doreen seemed glad of someone to talk to. She brought in a tray of coffee and biscuits, with some juice for Daniel. They chatted about weddings and babies for quite a while.

'I've just thought, why don't we meet up regularly. I could help jog your memory. Remind you about our school days, it might help.'

'That sounds a great idea. I'd love that.'

'I didn't ask you, but why did you knock on our door?'

'There *is* something you could help me with. I'm looking for my other mother. I wondered if she lived next door? There is a young girl Tania Walker next door, but she would be too young, she's only in her twenties.'

Doreen remembered Jade from primary school. Her filthy clothes, how no one wanted to sit next to her. What mother would send her to school looking like that? All that began to fall into place. Doreen remembered her mother showing her the photographs in the local paper. She pointed out the photo of Jade, as someone at her school, a victim of a vicious assault. Her mother had fractured her daughter's skull and was sent to prison. The woman that she'd always thought was Jade's mum, was a smart Irish lady. So that *wasn't* her *real* mum. Doreen didn't know what to say.

She hesitated, then said, 'I'll see what I can do.'

She was bluffing. She knew that would be very little. There was no way she wanted to get involved with a woman like that. The paper had said that the daughter was in a critical condition. If she died, her mother would be convicted of her murder. She remembered the story now, it all began to fit. Especially with Jade's memory loss. The memory of her awful mother, was one that Doreen knew she would *not* help her to retrieve.

Chapter Forty Six

'What sort of a day have you had? Did you find the park okay?'

'Daniel's been fine. I found the park, and guess what? I found an old school friend, Doreen Baker.'

'You remembered someone from your school days?'

'No, not exactly, she recognised me. I told her about my poor memory and she's offered to try and help me remember our school days. Apparently we were in the same netball team. Doreen helps her mum look after her disabled dad. But I expect we can find some time together.'

'I'm really pleased babe, you've found a friend; especially since you lost Lois when she moved to London.'

'I can't see her next week. Next week, I am going to the hairdresser. Your mum promised to come over and babysit,' she said, fingering the paper with the address of the flat, in her pocket.

'How you doing?' asked Jeanette. 'I can see you are walking fine now.'

'Yes, at first it was good to be able to hold on to the handle of the buggy, to steady myself, now I can go it alone.'

'That's brilliant. It must be three years since you were in hospital? You've made great progress. Stefan was saying that your memory is nearly back to normal.'

'I'm not sure it's back to normal. There are still a few gaps from way back. But I am beginning to remember teachers at school. I can remember their names, but can't remember what they taught? It's improving all the time. I'd better dash, my appointment's for two o'clock.'

Jade mentioned she would be in the hairdresser's for some time. But in truth she was only going for a quick trim, then make her way to what she hoped was Lena's flat.

As soon as she came out of the hair salon, her heart started to quicken. What sort of reception would she get? Would she recognise her mother? Would her mother recognise her? She was pleased that she had remembered her way to the block of flats. She tackled the stairs to the third floor, glad of the metal stair rail to hold on to. By the time she reached the front door, her heart was pounding. What would she find? She had a swift flashback and remembered having visited her mother prior to the wedding. Did she come to the wedding? She couldn't remember. She knocked again, harder this time.

A frail, scar-faced woman opened the door. There were severe dented marks across her brow and her eyelids were badly disfigured. It looked as though she'd had skin grafts. Lena had been badly beaten in prison. A prisoner had lunged towards her with a pair of opened scissors and plunged them into Lena's face. Despite several operations, they were unable to save her sight.

Jade's own scars on her skull had faded, her short blonde hair covered them. For some time after her brain operation, she was completely bald. Tess knitted her a skull cap with dreadlock-type strands of beads hanging down, to give the appearance of hair.

Jade broke the silence. 'Are you Lena Walker?'
'Yes.'
'Did you used to live at Fairfield Flats?'
'Yes, why?'

She was cautious. 'I think you used to know my mum?'

'I did know a woman in the flats, she had a young daughter, can't remember her name.'

'I was in the area, thought I'd call and see you.'

'That was kind of you. Come in. I'm afraid I can't see you. I'm blind.'

It was puzzling. Her voice was not the voice that she recognised. This was a soft, pleasant voice. Why had her flashback revealed a harsh loud voice? This voice was different.

'Have you lived here long, erm… Mrs Walker?'

'Not long.'

Lena didn't offer much information, so she asked, 'Why did you move from Fairfield?'

'I had to go away. I wasn't well.'

'You were in hospital?'

'Your mum has probably told you all about me. She came to visit me, after I was sent down. I did something dreadful. I realise that now.'

'You're saying you've been in prison?'

'In prison and in hospital.'

'When your mum came to see me, she told me she'd heard I'd killed someone. I don't remember, I was pissed out of my skull with drink. I haven't touched a drop since. I didn't think I could do it. But prison, in a way, helped me. Through prison I lost my sight, but it saved my life. I go every week to Alcoholics Anonymous now. They send a car round to take me. I've met some really nice people there. One of them insists on doing my weekly shop. She probably thinks I'm going to nip in an off-licence. No way, I'm dry now and intend to stay that way.'

'Would you like me to make you a cup of tea?'

'That would be nice, thank you. There are some biscuits in a round tin, in the first cupboard on the left.'

Wandering out into to the kitchen, she found everywhere spotless. The kitchen floor had a mock tiled effect that shone. The kitchen surfaces were clean and tidy, the stainless steel sink, gleamed. In the corner was a new washing machine and drier, clothes and sheets were tumbling. She stared at the clean microwave and toaster on the far counter. Opposite the kitchen, a door led to the bedroom. She could see that the bed was made up with a white fitted floral bedspread. Everywhere looked light and airy. She noticed the bedroom curtains had been opened. It was then she experienced a flashback to the home she first remembered. The curtains were *never* opened. It was gloomy, smelly and oppressive. Discarded cans and bottles littered the bedroom and kitchen. The smell was overpowering. In her mind she could hear raised men's voices. Lena screaming abuse at her. Men grabbing Lena, then grabbing her. She saw herself fighting a man off. Scratching him, biting him. Then a misty picture of Tess appeared. Tess put her arm around her and bundled her in the car away from all the squalor and aggression.

Immediately Tess's home smelled of fresh flowers, it was clean. There were clean clothes. Clean bed. Plenty of food and friendly faces. Until she went there, she didn't realise what an awful smell there was at her own place, or how neat and tidy a house could look. She had to pinch herself. Was this the same person? She carried in the tray of tea and biscuits.

'Thank you. You haven't told me your name?'

'You know my name.'

'No, I don't.'

'You gave it to me…it's Jade.'

'No. NO!' she shrieked. 'Why did you come here, for revenge? You must hate me! Didn't Tess tell you what happened at your wedding?'

The dark cloud started to lift, underneath, she could see a snapshot of the incident in the hotel.

'No. No one told me the finer details. I expect they were trying to shield me from the truth. All I knew was that someone who was drunk, hit me over the head with a bottle of wine. It never entered my head until now, that it was my *own* mother.'

'I am so sorry. You must hate me. You must hate me,' she whimpered.

'Mother, I *always* knew you hated me. Because you said it all the time.'

'It was the drink talking. It was the drink,' she wailed.

'Listen, I don't hate you. I don't hate anyone. It's not in my nature.'

'I am so sorry.' Lena burst into tears. 'I know it's a poor excuse. But I've never learned how to love anyone. My parents never loved me. And because of my father's horrendous behaviour, I eventually went into care. I know it's a poor excuse and I don't expect you to forgive me for what I did. Or how badly I treated you.'

Jade walked over to her mother and put her arm around her.

'I can teach you how to love, Mother. Had Tess not taken me to her home, when you were an alcoholic, I could have found it difficult to love someone, but it can be learned Mother, I can show you.'

'I don't deserve you. I was wicked to you.'

'You were sick, Mother. You had an addictive disease. Alcoholism and drugs. You needed help.'

For the first time, she hugged her mother tightly and kissed her. They both wept.

'I have to go now, I have someone looking after my son Daniel. One day I'll bring him to see you. Not next time, because I think we need time on our own, to get to know each other better.'

'I can't believe what has happened this afternoon Jade. I can't thank you enough for coming to see me.' Tears trickled down her scarred face. 'I really don't deserve you.'

'I'm your daughter Mum… everyone deserves a second chance.'

Chapter Forty Seven

'Where have you been? Mum and I have been going frantic. Mum even phoned the hairdresser. She said you hadn't even been there or made an appointment.'

'Where were you?' asked Jeanette. 'Did you get lost somewhere, love?'

'I went to a different hairdresser.'

'There you are, Stefan, I told you there was nothing to worry about.'

'I'm sorry. As long as you are safe, babe, that's the main thing.'

'Has Daniel been any trouble?'

'No problem at all dearie, he's been fast asleep.'

'I'll see you both at the weekend for lunch. Or is it Tess's turn?'

'It's our turn to have you all here for Mother's Day.'

'Thank you. That will be lovely.'

How would the family take to her visiting her birth mother? She knew she would have to wait for the right opportunity to present itself. She was more worried now, as to how her mum would react? Would she resent her seeing Lena? Would she be bitter after all the help, love and guidance she had given her, to go and seek a mother who hated her. After a sleepless night, she decided to go and see her at the first opportunity. She would try to explain her reasons for visiting her birth mother.

She set off the next morning, still feeling guilty after all that had been done for her, especially now that she had found out that it was Lena, that had assaulted her at the wedding and fractured her skull.

'Hi Mum.'

'Hello darlin' and how is our little Daniel?'

'He's fine. He's starting to pull himself up now and he's trying a few steps.'

'Ye don't usually come to see me on a Wednesday. My talk was postponed this morning, but working part-time now, ye're in luck. Something is on yer mind I can tell. Come on what's the problem? Ye had a row with Stefan?'

'No, nothing like that…not yet.'

At least not until I have told him about Lena she thought.

'Come on then, what is it?'

'Would you be angry if I said I had found out where Lena lives and I went to see her.'

'Saints preserve us, ye did WHAT?'

'I saw her yesterday.'

'I can't believe it. I can't believe ye would do such a stupid thing. Ye didn't go on yer own did ye?'

'Yes. Mum, I'm not asking you to understand my decision – just to respect it.'

'But darlin' she's dangerous. She could have turned on ye.'

'She wasn't and she didn't. She's blind, Mum, and her face is awfully scarred. She was attacked by a prisoner.'

'Was she still drinking? On drugs?'

'Nope, none of that any more. She goes to Alcoholics Anonymous every week.'

'Ye took an awful risk.'

'Yes I know now. I didn't realise it at the time. I didn't know it was her, who hit me at the wedding.'

'She told ye?'

'Yeah, she told me at first she thought she'd killed me.'

'Well at first we thought so too, when ye were in intensive care.'

'Mum, that was a long time ago. She's been punished for it. She's lost her sight. But at least she's come off drugs and alcohol.'

'How do ye know she's telling the truth?'

'She's different Mum, she's different. Can you believe it, her place is pristine. I couldn't believe it. Not a thing out of place.'

'It needs to be if she is blind.'

'You're angry with me.'

'I'm worried for ye. I don't want ye to be taken in by her. She's very devious.'

'I don't think she's like that now. With losing her sight, she would have every reason, in frustration to turn to drink, wouldn't she? But she hasn't. Mum, she actually burst out crying. I've never seen her do that before.'

'Well, that *would* be a change of heart. She was too hard a person to shed a tear before. Did she apologise?'

'Yes. She did.'

'Well, miracles do happen.'

Tess had seen amongst some of her young mothers, how having a child of their own can sometimes pull them towards their blood relative. Regardless of how they had been treated in the past. They find they have a strong longing to turn that situation on its head, a yearning for that parent to eventually love them.

'I don't know how I'm going to tell Stef? He'll go mad. He'll be furious with me.'

'That, my dear, is because he loves ye. He cares and worries about ye. I tell ye what, leave it with me. Stefan rang me on Monday, to say about a Mother's Day celebration on Sunday.'

'Yes, he's bought a cake.'

'With the right opportunity, I'll break it gently to everyone on Sunday.'

'Oh thanks. I was so worried what you would think?'

'I still think ye took an enormous risk, ye should have had Dad with ye. But ye've done it now. I hope ye didn't say that ye'd take Daniel to see her, did ye?'

'I said I might do one day, that's all.'

'Is that chicken done babe?'

'Nearly, a few more minutes. The roast potatoes are done and veggies are ready.'

'They'll be here in a few minutes. I'll get the wine out of the fridge.'

There was soon a buzz of conversation as both couples arrived together. Daniel was the centre of attention, with the grandparents watching him holding on to the sofa and trying to walk around the room. Stefan poured the wine and Jade placed the food on the table.

'Would you all like to come to the table?'

'This looks lovely. You have both worked hard,' said Felix.

Jade kept passing glances to her mum, wondering when she would broach the subject of Lena. After the meal, they all sat in the sitting room enjoying cake and wine. Tess had chosen a soft drink as she would be driving. She also felt she needed a clear head to mention Lena's visit.

'Where there has been a rift in the family, I like to think that Mother's Day is an opportunity for sons and daughters to forgive and forget,' started Tess.

Jade took in a deep breath. Here we go she thought. What mum has to say could cause a rift in *both* families.

'That's true, said Jeanette. 'But we're very lucky, we don't have that problem in either of our families, do we?'

'That depends on yer point of view.'

'What do you mean?' questioned Michael.

'This week Jade had a huge problem.'

'What sort of problem?' said Michael.

'When she became a mother herself, it is very common for people in her position to want to seek out their birth mother. She was tormented with this. She found out where her true mother was living and…'

Michael sat upright. He glared at Jade and interrupted, 'I hope you're not going to say you went to see her.'

'Yes I did.'

A gasp of horror, radiated around the room.

'Are you MAD,' Michael shouted. 'Did you know what you were doing?'

'You could have got killed,' said Stefan.

'Calm down everyone. How was she to know, with her amnesia problems? We all agreed didn't we, that we would keep the truth about her head injury from her,' explained Tess.

'That's true,' said Jeanette.

Michael was furious. 'So, wasn't Tess a good enough mother for you? Tess has given you everything, and I don't mean money. Her time, her love, her home.' said Michael.

'I've never said… I'm not grateful. Or that… I don't love you both.' Jade dissolved into tears.

'Well why did you have to open up old wounds then?'

'Dad, I… I… I could not remember,' she sobbed, 'what my birth mother was like? I had this nagging feeling of guilt.'

'Come on Jade, tell them what ye found, and how it helped ye come to terms with the past.'

Jade took a deep breath. 'I was shocked to see this little woman, her face severely scarred. When she was in prison, someone attacked her…'

'Serves her right,' said Michael.

'Someone attacked her, with a pair of open scissors. Stabbed her in the face. Blinded her.'

Michael was fuming. 'After what she did to you! You were within a whisker of leaving this life, she deserved what she got.'

'Dad, she was an alcoholic. She doesn't remember what happened.'

'Oh yes…very convenient.'

'You don't seem to realise, we nearly lost you,' said Stefan.

'She has someone to take her to AA every week. She's a changed woman.'

'Huh! How often have I heard that?' scoffed Michael.

'Give her a chance darlin'. Try and see it from her point of view.'

Michael scowled. 'I've heard enough,' he thundered, 'I'm going home.'

With all the raised voices, Daniel started to cry.

'Now look what ye've done. Ye've woken the baby up.'

Jade went over to pacify him.

'I think it's time we all went home,' said Jeanette. 'Thank you both for a lovely meal.'

They all moved towards the door, took their coats ready to leave. Jeanette, herself adopted, had some sympathy for Jade. She went over to her, gave her a hug and whispered something in her ear. She nodded and thanked her. Tess did the same.

'The meal was delicious, thank you,' said Felix.

Michael stormed out ahead of the others and sat in the passenger seat of the car.

'Mum, I'm so sorry. I've spoilt everything and dad is furious with me.'

'That's the angry policeman coming out in him. He'll calm down. It's because he was so worried for ye.' She hugged and kissed her.

'We wanted it to be a lovely occasion. It was a disaster. Please believe me, I don't love you and dad any less, because I looked for my original mother. Whatever happens, you'll always be my mum.' Jade started to cry again.

'I know that darlin'. Tess put her arm around her. 'Listen carefully, in this life ye will find there are all types of mothers. To me, ye are my daughter; I couldn't feel any closer to ye, if I had given birth to ye myself. Nothing will *ever* change that.'

Chapter Forty Eight

The journey home was silent. Michael was still seething. Not until he got indoors, did he begin to speak. 'You opened a right sack of snakes, with your forgive and forget speech.'

'Coffee dear?' said Tess.

She knew it was best to say very little, when he was in a right paddy. She didn't comment. Instead went into the kitchen and made a hot drink. She placed the steaming mug of coffee, on a nearside table and waited for her husband to calm down. Back in the kitchen she started to wipe down the work surface.

'Did you hear what I said?' he called from the other room.

'Yes I did.'

'What the hell was she playing at?'

'I did say to her that she should not have gone alone, that ye could have gone with her.'

'Huh!'

She came back into the sitting room, with a hot chocolate drink for herself.

'Michael we have to take what she has said about her, at face value. She has said how clean and neat it was everywhere. Lena's attitude. It all points to the fact that she *could* be off alcohol and drugs. If so, she sounds pretty harmless to me.'

'Is she intending to go again? – I hope she's not thinking of taking the baby with her?'

'She told Lena, she'd take Daniel to show her, but *not* yet. The day she went, the lift wasn't working. She could hardly think of carrying the baby and buggy up three flights of stairs could she?'

'True. Next time I'm going with her.'

'Now can we change the subject, we have had this *all* afternoon?'

Michael reached for his coffee. 'Mm. Nice coffee. What's in it?'

'It's Irish coffee. I put cream and a drop of whisky in it. Sure if I had a couple of Valium I'd have put them in it instead, or taken them meself!'

'All right…all right, let's call a truce. I won't mention it again.'

'Grand.'

'Has she said when she's thinking of going again?'

Tess took the tea towel and wrapped it round his neck in mock strangulation.

'Okay, okay just kidding,' he chuckled.

Back at the young couple's flat, they were both locked in a heart to heart discussion.

'Can't you see babe, you took a terrible risk. It was not as though she was an ordinary mother… like…'

He was about to say like mine, then remembered she was a fifteen-year-old schoolgirl.

'But how was I to know it was a risk? I couldn't remember her. My childhood has been a complete blank, that is until I walked in there. Bit by bit the pieces of the jigsaw began to fit into place.'

'I know before, you would never visit her or take me there. You would say it was too terrible. What has changed?'

'It's a long story.'

'Well, tell me some of it. It might help me to understand some of your quirky behaviour.'

'Quirky behaviour?'

'You know what I mean. Obsession with cleaning. Your initial aversion to anything to do with sex.'

'Stefan, my place was the pits. Filth everywhere. Not just dirt, a different type of filth. Sex with a capital S. Lena used to take in her so called 'lodgers.' As I got older I realised that she was a prostitute and was running a brothel. At first I used to stay with mum weekends and holidays, but had to go back to Lena in the week. Later on I found out the only reason she needed me back, was so that she could claim her benefits as a single parent. One time, when I was about twelve or thirteen, one of her men friends grabbed me…' she hesitated. 'It wouldn't take much imagination to know what *he* wanted.'

He put his arm around her. 'Stop… I think I can guess what happened. Don't upset yourself. There has been enough upset here for one day. It's still light until about half six. Wash your face, let's take Daniel to the park for an hour.'

'I feel better now,' said Jade taking Daniel out of the buggy and removing his coat after the walk.

'If you want me to go to Lena's with you some time, let me know.'

'That's sweet.' She kissed him.

'You never know I might get the urge one day to find *my* birth mother. She's probably married with heaps of kids.'

'You always said you wished your adoptive parents had adopted another child. Just think, your birth mother's children would be your half brothers and sisters.'

'That's interesting, of course they would be. Are you trying to get me on the trail of searching for my birth mother? We've got enough with *your* problems. Not yet anyway. Not without my parents' agreement.'

'If you did, how would you go about it?'

'I think you can go to some sort of Adoption Agency, get the details of where the mother lived at the time and start searching from there.'

'Seriously, do you think you would start looking for her?'

'I might one day. If I did decide to, would you come with me?'

'Of course I would, you know that.'

Jade had certainly got the families discussing about birth mothers. It continued with Jeanette and Felix at their house.

'I hope Stefan doesn't get any crazy ideas of looking for *his* biological mother Felix?'

'I don't think he would.'

'How would he go about it?'

'I don't know. I don't expect even with UK easing of the adoption laws, he'd find it very easy to trace *his* birth mother. Not through the Catholic Adoption Society, we know how tight lipped they are.'

'How did you manage to find out about your real mother Jeanette? You never really told me the whole story.'

'Unlike Jade, I never knew my real mother. She was killed just after the war. I was only a baby. Three kids were messing about on a bomb site in Hackney. My mum noticed they were jumping on something. As she got nearer she saw it was an unexploded bomb. Evidently, she leapt up onto the bomb site and tried to drag the kids away. She got two of them to safety. Then when she went back for the other boy, it was too late. The bomb exploded, killing my mother outright, together with the seven-year-old boy.'

'What happened to you?'

'With the blast of the bomb, my pram was hurled across the road and landed upside down. I was still strapped in. I found all this out from my gran before she died.

She told me what happened. The two boys my mother saved, were brothers, they turned the pram over, found I wasn't badly hurt, just cuts and bruises on my face. That's this scar here.' She pointed it out to Felix. 'They wheeled the pram home to their mum. Once word got around about a woman and child being killed leaving the baby in the pram, they soon found my gran. At first she tried to look after me. But after a while it became too much of a struggle. Gran wasn't a fit woman, she found it hard to look after me as well as dad. He was wounded in the war, lost an arm and a foot. He still had a piece of shrapnel in his skull. At the time when all this happened I was six months old. The boys and their mother kept in touch with my family. After gran died, I found a newspaper cutting, calling the two boys heroes for rescuing me.

When it became too much for gran, the boys' mum offered to take me into their home. Later on they adopted me. They told my gran it was the least they could do, as my mother had saved her boys' lives. You've met my older brothers Felix?

'Yes I remember meeting them, they came to our wedding.'

'Well because they found me, they always made a fuss of me. They reckoned I belonged to them… *finders keepers* they used to say. Consequently as a kid, I could do no wrong, they would step in and cover for me.'

'I never knew all that. I knew your mum had died and you were adopted, but I didn't know the whole story. What happened to your dad?'

'He lived with gran and me until she died. Then he went into a British Legion Home. I used to go with my brothers to the home to see him. At first he didn't understand who the boys were? Later he didn't recognise me. Or remember his wife. He was in his own world. He would have nightmares about the war. Thought the enemy was coming after him. In the end they had to sedate him. It was a sad ending for him.'

'How long was he there?'

'He wasn't there very long. About a year and he died. I remember the day my mum came up the school. I was in the gym, having PE. The teacher told me to get dressed. I thought I done something wrong. She usually only said that to girls if they'd been mucking about. The PE teacher Miss Sims, told me to go to the headmistress's office straightaway and that my mother was in there with the headmistress. Miss Hill the headmistress, told me that my mum had something serious to tell me. Mum didn't seem too upset, so I guessed it couldn't be the boys. Then she broke it to me that my dad had died. I burst into tears in the office. I remember my mum put her arms around me and said, 'Come on Jeanie,' she always called me Jeanie, come on dear, I'm taking you home.'

'I didn't know any of that Jeanette. Especially about *your* own mum, rescuing your brothers, that's an extraordinary story.'

'I'm sure Felix, there was lots of similar stories like that, during and after the war.'

'You're right, I'm sure there were.'

'When dad died, I was heartbroken. I went to his funeral. He had a proper regimental funeral. It wasn't until the trumpet played the last post at the cemetery, that it dawned on me. This was the last link with my real family…and it had gone. I didn't go back to school after that. There was only one more term to go – couldn't face my friends. It took a long time but slowly that great void I felt inside me, became easier to cope with. I found I could start talking to people and going out with friends again. Then when some handsome young man came along everything changed.' They looked at each other and grinned.

'I discovered for the first time, what it meant to fall in love. I know we were both young to get married, but I've never regretted it.'

'If we could have children when young,' said Felix, 'that could have proved stressful for us. Look at friends we know that marry young like us. Had families straight away. Few are still together.'

'That's true, dear. It was meant to be. I thank God for bringing us together. We met and fell in love. I know we've had a few ups and downs, no marriage can be a hundred percent perfect. But we both found the right person to spend the rest of our lives with. Now God has blessed us with a gorgeous little grandson.'

Chapter Forty Nine

Year 2000

All three families celebrated the Millennium in their own way. Apart from Felix panicking that the computers in his travel agencies might crash, otherwise they were happy to say goodbye to the old year and welcomed in the new.

Tess, Michael, Maura and her husband, decided to go to their local hostelry to join in the festivities. Daniel went to a friend for a sleep-over, allowing his parents to join the party with the Travel Agency. After the celebrations, life returned to some form of normality.

Jade took her husband to meet Lena. He was able to reassure both families that Lena did seem a different woman. She appeared to have paid in full for her actions and for the first time in her life felt remorse. He also met the woman that helped her with shopping and took her to the AA group regularly. She seemed a very pleasant helpful lady in her late thirties. He found it hard to imagine that she, too, had been an alcoholic. Jade was right, there didn't seem to be a sniff of drugs or alcohol in the flat. He was able to verify her description of the flat. It was very clean, with an absence of clutter.

Lena was registered totally blind and now had a woman call in three days a week to help her clean and tidy up, make the bed and sort out the washing together. The young person who had befriended Lena at the AA meetings, instead of bringing in the shopping, had started to take Lena to the shops. Every week, a support worker called in. Audio books were organised, delivered and collected. Sometimes her AA friend took her to the library where they had a selection of audio books she could choose from. The Royal National Institute for the Blind, offered advice and encouraged her to go along to a support group to meet with others who had sight impairment.

Lena's face was a mess. Being blind, she was unaware of how badly scarred she was. Her older sister had started to visit her, she too had started to go to AA herself, at a different group. The sisters addiction, re-affirmed the saying: *the sins of the fathers were being visited upon the children*. Now that Daniel was ten and full of self-confidence, Jade was free to concentrate on her business plan. She was able to branch out from the beauty salon where she worked. With family financial help, she was able to rent and convert a disused shop, into her own hairdressing and beauty salon. Once established, she was gradually able to employ qualified hairdressers. They each rented a chair in her salon. As the business thrived, Jeanette, who had always done her husband's bookkeeping, agreed to manage the salon's books as well.

'This flat is beginning to look like a menagerie. We have rabbits munching away in hutches. Hamsters running mindless around wheels. Now Daniel has just brought home something else. What are you cradling in your hands son? Let dad have a look.'

'It's a chick.'

'Yes, I can see it's a chick. But how the hell can you keep a chick?'

'I can feed it. Give it water to drink. I'll look after it Dad.'

'Don't be silly Daniel, how long do you think it is going to stay that size. It will grow into a full sized chicken in no time,' said his mum as she carried on ironing.

He pulled a face. 'What's wrong with a having a chick. I WANT a chick.'

'Well you can't have it. Give it to me. I said, give it to ME!'

He snatched the chick out of his hands and took it down the garden and promptly pushed it through a gap in the fence and marched back into the kitchen.

'I've had enough of this animal nonsense,' he said with a deep sigh.

Daniel had already stomped up the stairs to his room.

'A chick for goodness sake. What next will he bring in?'

'You *were* a bit harsh with him weren't you. He's only a kid.'

'You were too busy working, to see what he brought in *last* week!'

'What was it?'

'Only a hedgehog, teeming with fleas, I've been scratching myself ever since.'

Jade started laughing.

'It's not funny. I had a fight on my hands with him yelling, *it's mine, it's mine. I want it.*'

'What did you do with it?'

'The same as I've just done with the chick, pushed it through next door's garden. That kid's got animal mania. I'm sick of it. I'm the one that has to see to all the animals round here.

That boy has either got his head in a book, watching television or playing video games. He's nowhere to be seen when it comes to feeding and cleaning out *his* animals.'

'Calm down.'

'I won't calm down. I'm fed up with it all.'

'Fed up with me too?'

'Mm, sometimes. It's always me that has to take a firm hand with him. You're always too busy, too tired, or turning a blind eye to what he gets up to.'

'So would you be, if you had half your staff about to leave and set up their own businesses.'

'I might have known it was the salon getting you down. Look at the hours you work? You're always saying you're too tired. I can't remember when you last cooked an evening meal. Either I have to do it, or it's a take-away. You'd better start advertising for extra staff.'

'When I started training for hairdressing, the beautician side really appealed to me. I don't want to have to close down the beautician service and go back to hairdressing again. All that hair falling into my bra and pants, covering my body.'

'That would be about the only thing that would have access to your body these days, it's always, the cry, *I'm too tired*.' he said, with a squeaky high pitched voice.

'That's enough.'

She stormed off to the bedroom. A few minutes later she came back into the kitchen.

'I've an idea. First, let's all get ready and go to McDonald's. Then I'll tell you my idea.'

'Are you supposed to be eating those fries Daniel, or playing with them?' asked his dad taking one from his plate.

'I'm full up.'

It was on the tip of Stefan's tongue to tell him he had just eaten a grown-up chick. He bit his tongue and thought if he was not careful Daniel might come out with, *Okay Dad, I'm not eating anymore animal flesh*, and with a freezer bulging with chicken nuggets and fish fingers, now, was not a good time to upset the *veggie* cart.

'Are you listening? When you were in the kitchen, I rang Doreen. She used to work at *Snips* hairdressers in the High Street, before they closed down. I know Doreen's got the baby now, but she reckons with Dave's shifts, she could work part-time. It would be a great help. I get on well with Doreen. She's not the sort that would keep taking other staff's clients, like the other two that are leaving.'

'Sounds good. When can she start?'

'Monday, it's always quiet on a Monday. It would give me time to show her around. We get on well together, we always have a good laugh.'

'It should lighten the load then, hopefully it will help lighten your mood too.'

'Yes, it'll be good.'

Doreen quickly settled into the salon. Before she married Dave she had lost both parents. They had both suffered ill health for many years. After a while they were able to move into her parent's cottage. Jade and Doreen worked well together. Three years later, Jade was considering offering Doreen a partnership in the business. On Doreen's day off, thinking Jade would be there, Doreen called round Jade's house at midday. Stefan had dropped in to make himself a sandwich for lunch. He was surprised to see her.

'Hi Doreen. Jade's not here, she's at the salon.'

'I wasn't sure. She said she was going to the dentist in the morning. I thought she might take the rest of the day off.'

'You know her, it takes a lot for her to stop working.'

'Oh well I'll ring her later then.'

'You may as well stay for a snack while you're here. I've just made some cheese sandwiches. Would you like one?'

He brought in a tray of sandwiches and a couple of glasses of wine.

'Thanks. I don't usually drink, except at weekends with my husband. We usually go for a pub lunch at the Red Lion.'

'Let me take your coat.'

After they had eaten, he returned to the kitchen and brought in the rest of the wine.

'We may as well finish it off Doreen, it will only sit in the fridge for days.'

He topped up her glass and sat beside her on the sofa.

'Your hair looks nice. Do you do each other's hair?'

'Yes, usually, on a Monday, when it's quiet.'

He leaned over to touch it. 'It feels lovely and soft.' On impulse, he kissed her and immediately felt guilty. She responded with a full-on, passionate kiss. Slowly he unbuttoned her blouse and placed his hands gently on her breasts. He whipped off his shirt and, in kissing, manoeuvred her so that she lay down on the sofa.

They didn't hear the sitting-room door open. Daniel stared for several minutes at first unable to comprehend what he was seeing. Then slammed the door in disgust. He was angry. What the hell was his father doing with Doreen?

'Who was that?' asked Doreen.

'It must have been Daniel.'

Shocked, they both leapt up. Hastily they tried to get dressed. Flustered and blushing he said, 'I am so sorry Doreen, I don't know what came over me. It must have been the wine.'

'I am as much to blame Stefan. It was stupid. I'm going.'

'As far as I'm concerned, it never happened. I'm not saying anything,' he said. 'And if Daniel knows what's good for him, he won't say anything either.'

Chapter Fifty

But it did happen. What took place between Stefan and Doreen, didn't take long to surface. Daniel was nearly fourteen, and a secret with a teenager is not often a secret for long. He was soon to reveal his observations to his mother.

'Mum, how long has dad been having it off with Doreen?'

'What do you mean?'

'When I came in lunch-time he and Doreen were *at it* on the sofa.'

'Don't be silly, what was Doreen doing here?'

'I don't know. All I know is dad had his shirt off, and Doreen's, was undone. They were over there having sex on the sofa.'

'This is not one of your stupid jokes is it? To say something like that is not funny and can cause a lot of trouble.'

'Mum, come off it, I'm not stupid, I know what I saw – it was disgusting!'

Jade started shaking. She could not believe what she was hearing. It was not possible. If he had been the sort of guy that flirted with any woman in a skirt, although she wouldn't condone it, she could believe it was possible.

'Go on Daniel, off to school. Done your homework? Got everything? Go on then. Your mate's at the door.'

'Bye, Mum.'

She sat down. She couldn't stop shaking. Like an ear worm constantly repeats a familiar tune in the brain, so question after question repeated themselves and tormented her. She came to the conclusion that it must be true. How could Daniel invent something like that? Yet she didn't want to believe it. She thought of approaching Doreen first; if Daniel was mistaken, why break up a good friendship? What was Doreen doing in the flat, in the first place? Had she been there before, on her day off? Common sense told her she should have it out with Stefan first. Then the thought came again, why destroy our marriage? Why lose trust in her husband, if the whole thing was a figment of Daniel's vivid imagination? Would he try to shock her like kids of his age do, just for attention? Is it all that sex education they are getting at school?

She contemplated waiting until Daniel came home from school and challenging him again. Doreen would be back in the salon after her day off. They would be working together. Would her body language or attitude, give her away? Would she look guilty, not her usual happy-go-lucky self? Probably not, if she'd been having an affair with her husband for some time. Whilst all these questions were tormenting her, Doreen rang in sick.

'Sorry to let you down, I think I'm going down with something.'

If Daniel was to be believed, she was definitely going down with something. Down in Jade's estimation of a trusted friend.

Questions began to buzz round and round in her head in the same way a bluebottle, constantly buzzes around the head. Thoughts of confrontation – explanation – humiliation. She couldn't switch off. Questions, decisions, conclusions, constantly interrupted her thoughts. Doreen going off sick, was that indicative of guilt? Did that meant she couldn't face her this morning? As the morning wore on, she began to believe her son. She was convinced that something had definitely taken place between Stefan and Doreen.

By lunch time, she was so stressed, she had started to make small mistakes. She decided to go home. At least that was her intention. Her mind switched from Stefan to Doreen. She had made up her mind, she would have it out with her first. As she knocked on her door, she felt nauseous. One look at Doreen's face and she had her answer. Red, puffy eyes, blushing with shame. Jade felt sick. Intense anger surged and surfaced. Before she could utter a word, Doreen started crying.

'I'm so sorry Jade. I don't know how I can live with myself with what happened.'

'You'll be sorry when I've finished with you. Go on. Tell me what happened?'

Doreen was choked, unable to speak.

'Okay if you can't speak. I'll tell **you** what happened. **You**, **you** a person I trusted and thought was a dear friend, had **SEX** with my husband. Not only that you had **SEX,** but you even had the temerity to have it in front of my **SON!** How dare you. How **dare** you. I'm the one that should be crying. You have shattered the trust that I had with my husband.'

'I'm so, so sorry,' she snivelled. 'It just… just happened.'

Instinctively, Jade lashed out. She slapped Doreen hard on both cheeks. Doreen reeled and flopped back on her chair.

'Just happened did it? **Just happened**, so if I was to come here and have **SEX** with Dave. That would be fine would it? I could tell you it **just happened**. That would make it all right would it?'

'I didn't mean it like that.'

'Then how **did** you mean it?'

'I went round to your place,' she said, putting a hand to her burning cheeks. 'I thought you would be there, you said you were going to the dentist and then going home. Stefan was making sandwiches for lunch. He persuaded me to stay…'

'Sounds as though you didn't need much persuading.'

'He brought in a glass of wine and then the bottle. I don't normally drink much at all, as you know. Stefan came on to me and to my horror I found myself just falling into a trap. A trap that I couldn't seem to get out of.'

'So you're saying it was **all** Stefan's fault. He trapped you. He plied you with drinks, in order to take advantage of you? **RUBBISH**! I suppose you are going to say he held you down. It wasn't **your** fault. Now **you** tell me, what stopped **you** from doing what I've just done? It's not as though he's a big guy is he? You could have slapped him round the face. Got up and left. Which is what I'm going to do. It goes without saying, any thoughts of a partnership at the salon is over, as well as our friendship!'

Jade stormed out and slammed the front door.

She was so angry she was trembling uncontrollably. She wandered aimlessly and found herself in the park, sitting on a bench, in floods of tears. All her hopes had been pinned on Doreen saying that it wasn't true and that Daniel, like a lot of teenagers might do, had made it up as a joke. This was only the beginning of a devastating situation. The outcome for her marriage was in the balance. How can he deny it? He can't. Marriage, she thought, cannot survive on love, it has to be based on more than love. If they can't trust each other – it's over.

She slowly walked over to the park café, ordered a cup of coffee and sat back on the bench. People were walking through the park looking at the lake. Usually it was bustling with swans and pedal boats. She glanced at the still, silent lake, in a daze. Everything seemed unreal. A light scattering rain, began to dampen the wooden table. At first she was unaware of it, until spots of rain began to make circles in her cup. Her thoughts turned to pebbles dropping and making circles in the lake. Now she could understand how a severely depressed person wanted the lake to encompass them, blot out what lay ahead. She stood up. She knew she had to go home at some point. Somehow, she had to weather the storm that was approaching. She had to confront Stefan. Once again, she changed her mind, pulling her scarf over her head, headed towards Tess and Michael's house.

Chapter Fifty One

'Darlin', what's happened to ye?' Jade fell into Tess's arms on the doorstep. It's over Mum…it's over!'

'What is?'

'Stef and me.'

'Why what's happened?'

'I don't know what to do.' She started to cry.

'Calm down darlin'. Come in. Sit down. Don't say anything yet. Let's have a cup of tea and we will talk things through.'

'Who was at the door?' Michael came into the kitchen. He could see Jade had been crying.

'What's the problem dear?'

'It's okay Michael, we'll come in the other room in a minute. I think this could be women's problems.'

Michael nodded and retreated behind his newspaper, in the sitting-room.

It took a while before she could open up and tell her mum the situation. She then found herself blurting out what had happened.

'It's Stef and Doreen. Daniel saw them having sex on the sofa.'

'Oh no, surely not. Stefan's got more sense than that.'

'I thought Daniel was making it up at first. Then I went to see Doreen.'

She started to cry again. Tess put her arms around her.

'Darlin', sure we can sort all this out.'

'It's over. It's over between me and Stef.'

'Is that what Stefan says?'

'I don't know.'

'What do ye mean, ye don't know?'

'I haven't spoken to him yet.'

'Well ye've got to speak to him. Give him a chance to speak for himself. Haven't ye?'

'I can't forgive him. I shall never forgive him.'

'Sure ye will. First ye have to hear his side of the story. Have ye eaten anything today?'

'Mum, I can't eat, I feel sick. I thought I was going to vomit everywhere when I got to Doreen's place. Guilt was written all over her face.'

'Ye can't tackle a battle on an empty stomach. Here, I've made ye some toast. Eat it.'

'Mum can you come with me to face Stef?'

'No, sorry but this is one fight ye have to put the gloves on for yerself. Not as though ye are a child anymore. Ye are a thirty-one-year-old mother. Ye know ye have my support, whatever ye decide to do. But this is a dilemma for Stefan and ye to sort out. It wouldn't be right for me to interfere. Ye have to brave it alone.'

Before turning the key, she hesitated. His car was outside. She took in a deep breath, said to herself; if I can confront Doreen, I can confront Stefan.

'Hi babe, busy day?'

'You could say that. Not nearly as busy as you and Doreen on our sofa.'

'What do you mean? What are you getting at?'

She fought to stop the tears flowing. 'You and Doreen having sex *here*.' She pointed to the sofa. 'Yesterday.'

'Where did you get that nonsense from?'

'Nonsense was it? Daniel told me this morning.'

'Oh for goodness sake babe, you know his imagination goes wild sometimes.'

'No it was *you* that went wild with Doreen.'

'You're crazy it must be your memory problems, playing tricks on you?'

'Oh no. No, you can't use that, to try and excuse your behaviour. It won't work.'

'Calm down girl.'

'Don't treat me like a child. You explain yourself.'

'Okay, Doreen and I sat on the sofa together and we just joked about, that's all. Daniel's making more of it than it is.'

'So you joked about, without your shirt on, and with Doreen's blouse undone did you? Stop these lies at once and tell me what really happened.'

'I've told you, babe nothing happened. Daniel has got confused.'

'So everyone else is confused except you? I'll give you one more chance to tell the truth. But first I'll tell you this. I've been to see Doreen and she has told me everything.'

He was stunned into silence. His eyes began to fill up with tears.

'I'm so sorry Babe. Doreen came looking for you. I gave her some lunch…'

'And then you had sex for dessert? Did you?'

'We had some wine. It must have lowered our resistance. One minute I was asking whether you styled her hair and the next … well it all happened so quickly. Well let's face it a man has certain needs. When was the last time *we* made love?'

'Oh it's *my* fault now is it? Not the wine? Not an opportunistic encounter then?'

'You are not listening.'

'Oh yes I am. It's a load of lies, blame and excuses. You'd better sleep in the spare room tonight.'

She took herself up to the bedroom, flung herself on the bed and sobbed. Two hours later, a knock came on the bedroom door.

'Can I come in?'

'I suppose so.'

He tried to pacify her. 'I am really sorry Jade, it won't happen again.'

'How can I ever trust you again?'

'You have to believe me. Please believe me. Give me another chance. When I say it won't ever happen again, I mean it. Doreen doesn't mean anything to me. It's *you* I love. You know it is. I'd do anything for you.'

Then in a last minute ditch, something pierced her heart.

Crying, he said, 'You forgave Lena, you gave her another chance. Everyone deserves another chance, you said, can't you do the same for me?'

This was different. Could she do the same, after what he had done?

'We'll talk about it in the morning. Close the door after you.'

Was the door *really* closed on their marriage? He was deeply troubled and couldn't sleep. The following morning they ate breakfast in silence. She couldn't even glance in his direction. He left for work without a word spoken. Once he'd left for work and Daniel for school, she telephoned her manager.

'Once the staff have finished with their clients, I'd like the salon to be closed today please. Thank you.'

No sooner had she replaced the receiver, when the phone rang. She hesitated. Could it be Stefan? Doreen? She didn't pick up. Then she worried, had something happened to Daniel? It rang again.

'Ye alright darlin'? I've been so worried since yesterday.'

'I feel better now Mum, now I've got it off my chest. It's not resolved of course.'

'I'll come round. I didn't think ye'd be going in to work this morning.'

'Thanks Mum. See you later.'

'Come on, get ready. Let's go to that favourite café near the beach at Leigh on Sea for a coffee and a good old natter.'

'I don't feel like going anywhere.'

Tess was able to reluctantly persuade her. 'Ye'll feel better out in the fresh air.'

After they arrived at the café and had coffee and a toasted teacake, she began to relax, and told Tess what had happened.

'He was bound to fight his corner. He wasn't going to give in just like that. He thought if he could make ye believe that nothing happened, then all would be well. That's typical of men dear, they bury their heads in the sand. Until they find the only way out, is to come clean and tell the truth.'

'I suppose you're right.'

'What he said about forgiving Lena, makes sense doesn't it?'

'But it's hard to forgive something like this.'

'I don't agree. What he did was one stupid incident. A lack of will power, a sudden weakness. With Lena, ye were forgiving her, not for the time she nearly killed ye. But for years and years of neglect and hatred that she had for ye. This is totally different isn't it? Remember that ye two have something special. Many couples think they have, but still struggle sometimes to find it. Ye have an overpowering love for each other. Anyone can see that. They only have to be in your company for a few minutes to notice it. Surely that must be the great healer in this situation? The love ye have for each other can overcome this can't it?'

'I hope so.'

'Would ye like me to contact a counsellor; I know one that works for the Marriage Guidance?'

'Would you? Do you think he would go?'

'If he thought his marriage was on the line, I'm sure he would.'

'What do you think Stef?'

'About what?'

'The Marriage Guidance appointment next week, are you going to come with me?

'I said I would didn't I?'

'Stefan and Jade, please take a seat, my name is Luke. Don't look so worried. First I would like to ask you, where you would hope to see your marriage by the end of counselling?'

Stefan thought for a few seconds.

'Back on track, I suppose?'

'And Jade?'

'To be able to express my emotions. Better communication I think.'

'Can I ask you, do you avoid talking about difficult subjects?'

'Sometimes,' they both said together.

'How did you two meet?'

'We met at a youth club,' she replied.

'Under a table tennis table to be precise,' he grinned.

They looked at each other and remembered how it was love at first sight, and both gave a half-hearted smile.

'In order to improve your relationship, you cannot control what changes *your* partner makes. Marriage therapy is not meant to fix *one* partner. You need to concentrate on what is within *your* control and look at any barriers to those changes. Over the next few weeks I need you to look at where you are both coming from. When you were growing up, what was your home life like? Did you witness arguments or unhealthy relationships within the family?'

Jade nodded agreement to both. Stefan shook his head as if to say he'd never heard of any problems in *his* family.

'As you grow up, you develop a lot of ideas of the world, about yourself and other people, based on what your experiences were as a child. I will need to know your personal history, past relationships and so on. You will need to be open with me. I would like you both, when you get home, to write down what you consider to be your partner's strength and weaknesses. Is that all right with you both?'

They looked across at each other, 'Yeah fine' said Stefan. 'That's all right with me.'

'Next week we will focus on your current problems. Meanwhile I want to take you back to when you first started going out together. You say you didn't have sex for a long time. So that is where you need to start. At home, start at the very beginning with no sex.'

They both turned to look at each other. Stefan had a startled expression.

'I want you to start with a kiss. Nothing amorous, just a peck on the cheek. Start with a peck and gradually work up to the passion over one week. If possible no making love until we discuss how you got on, next week.'

When they left the room they were smiling. Until Stefan recognised someone making enquiries at the receptionist's desk.

'Mum, what the hell are you doing here?'
'I could ask you two the same?'

'Personal reasons Mum.'

'Exactly Stefan, personal reasons. That's why people come here.'

Jeanette disappeared through the exit door, before he could ask any further questions. On their way home, he seemed more concerned and puzzled over what his parents' issues were than their own.

'For goodness sake, forget your parents for a minute, we have our own problems to sort out, without worrying about other people's.'

Chapter Fifty Two

Whilst the young couple sat down to write their partners' strengths and weaknesses lists, Jeanette meanwhile had decided to go and see Tess. Despite Tess's own lack of marital problems, she seemed to have acquired the role of family confidant and advisor.

'Come in Jeanette,' she called out to Michael. 'It's Jeanette, Michael. Are ye in the study? We'll go in the sitting room then. What is it Jeanette? The kids are all right aren't they?'

'I haven't come to talk about them, it's Felix.'

'Oh why? What's wrong with him?'

'I found out that his travels abroad, are not quite as innocent as he'd have me believe.'

'What do ye mean?'

'He has another family in Greece.'

'I know ye told me he has family, a brother in Rhodes, wasn't it?'

'Yes. But he also has another wife in…'

'What? No, not Felix surely?'

'How did ye find out?'

'When I was clearing out the shed. I found a box of photos and letters. One photo showed him laughing with this woman. But the worst one, was the wedding photo I found of them…getting married.'

'Are ye sure? Could it be his brother?'

'At first, that's what I hoped. I remembered I'd met him, and Tess, they are not a bit alike. He looks more Greek than Felix; much darker complexion. Then I found these, some letters addressed to him. I don't know which way to turn. I went to the Marriage Guidance today, to see if they could help me. They referred me to a solicitor that can deal with this. Stefan saw me talking to someone at the reception. It seems as though our whole family is in a turmoil.'

She started to cry.

'Calm down, Jeanette, I did know that they had a few problems. I suggested the Marriage Guidance Bureau might be able to help them. I can't lie and pretend I didn't know they had problems with their relationship. Ye would need to ask Stefan about it. I can't divulge something that I have been told in confidence.'

'To be fair, it's a good thing they didn't come to me. What advice could I give them, when my own marriage is about to fall apart, after thirty-six years?'

'Try not to get upset again Jeanette.'

Tess put her arm around her. 'Let me make a coffee for ye. Sure there's bound to be a perfectly rational explanation?'

'What happened with Felix, when you told him what ye'd found?'

'I found them three weeks ago, when he was away. He only came home yesterday. I couldn't face saying anything. He was so happy to be home.'

'Jeanette ye cannot delay it any longer, it will make ye ill. Ye will have to speak to him about it.'

'What are you trying to say? Our marriage is over? Photos? What photos?'

'Ones I found in the shed when you were away.'

Jeanette showed him the photos. 'There's a few there of a wedding. *Your* wedding!'

'Jeanette don't be ridiculous. How could I marry someone else? We have been married since we were both eighteen.'

He took another look at the wedding photos.

'There, if you look again, it's a picture of my brother's wedding.'

'No, you've forgotten. I've met your brother. He was best man at our wedding. You know that you don't look a bit alike. All those trips to Rhodes. On behalf of your travel business? When you were with *that* woman.'

'That's stupid. Why would I do that?'

'I don't know, you tell me?'

'You're paranoid woman, it's all in your head.'

'No it's *not* in my head. It is in these photos. Look! What about these letters?'

'What letters?'

She thrust them in his hand. Felix gave a quick glance at them.

'This is becoming ridiculous. Who is she? I don't know who she is?'

He promptly ripped up the letters and tossed them at Jeanette.

'I suppose you think you have destroyed the evidence.'

'What evidence? I haven't done anything.'

'I went to the Marriage Guidance Office, they recommended a solicitor, Julian Masters. He deals with marital problems and divorce. He specialises in bigamy.'

'*Bigamy*? Are you mad? Now you've really lost it!'

'I haven't lost the evidence – you haven't destroyed it.'

She bent down to pick up the scattered, torn letters off the floor.

'Mr Masters, photocopied them all.'

'I can't believe you are saying all this.'

'My solicitor is taking it further. He's contacted a friend of his in Greece. His friend is a lawyer. This lawyer has promised to find your wife. He's already searching the Greek marriage records.'

'I've had enough of this nonsense. I'm going out.'

'You can't run away from this Felix.'

He snatched up his jacket and with a heavy slam of the door, was gone. He returned after midnight.

Both father and son now found themselves relegated to the spare room. The next morning, Jeanette looked in his wardrobe. He had packed his usual going abroad suit and shirts, together with his shaving gear. He had left her.

At first she took some comfort from the fact that the arguments had been placed on hold. The magnitude of the situation she had found herself in, began to sink in. Her marriage was a sham. Jeanette was distraught. She fell back on the bed and wept.

Later she felt she must be strong and face the conflict ahead. She showered and dressed. Prepared some breakfast, found she had cooked for two. She pushed it away. She felt ill. How could something like this happen? She had always thought that theirs was a very happy marriage. She had seen marriages of friends flounder and go through the divorce courts. Very few marriages, she thought, seemed to last into old age. Marriage for some youngsters, being looked upon as being old fashioned – out of date. How often had she heard young people say,

'What's the point of a piece of paper?'

True, they'd had a few arguments over the years, who doesn't? But it never occurred to her that they wouldn't retire and grow old together. It was inconceivable, that she would be left on her own. What would she do? Would Felix be made to support her? If he refused, would the courts see to it that he did? She had always supported her husband in his travel business, done his bookkeeping. Kept the accounts. Made appointments with the accountant. Would she, at her age, be expected now to go out and get a job and support herself?

Chapter Fifty Three

'Did you write down your partner's strengths and weaknesses? Have you brought them with you? Good. I'd like you to swap over what you have written. Perhaps you would like to go in a quiet corner on your own and slowly read them.'

After having read them, they returned to their chairs and faced Luke, the counsellor.

'Were there any surprises there?'

They both nodded and murmured agreement.

'I noticed that on both of your lists, the strengths far outweighed the weaknesses. Now, I have written four questions for you both and I would like you to go back again into a quiet corner and write down your answers.'

They both went in separate corners of the room with the list of questions.

What are your goals for your relationship?

What do you think your relationship would look like if your goals were achieved?

What are you willing to do, to improve your relationship?

If your relationship improved; how do you feel the two of you would behave differently?

They glanced over at each other. Gave a wry smile and started to write. After they had completed their answers and returned to their original places, Luke asked another question.

'I would like to ask you, what made you seek guidance?'

They looked at each other. Neither spoke.

'You will need to speak openly about your problems. Do you think you just can't get along? You feel you have drifted apart? Don't want to be married anymore?'

Within a few moments they both opened up and discussed what had happened. Stefan tended to blame his wife for what had happened.

'It's because of her working long hours. She's always feeling tired and making excuses and turns away from me when I wanted to make love.'

When they left, they were instructed to kiss each other passionately every day and go no further.

To the amusement of the waiting clients, when they got outside the room, Stefan felt he would start the therapy straightaway. When the waiting clients observed the couple following instructions, one man nudged his wife and said,

'What tablets has Luke given them? We must ask for some of them.'

That night they broke the rules. They slept together and made mad, crazy, uninhibited love.

'Shh! Stef, they will hear us in the flat above.'

'They're only jealous. I love you Mrs Rondo.'

'I love you too Mr Rondo.'

The next morning he posed the question. 'Do you think we need to carry on with this marriage guidance stuff?'

'Yes, we should. I think Luke will give us answers as well as questions next time.'

Jeanette was also awaiting answers. Felix had been gone for two weeks. She had no idea where he was? He had not taken his passport. The phone rang. It was the solicitor, would she call in the office? He had received some news from the lawyer in Greece.

'Mrs Rondo. I have confirmation here that you husband was indeed married to a woman in Ródhos. But it is not as simple as that. You were married in 1964. This marriage in Greece, took place in 1963.'

'So what you are saying, we were never married legally in the first place.'

'Precisely. According to the shipping register, he left for England on the same day that they got married. A cabin was booked for two people, but according to the shipping records, he set off alone. He was only seventeen at the time…..Mrs Rondo, I feel I should point out that this could have been an arranged marriage, which in the event, he wanted no part of.'

'I understand what you are saying, but that doesn't make me feel any better. I have been living with what I thought was my husband for all these years, in fact what you are saying we were living a lie; we were never really married in the eyes of God.'

Two weeks later and Felix had not made any attempt to contact her. Jeanette was beginning to worry what had happened to him. Then the call came, not from Felix himself, but to her surprise from Luton and Dunstable Hospital in Bedfordshire.

Felix had been found collapsed on a park bench. According to the hospital, he was unable to give an account of why he was in Bedfordshire. Apart from knowing Luton Airport, he had said he didn't know anyone in the area.

Jeanette asked Stefan to drive her to the hospital. According to a witness, he had been attacked by two men. They had beaten him up and taken his wallet. On arrival, Jeanette spoke to the duty doctor on the ward.

'When your husband came in Mrs Rondo, he was unconscious. He has suffered from concussion. He is now able to give an account of what happened. You can ask him to tell you.'

Felix looked thin and drawn. Jeanette leaned over and kissed him. He immediately grasped her hand and held it close to his chest.

'A couple of thugs came from nowhere and set about me. Apparently, a Salvation Army woman found me. They said she got an ambulance and came with me to the hospital.'

Jeanette was so glad to see him, she didn't bother to ask him to explain – why Luton?

The ward sister had some good news. 'Mrs Rondo, your husband can possibly be discharged tomorrow. The consultant will see him on his round first thing tomorrow morning. All being well, he can go home.'

'Mum, we could stay at dad's hotel in Luton tonight.'

'What do you mean *his* hotel?'

Once again she found her thoughts going into overdrive. His hotel? How often had he stayed there and with whom?

'It's not his yet, but the Travel Agency is thinking of buying it. Dad thought it would be useful to have his own hotel. Travellers could stay over, before getting their flights from Luton Airport. Or if their flights were cancelled or delayed.'

Jeanette let out a sigh of relief. Maybe, he had been staying there, for the last few weeks.

Once home, Felix was rather withdrawn. After a few days, she sensitively asked him a few questions.

'Do you remember why you left here?'

'Yes. I do.'

'Since then Felix, I have met with Mr Masters the solicitor.
'Huh huh.'

'He has found out that you married someone called Maria Demetriadou in 1963. Then you left for Britain the same day. I think it would be a good idea if we both went to see him together. You have to realise Felix, we have lived a lie.'

'Mr Rondo, why don't you start at the beginning,' prompted the solicitor, 'because I think I may be able to help you both. Start at the beginning and tell me why you married Maria Demetriadou?'

'I was hoping that Jeanette would never have to learn about this. Because when we got married,' he turned to Jeanette, 'I thought you would never understand. In the end I just closed my mind to it. Pretended it didn't happen.'

'But it did happen didn't it, Mr Rondo. Shall I remind you what happened. My legal friend in Greece, did a lot of digging. He found out that it was an arranged marriage. Instead of a dowry from your father to the bride, it was the other way round. Why was that?'

'Okay, I'll tell you. Maria was expecting a child, and before you say anything, it was nothing to do with me. I never touched her. I had only walked out with her once and that was chaperoned. When her father found out she was carrying a baby, he was furious. He knew my father's business was in difficulties and decided to bribe him into making me marry her. He gave him 20,000 Drachma. The money for him was too tempting. So he made me go through with the wedding ceremony. The honeymoon was already booked for us to sail to England. I planned to study at a London Business College and had already made the necessary applications a year before. So I planned to make my escape and go alone. When I reached England, I completed my enrolment in the college and commenced my studies.

When I started the travel agency, I foolishly made arrangements for tourist operators in Greece. Maria learned of my business and started to send threatening letters and photos.'

'However it's wrapped up. Felix, you committed bigamy.'

Jeanette swivelled around in her chair to face Felix.

'You could go to prison for bigamy couldn't he, Mr Masters?'

'It is not quite like that in law, Mrs Rondo. The fact that Felix left his bride the same day, and did not spend the night with her, one would presume that he did not consummate the marriage. Is that correct?'

'Yes, that's correct. I never touched her. I only kissed her when told to by the priest.'

'Quite, and that the bride was pregnant by another person.'

'I feel I should say something here Mr Masters. One thing I *am* certain of, is that this woman's child could *not* have been Felix's.'

'How could you prove that?'

'We both had tests done when we found we couldn't have children. I couldn't conceive. I'd had both ovaries removed when I was fourteen and it was found that Felix had a very low sperm count. That is why we had to opt for adoption.'

'By what I have heard and read, I am pleased to say this would *not* be a case of bigamy. This was a marriage of convenience, not consummated and could be annulled. Once it is annulled it would then mean that you are married legally. I'll do the paper work for you and see that it goes to the appropriate courts.'

They both left arm in arm. Felix had carried a burden, that could have been settled years ago. The letters were found to have been written many years ago. Demanding letters for money, for Felix's fictitious son.

Chapter Fifty Four

The Rondo families had once again started to trust each other. Stefan and Jade patched up their marriage. After a course of therapy, Jade forgave Stefan and did give him another chance. They agreed his indiscretion with Doreen was partly down to the alcohol having removed his inhibitions. Although reluctant to admit it, she did reveal to Luke that she wasn't entirely innocent. She *had* deliberately avoided and rejected making love with her husband for far too long a period of time, and should have sought counselling earlier. Having forgiven him, she felt she should do the same for Doreen.

'I feel I should go and see Doreen.'

'Really?'

'Well, yes. It took two. So if I can forgive you, I should be able to do the same for her, shouldn't I?'

'That's up to you babe. Like Luke told us, we all make mistakes, it's whether we can heal the wounds and start again?'

'I think I should heal a few wounds today. I've been thinking, I might sell the shop.'

She had originally rented the salon, until Felix bought it for them both, as an investment.

'Why not rent it out?'

'I suppose I could do. Hairdressers are always looking for premises. I might ask Doreen, as a sort of olive branch.'

'What would you do with yourself?'

'I'm not sure yet, I thought I might go in for fostering.'

'Good idea.'

'I expect I'd have to go for training?'

Doreen was visibly shocked when she opened the door, to see Jade standing there.

'Oh! Jade. I didn't expect to ever see you again. You'd better come in.'

Initially conversation was stilted, but within a short while they were chatting normally.

'I didn't get a chance to tell you, that Dave and I had been going through a sticky patch in our marriage. I'm not trying to make excuses for what happened. But at the time Dave seemed to be shutting me out. Not speaking. Not wanting to make love. He put it down to pressure at work. The business was in difficulties, there was talk of liquidators being brought in. He's alright now. His job is secure. Our love life at that time seemed to be in a wilderness.'

'We went to Marriage Guidance, Doreen. It would seem, that like your Dave, I have to take a small part of the blame. When it came to making love, I was always too busy, too tired, too disinterested. Anyway let's not talk about it anymore. I am thinking of renting out the salon.'

'Sounds a good idea, but what would you do?'

'I'm not sure yet. I thought about doing something with children. Working in a nursery, or training to be a foster mother, I love children.'

'Sounds a good idea.'

'I have also given some thought about the salon, if I rented it out, I would still own it, but I would like to have an experienced manager to take it on. How would you like to take it on Doreen? Would you be interested in coming back as a manager?'

'Are you serious?' Doreen was stunned at the proposal.

'I could always be on hand in an emergency; but I would be renting *you* the salon. You could run your own business?'

'I can't believe I'm hearing this.' She felt choked with emotion. 'I would love it. To rent it and run my own business. It's something I have always dreamed of.'

They hugged each other. Tears trickled down Doreen's face.

'I'd love it. Thank you. Thank you so much.'

Before she left, Jade handed her the keys of the salon.

'There you are Doreen, it's all yours. We can talk about drawing up a contract and the rent later.'

As she left Doreen's house. It felt as though a load had been lifted off her shoulders. Not only handing over the salon, but the act of forgiveness. She felt she had cleansed her soul. She could start life afresh. No grudges. The anger stored up over past weeks, had gone. On the way home she called into Social Services offices and picked up a leaflet on fostering.

'What do you think?'

'It's up to you babe.' He read it and handed it back to her. 'Do you think you could do it?'

'I think so. Remember I was privately fostered.'

'I was adopted. You were fostered, we're an odd pair.'

'That reminds me I ought to go and see Lena. I haven't been for ages. Last time I was there she was going for training, so that she could have a guide dog. First they have to go and train with the dog. See if they are compatible.'

The instructor spoke to Lena. 'Lena I would like you to get inside the van with your dog.'

'Oh good, the dog is licking me. He must like me already.'

'No Lena. He is trying to let you know that you are treading on his tail.'

'Oh dear, sorry Ben.'

'We are at the railway station. We are on the edge of the platform. Now Lena, I want you to give your dog the instruction to go forward.'

'What! Should I really do that?'

'You need to be able to put your complete trust in the dog. Ben has been trained in this situation to protect you and do the right thing.'

'Oh dear,' she sighed, 'here goes.'

Lena hesitated and gave a clear instruction for the dog to take her forward. To her relief, the dog refused her command. Ben manoeuvred her to move away from the edge of the platform and firmly sat down.

'That's amazing,' she patted the dog on the head. 'You are a wonderful dog. I've never had a dog before.'

'This dog, Lena, is going to be your eyes. Ben is also going to be a true companion.'

Lena was delighted to show Jade, how wonderful Ben was. As soon as she put on his working harness, the three of them strolled along to the local park. Jade reflected that this was the very first time, that her birth mother had ever taken her to a park. Unlike Tess, she had never played with her. It made her realised how much she owed to Tess for all the love and affection she had showered on her over the years. If she went into fostering similar children, she'd had an ideal role model. The difference being that Tess had fostered her, with no thought of any monetary reward. Had she stayed with Lena, she knew it would have stolen her childhood. It could have led to a destructive life, like Lena's.

'Are you still thinking of fostering?' Stefan asked her.

'Yes. I'm going to fill in the application form. Meeting up with Lena made me realise what an impact a foster parent can have on a child's life.'

'Did you ever find out who your father was?'

'No. Judging by the horrible men that used to be in her life then, I don't want to know. Do *you* know?'

'I told you, my birth parents were only school kids.'

'They wouldn't be school kids now, though, would they? Why don't we look for them?'

'I've been thinking about it. In fact I mentioned it to mum and dad and they were happy for me to try and trace them. They didn't hold out much hope, as it was through the Catholic Adoption Agency.'

'We could try ourselves. Birth records, marriage records and so on.'

'All right we could have a go next week.'

Chapter Fifty Five

'Where do we start, Stef?'

'Well, according to mum, I was found in the back of a bus, wrapped up in a school jumper with a Catholic medal attached. That's all we have to go on.'

'Ah, but we do have your date of birth.'

'True, and a rough idea how old my mother was at the time. I believe she was fifteen.'

At the local library, the librarian helped them look through the archives. Then Jade hit on a good idea.

'You were found on Christmas Day, the day you were born. I imagine a day or two later it would have made headline news in a local paper somewhere?'

'All we know is, that it was somewhere in Essex.'

They found a reference to a baby being abandoned on a bus in Romford. Having the correct date of birth, they decided to drive to the Romford Newspaper office. They were able to track down the recorded story.

'Hey look, Babe, in the Romford Recorder, it actually says which school was indicated by the jumper. Police were trying to trace the mother. Keep looking, we may find where the police found her?'

'Look, there's a picture here of me in the jumper; it's when the police made an appeal for the mother to come forward.'

The archivist official went over to the table to speak to them. 'I'm sorry we are closing now. We close at four o'clock on Saturdays.'

Stefan felt frustrated. 'Just as we were beginning to get somewhere.'

'I can get in on Monday. I'll carry on where we left off.'

'Stef, Stef, I've got an address. Well sort of,' she rushed in the flat. 'I've got the name of the close, where her mother lived. It says, *the grandmother of the baby had no idea that her daughter was pregnant.* No name of your mother. We could go and see if anyone remembers the birth and the family?'

'Slow down, I've got to think seriously about this.'

'You're not backing down now are you? Not now we've gone to all this trouble?'

'No, no I am not. I just need time to work out the consequences, if we should find her?'

'Don't be a wimp. I went to find Lena. Take it easy, I'll be with you.'

'Okay, when shall we go?'

'Let's see. She could be working, so how about Sunday?'

They set off to Romford, the area they were looking for was Hornchurch. After buying a local map at a newsagents, they found the cul-de-sac and started to knock on doors to the neat terraced houses. Stefan was left to explain.

At the first house, there was a woman too young to have known the schoolgirl. The next a middle-aged woman. 'Sorry I have only lived here two years.'

At another, an elderly gentleman opened the door. 'I'm sorry to trouble you. Can I ask how long you have lived here? Only I am trying to trace a girl who used to live in this close.'

'If she lived here in the last forty-five years son, then I would probably know the person. What name did you say?'

He ignored the question. 'She used to go to the convent school.'

'Let me see, I've known a few kids what went to convent schools that lived in this close. When, long ago?'

'Around about 1968/69.'

'Ah,…that would be round about when little Renee, our granddaughter was born. Oh yeah, I remember there was a young girl. Mary, Mary something…?'

He turned round and called down the hallway to his wife.

'Joan, what was the name of that convent girl? She can't hear me, she's probably down the garden, you'd better come in.'

The elderly man took them into the kitchen. His wife was taking washing out of a tumble drier.

'Joan, this young couple are looking for that convent girl, what used to live down 'ere. You know, that one what caused all that scandal. Abandoned her baby. What was 'er name Mary…Mary something?'

'Mary Lynch.'

'That's it, Mary Lynch. I knew the first name was Mary. That's the one. 'ow could we forget? News reporters, photographers. Joan, you remember, when they took that photo of our road. She was more concerned, that all the neighbours could see 'er washing on the line. Believe me, swarming around 'ere they was. More bobbies, than bluebottles round a jam jar.'

'She lived next door but one. They moved years ago,' said his wife.

'Where did they go to, love? Your sister knew 'em didn't she? They moved to the coast, somewhere near Sarfend.'

'Westcliff? Leigh-on-Sea?' Stefan prompted.

'Yeah that's it, Leigh-on-Sea.'

Jade and Stefan looked at each other and grinned.

'Wait on, my sister may 'ave the address. She kept in touch with the family.'

After weeks of door-knocking and phone calls in Leigh-on-Sea, they eventually found the girl's mother. Mrs Lynch was reluctant at first to talk to Stefan, saying she needed to speak to her daughter first. Mary, her daughter, she said, was married with three children.

'I quite understand Mrs Lynch. I really don't want to interfere, but could you just ask her, if she would like to speak to me please?'

He gave Mrs Lynch his contact number. He felt despondent. He didn't hold out much hope he'd hear from her.

'I bet her mother has probably binned my number already. Hey babe, her mother that we've just been talking to, that's my grandmother isn't it? Well, we can't do any more, let's go home.'

At first he waited in anticipation. But as month turned to month, then to a whole year, it turned once again to a feeling of rejection.

'Never mind Stef, maybe it wasn't to be. We don't always get what we want in life. You just have to accept that Mary has made her own life, with her husband and children. She may not have told her husband that she had a baby when she was at school. You turning up on the doorstep could cause real trouble in her family.'

'That's true. But everyone wants to be acknowledged for who they are. It leaves a big hole when you don't know where you came from. All I'd like is for Mary to acknowledge that I'm her son.'

A few days later, his prayers were answered. A husky voice contacted him.

'Hello, is that Stefan? This is Mary, my Mother contacted me. I understand you would like to speak to me?'

He was silent, he could hardly believe what was happening. This was the voice of his real mother. A shiver went down his spine.

'Stefan are you there?'

'Yes, yes. I'm here. I can't believe I'm hearing your voice. It's great.'

'It's wonderful to hear you too. I never dared to hope that you would find me? I want to say I never ever stopped thinking about you. Especially on your birthday which, of course, is on Christmas Day. I wondered where you were? Did your adopted parents look after you properly? Were you happy?'

'I thought about you too. Yes, my adopted parents have been wonderful. My dad…'

His throat dried with nervousness and emotion. Tears cascaded down his face. 'I'm sorry, Mary, I'm overwhelmed, this is so emotional. I didn't think I would react like this.'

'Don't worry, Stefan, I'm the same here.' He could hear the break in her voice.

'I'm sorry it has taken me so long to contact you. It's not that I didn't care about you. I needed time to get my head around it. Because I abandoned you, I didn't think you would ever want to speak to me. What mother I thought, could *do* that?'

'A frightened schoolgirl mother, Mary.'

'Yes, that's true. We have a lot to talk about and I'm dying to meet you. Would you want to meet me?'

'Of course. I'd love to.'

'Let's make some arrangement now. I don't think it's wise to meet my family just yet.'

They discussed a time and place. They were both reluctant to let go and terminate the phone call. They were elated in the knowledge, that they had acknowledged each other, and excited that soon they would meet for the first time.

Chapter Fifty Six

Mary had tears in her eyes when she came off the phone. Her youngest daughter Laura, looked concerned.

'What's wrong Mum?'

'Nothing's wrong.' Mary took in a deep breath. 'I have just spoken to your brother, he is called Stefan.'

'What do you mean my brother?' asked Laura.

'It's something I've never told the family except your dad, he knows all about it.'

'Knows about what Mum?'

'Sit down I have something to tell you.'

Mary explained how she had met her first boyfriend when she was thirteen. She was on the bus going home from school. They got chatting about their different schools. He was at a comprehensive school, she was at the convent. They were soon talking about the subjects they liked – and the teachers they didn't. He made a habit of looking out for her each day and soon she would save him a seat on the bus. Within a few weeks they were meeting up and going to the cinema or swimming. Her parents thought it was just a schoolgirl crush, but the more the two of them met, the stronger their affection grew.

On Mary's fifteenth birthday, her boyfriend, who was a year older, announced to her parents that they had just become engaged. Mary was thrilled and proudly showed off her ring, with its small, pale-blue zircon stone. Her father was furious.

'It's ridiculous, you're only kids. I don't know what the pair of you were thinking of?'

Her mother was more understanding.

'I know you two have known each other for some time, and you're a nice lad, but for a start, you are not a Catholic are you? That would cause enormous problems.'

Her boyfriend was adamant. 'Not when we love each other Mrs Lynch.'

'Love, love?' scoffed her father. 'What does any kid of your age know about love? I think you'd better go home now sonny. My wife and I need to have a serious talk.'

'I was just leaving anyway.'

Mary went with him to the front door. 'Don't take any notice, they are both a bit shocked that's all. They think we are too young to know our own minds.'

'I don't think it's only that. I can never see your father accepting me. For a start, I'm the wrong religion.'

They kissed in the hallway and waved goodbye. She was upset and went to her room. She could hear her parents arguing. Their raised voices could be heard upstairs. She heard her father shout. 'Bloody stupid if you ask me. They're only kids. There's no way I'm going to allow her marry a proddy.'

Mary's daughter was amazed at her mother's revelation.

'So you were really engaged Mum, at fifteen, that's cool. Did Grandad let you see your boyfriend after that.'

'I had to give the ring back and we were forbidden to see each other. But it was true what my boyfriend said to my dad, that we loved each other. As far as we were concerned, no one was going to split us up. We still met every day, on the bus going home from school. His parents were happy for us to go out together. In a way, they encouraged it. We didn't tell them that my parents disapproved. In order to be able to see him. I invented a best friend '*Donna.*' I would tell my parents that it was Donna I was going to the cinema with. Sometimes my boyfriend's parents would invite me over for meal, and on a couple of occasions to stay over at their house.'

'When you were really staying at your boyfriend's house.'

'Yes.'

'Sleeping with him at weekends?'

'Certainly not! When I stayed over I had the spare room, nothing like that happened.'

'Go on Mum.'

'One evening his parents were going to the theatre. That night, we found some cider in a cupboard, we thought it was *Cydrax*, a non-alcoholic drink. We were drinking it, sitting on the sofa, cuddling up, watching TV, when it happened. Like a lot of romances with young people, I know now, it can get out of hand when the hormones kick in. One morning I did have some sickness, but I put it down to something I ate. I never dreamt I was having a baby. It was one thing to get engaged at fifteen, quite another to have a baby. In those days, we didn't have sex education at the convent school. I didn't have a clue. I didn't think I could get pregnant when we'd only made love that one time.'

'But Mum, you must have started to show.'

'No, I didn't really show at all.'

'You must have known something Mum? Surely you can't be pregnant and not know anything?'

'Nothing. Right up to the day I had the baby. But then I read in the paper, that the baby only weighed two and a half pounds. So, it's not surprising that I didn't look pregnant.'

'That's unbelievable.'

'It was Christmas Day, I had been invited to *'Donna's* for tea. I had a few pains, after tea, but put it down to having eaten too much during the day. Afterwards we went for a walk. We were just passing Romford Bus Station, when I had this terrible pain. I was doubled up. My boyfriend suggested we sat down in one of the empty buses. Being Christmas, they were all parked up. There were no buses running that day. We went in one and sat down. At first I thought I'd wet myself, I was so embarrassed, but now I know that it was my waters that had broken. I had this pain and the baby was born on the seat of the bus. It was very tiny, I didn't think it could live.'

'Weren't you scared Mum?'

'I was in a right state, I was so glad my boyfriend was with me, I didn't know what to do. Fortunately, he was a cadet in the St John Ambulance Brigade, although he told me afterwards he'd never seen a baby born before. He took a white shoe lace from one of his sneakers, cut off two pieces and tied off the baby's cord in two places. Then he cut the cord in the middle with his penknife. He was marvellous. He took off his T- shirt and wrapped it round the baby. Being winter, I had a school jumper in my bag, I put that on him and pinned my Catholic medal to it. Afterwards we went to a call box, and rang Romford Hospital. We told them, we'd found a baby in a bus. So we knew he wouldn't be there for long.'

'Why didn't you take the baby home?'

'It was freezing cold, he probably wouldn't have survived. Nor would I, my father would have killed me – thrown me out on the street. We were both scared out of our wits. We didn't know what to do. It all happened so quickly, we didn't have time to think. I remember thinking afterwards, thank goodness it didn't happen at school. Heaven knows what the nuns would have done to me. We didn't tell a soul. We went back to his house, his family were watching a variety show on television. I sneaked upstairs and had a quick bath. David pinched some underclothes from his mum's drawer, a top and skirt from the wardrobe and I nipped off home. Fortunately my parents were glued to a programme on the telly, so I was able to slip upstairs and quickly change into my own clothes.'

'I can't believe how you got away with it Mum?'

'A couple of days later, we read about it in the Romford Recorder so we knew the baby had been found and had survived. They showed a picture of it. Now Laura, that little baby is in his thirties and has been looking for his birth mother. That was him. Stefan, my son. I have been speaking to him on the phone.'

'Mum, that's amazing. What happened to your boyfriend?'

'A couple of years later he emigrated with his family to Canada.'

'That's where my dad comes from. Mum, you said *he* was an old school friend…he wasn't … was he … is he?'

'Yes, your dad was the boyfriend I fell in love with all those years ago. He returned to England, after he had lost his wife. Your sisters, Kayley and Naomi's dad, had also died. Ian set about trying to find me. Yes Laura, he is Stefan's father. I haven't told Stefan about his dad yet'

'Wow, that's amazing.'

'Yes, and it's all true darling. I can't wait to tell Ian when he comes in tonight. He'll be thrilled.'

'I'd love to see his face Mum, when you tell him, that his son has been in contact.'

'Stefan is not only related to your dad and me Laura. He is also *your* brother.'

'Oh yes, so he is. That's cool, Mum.'

Stefan looked at his watch, they had been on the phone for an hour.

'Wow, that was Mary, my real mother.'

'I rather gathered that.' They flung their arms around each other.

'We are going to meet each other. On our own at first. Later we will both introduce our families. To think we could have passed each other in the street.'

'That's great,' said Jade. 'I'm really pleased for you.'

A week later Stefan was on his way to the hotel where they'd had their reception. It was under new management and had been refurbished. Neither had been back to the scene of the assault. He felt this was going to be a pleasant occasion and that he could brush away any old ghosts that lingered from the hotel.

He arrived early and awaited Mary in a small light and airy lounge overlooking the grounds. He sat with half a lager looking constantly for any sign of anyone arriving. As the allotted time drew near, his hands became clammy, he felt sick. The door of the lounge opened. A petite, fair-haired woman entered, wearing a lemon coloured shirt, navy trousers and an anxious expression. She looked straight at him. He stood up. They quickly gravitated toward each other. Stefan was unsure what to do. Did he kiss her? Hug her? Shake hands? All questions like that vanished, as she threw her arms around him and hugged him tight.

'Oh Stefan, I can't tell you how long I have waited to do that!'

'I never dreamed I'd ever see you Mary.'

'Please Stefan, please if you can, call me mum.'

'Oh Mum.' They both cried tears of happiness.

'Let's sit down, what will you have to drink…Mum?'

'I'll have a white wine Son.'

Stefan was in a daze, this meeting seemed so unreal. After a drink, they went outside into the grounds of the hotel. They walked arm in arm. There was so much to talk about. They sat down on a bench in the grounds and talked non-stop. Mary wanted to know all about Jeanette and Felix, had they treated him right? What was his job? He explained about the family travel business. He felt too nervous to ask her too much. He would love to have asked about his biological father, but thought it wise not to ask just yet. It might be too painful for his mum to speak about it, one day she might tell him. They spoke at length about Jade. Mary was delighted to learn that she had a teenage grandson called Daniel. It started to rain so they retreated back inside.

'Would you like to stay and have some lunch here Mum?'

'Not today Stefan. Next time. Or …' she paused, 'next time, would you like to come to lunch with our family. Bring Jade and Daniel. Meet my husband and our three daughters, Kayley and Naomi your half-sisters and Laura your sister.'

He did not pick up on the mention of Laura, being his *real* sister. Stefan was busy noting that his mum had said *our* family and not *my* family.

'Yes I'd really like that. That would be great.'

They hugged, kissed and clung to each other. Did she think he looked like his biological father? His mum hadn't spoken about him. For the moment that could wait. It was anticipated that eventually, all the family would meet up. Mary had shown a great interest in meeting Jeanette and Felix. Stefan didn't expect to be accepted into the bosom of Mary's family; just to be able to make contact with his mother was sufficient. Who knows what the future could hold? For like Jade, he too had found acceptance and had been reunited with his birth mother. For years he had been tormented with a nagging feeling of rejection. That feeling had gone. Stefan… had finally found his roots.